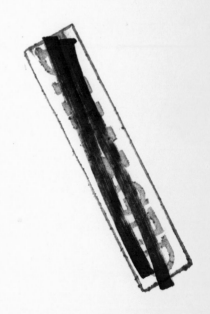

D1250823

DUTY FREE

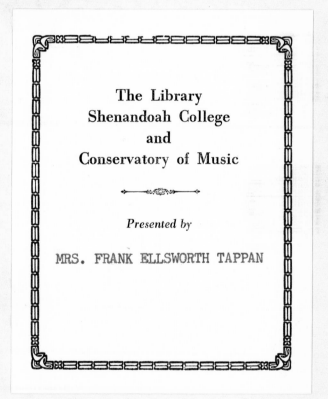

A CRIME CLUB SELECTION

With its spectacular site in the eastern Pyrenees, its smiling natives, its charming Prince, and its fairy-tale way of life—the principality of Sainte-Roche had everything. Everything except money. And that was why Robert Brown (valet to the Prince, Foreign Minister of Sainte-Roche, and the perfect gentleman's gentleman) determined to tap the wealthy benevolence of the United States.

Mr. Brown's ingenious scheme to obtain economic assistance, his embarrassing connections with some notorious jewel thieves, his Prince's champagne-and-caviar romance with a very beautiful and very rich American tourist, and the explosive cultural impact of American expense accounts and bulldozers on the inhabitants of Sainte-Roche—all add up (in true Manning Coles style) to a delightful chronicle of international urbanity and skulduggery.

Scene: the eastern Pyrenees

This novel has not appeared in any form prior to book publication.
(Chase & Adventure)

DUTY FREE

by

Manning Coles

Published for the Crime Club
by Doubleday & Company, Inc.
Garden City, New York
1959

All of the characters in this book are fictitious,
and any resemblance to actual persons,
living or dead, is purely coincidental.

Library of Congress Catalog Card Number 59–6987
Copyright © 1959 by Manning Coles
All Rights Reserved
Printed in the United States of America
First Edition

To
G.M.T.

Psalm xv, especially Verse 5.

CONTENTS

Robert Brown.
Prince André of Sainte-Roche.
The Six:
    Gilles d'Ecosse, Chancellor and Schoolmaster.
    Louis Durand, Postmaster.
    Marcel Avril, Editor of the Sainte-Roche *Bulletin.*
    Henri Tonnerre, Innkeeper of The Goat.
    Jean Latour, Farmer.
    The Reverend Father Denys, Curé.
Jules Gobain, Innkeeper of The Hunter.
The late Aristide LeBlanc, the Army.
The American Economic Mission:
    Morris M. Mathews, Economic Adviser.
    Edward K. Spenlow, Roads and Communications.
    Donald S. Farson, Housing and Education.
Adam K. Hopkins.
Betty Hopkins, his daughter.
Fishy Pike.   }
George.   } Crooks.

SCENE, the Principality of Sainte-Roche in the Eastern Pyrenees.
TIME, 1957.

DUTY FREE

CHAPTER I

Faraway Place

"It appears," said the English traveller in the hired car, "to be rather a long way."

"It does not merely appear," said the driver sourly. "It is. And if I have another puncture here, in this wilderness——"

The traveller looked about him. "I have always been an admirer of unspoilt scenery in spite of having spent most of my life in cities."

"If Monsieur likes scenery, there is so much of it here that if a man were to spend many years merely looking at it he would still not have seen it all. Me," said the driver, changing down for the fiftieth time since leaving Py, "me for the big cities."

"Have you ever lived in a city?"

"I once visited Perpignan," said the driver with some dignity.

The conversation dropped for lack of common interests and the traveller let pass some time and also some miles of the foothills of the Pyrenees before he spoke again.

"This place," he said thoughtfully, "must be as remote as Andorra."

"Andorra is not remote, not truly remote. People go to Andorra. Visitors, in cars and coaches. Everyone has heard of Andorra."

"And Sainte-Roche?"

The driver twisted his mouth and shrugged his shoulders.

"Monsieur wishes to go to Sainte-Roche, no doubt for some wise purpose. For myself, I cannot say anything about it since I have never been there."

"It is a Principality," said the Englishman in a tone of faint rebuke.

"Undoubtedly, monsieur," said the driver, and gave his undivided attention to the road, which had passed from poor to bad and was becoming simply horrible. "Not far now," he added.

They came over the crest of a ridge and descended to what was plainly the valley of a river, a wild mountain torrent which could be heard but not yet seen, so deep was the gorge in which it ran. Just ahead of them there was the first example of the work of human hands which the Englishman had seen for the past hour; it looked like a bridge but was not easily discernible because all that could be seen of it was an ancient and unbelievably solid archway built of large pieces of stone; upon either side was a stumpy tower. Fifty yards short of the bridge, by the side of the road, there was the weathered stump of what had been a stout post, and at this point the driver stopped the car.

"We arrive," he said cheerfully, and got out of the car.

"But——" said the Englishman.

"We arrive," repeated the driver, and waved a hand towards the beautiful, if rugged, countryside on the further side of the stream. "The Principality of Sainte-Roche, at Monsieur's service." He took the Englishman's luggage out of the car, carried it across to the post, and piled it up there. "This," tapping the post, "marks the frontier. They say it used to have a notice-board on it to say so, but it blew away many years ago. Before my time, monsieur. Now, if Monsieur will excuse me——"

The Englishman got out of the car and paid the balance of the fare, adding a tip. The driver thanked him, wished him a pleasant stay in the Principality, turned the car, and drove away without a backward glance.

The Englishman had expected to be met at this point but was neither surprised nor annoyed at finding himself alone. No doubt someone would come in due course, and in the meantime it was very pleasant here; the day was glorious, the air exhilarating, and the views of dropping valleys and soaring peaks such as to uplift the heart.

"Quite breath-taking," he said, and strolled on towards the bridge. To lean over the parapet of a bridge and look down at the water below is a natural human instinct. He passed under the archway and set foot upon the bridge approach.

But there was no parapet to lean upon; there was in fact no bridge in any practical sense, for the one arch which had leapt the stream was gone altogether and not even a wooden plank spanned the thirty-foot gap to the other side. Eighty feet below, the brown river roared among boulders and the limestone sides were nearly sheer.

"Dear me," said Robert Brown, and strolled back to the frontier post to sit down upon his biggest suitcase and light a cigarette. The air was not merely exhilarating, it was warm and smelt of wild thyme. The hillside was patched with clumps of bushes which gave off an aromatic smell, the spiky grass was starred with small flowers and was shrill with a chirping sound which took him suddenly back to his boyhood; he stooped down and looked at the ground. Grasshoppers, dozens of them, large active grasshoppers.

Presently a man came along the road by the way the car had come; he was on foot and wore the uniform of the French police. The Englishman turned at the sound of footsteps and, even as he did so, caught sight out of the tail of his eye of something moving in the bushes. He believed it to be the figure of a man; whatever it was, it disappeared at once and Brown turned his attention to the gendarme, who, for his part, was struggling with a sense of unreality.

There are very few people about in these parts and those who come are usually smugglers, since, besides the frontiers of Sainte-Roche, the frontiers of Spain also are not far away. When travellers are honest and upon legitimate errands, they are herdsmen in search of strayed beasts or hunters stalking the agile ibex, in either case countrymen in country clothes.

The gendarme's incredulous eyes beheld, seated by the frontier post upon a neat pile of luggage, a short but dignified figure in a well-cut town suit of dark cloth. He wore a white shirt with a stiff collar, a tie of modest pattern and controlled by a small gold safety pin, completely unnoticeable socks, and highly polished black shoes. In his hands he carried a pair of grey suede gloves, and against his knees there rested a tightly rolled umbrella. Upon his head this incredible person wore an excellent bowler hat.

The gendarme pulled himself together, marched up, and saluted smartly; Brown, who spoke French fluently, greeted him.

"Good day to you. A beautiful day, too, is it not? I hardly expected to see a gendarme in so remote a spot."

"The car passed me with two men in it," said the gendarme mildly, "and went back with only one, from which I deduced that somewhere here a gentleman would be waiting. May I see Monsieur's passport?"

"Certainly," said Robert Brown, and gave it to the man.

"Ah, Monsieur is English. Monsieur intends to cross the frontier into Sainte-Roche?"

"That was my idea, but there seems to be a certain difficulty. The bridge——"

"Ah, yes. The bridge is undoubtedly in a poor state of repair, Monsieur is right. He is, no doubt, expected? Yes, then, in that case someone will probably come."

"And repair the bridge?"

The gendarme laughed politely and took a pace back, saluted, and wished him a good afternoon.

"You do not, then, wish to examine my luggage?"

"There is no customs post upon this frontier, monsieur, nor am I authorized to act as customs officer. So far as France is concerned, Monsieur's baggage may pass unexamined."

"So far as France is concerned. And as for the Principality of Sainte-Roche?"

"I regret I have no information to offer." The man looked about him and smiled faintly. "There would not appear to be, here, the facilities for excessive frontier formalities, but no doubt Monsieur will find out in due course. I have the honour once again to wish Monsieur a good day and a pleasant journey."

The gendarme saluted again and walked away; in a few minutes his neat figure had disappeared over the crest of the rise.

"I think I have come to a dam' funny place," said Brown to himself.

Ten minutes later the bushes parted and a head looked cautiously out within six feet of him.

"Has that man gone?" it asked in a dialect so broad that Brown asked to have the question repeated.

"That man. Has he gone?"

"Oh yes."

"Good." The bushes parted further and a man stepped out, a young man of sturdy and athletic build with a mop of shaggy hair. He wore a belted tunic of homespun cloth, kneebreeches, and heavy shoes; the shirt which showed at the neck of his tunic was faded and ragged, but Brown noticed that the buckles of his belt and shoes appeared to be of silver.

"I do not like frontiersmen," he said. "Good day, monsieur. Are you the Englishman who is come to attend upon our Prince?"

"I am, yes."

"Good." The young man stepped back into the bushes and was immediately lost to sight.

Five minutes later he appeared again on the road nearer the bridge, and this time he was leading a string of three mules. He brought them up to the frontier post and immediately began loading Brown's luggage upon the last two in the string. Brown watched with some apprehension, which the young man noticed.

"They will be quite safe," he said. "This rope is good and the mules are good also. They always carry things. The first mule has a saddle for Monsieur."

"So I notice."

"His name is Perfecto."

"How nice. And what is yours?"

"Jean-Alphonse. Will Monsieur now mount?"

Brown glanced down at his trousers with an expression which might have been pity but mounted Perfecto without any demur. Jean-Alphonse took Perfecto's bridle, turned the cortege round in the road, and led them back towards the bridge.

"Has Monsieur a good head for heights?"

Brown was becoming used to the dialect by now.

"Reasonably good, I believe."

"It is well," said Jean-Alphonse calmly.

"What happened to your bridge?"

"It was the war. Somebody blew it up for us, the maquis— the Germans—who knows?"

"A little inconvenient, is it not?"

"At that time, we were glad. We did not want the war in Sainte-Roche."

"Very sensible of you."

"Neither the Germans nor the maquis nor anyone who wanted to fight anybody else. So when the bridge was broken they could not come. Good, very good."

Jean-Alphonse turned abruptly off the road down a bank so steep that Brown was not ashamed to cling on like a monkey. They entered upon a track which wound about among the juniper bushes.

"But is there no other road than this?"

"No. Why? One is enough."

"But the bridge——"

Jean-Alphonse grinned over his shoulder.

"When the bridge was there we used it, naturally. But when it is down during twelve or fourteen years one becomes accustomed, Monsieur understands."

"Perfectly. I assume that when things are wanted a mule train is sent for them."

"Eh?"

"People go with mules. Like this."

"*We* take the mules," said Jean-Alphonse, emphasizing the pronoun. "Or, if people are good walkers, *we* guide them. *We* know the tracks."

"Who is 'we'?"

"I and my father and my brothers and two of my uncles."

"Indeed. But does not everyone know the way?"

Jean-Alphonse stopped the string of mules by hauling back upon Perfecto's bridle and came round to stand at Brown's knee and emphasize the argument with a sinewy finger.

"Monsieur, we are the frontier guides. If everyone knew the way, should we be engaged to guide them? No. We have a right to live, no? To eat, to clothe ourselves, yes?"

"Yes, but——"

"All this we do by being the frontier guides. The Six are always saying that the bridge must be repaired, this they have been saying for many years."

"Then why don't they do it?"

"What would be the use? Only to let in the outside world, and, monsieur, we are quite happy without the outside world. I am not ignorant, I have heard what it is like outside, the curé and others have told me. The things people want! They even tell me that people are taxed outside, yes, as much as one tenth of what they have. Why should we be taxed? So it is better that the bridge is not mended. Understood?"

"There is indeed something in what you say," said Brown.

"Naturally," said Jean-Alphonse, returning to Perfecto's head. "Now let Monsieur hold on tightly, and if he wishes to shut his eyes it will not matter. I, Jean-Alphonse, am in charge of him. *Allons*, Perfecto."

They turned towards the edge of the ravine. The next twenty minutes were such as Brown only dimly discerned and later

23

did his best to forget. With eyes which would fly open when he most desired not to see, horrid pictures were printed upon his mind of swaying upon the brink of chasms while the mules skipped like goats from ledge to ledge and finally slid on their tails to the water level, where they stopped. Brown was pleasantly surprised to find himself still alive and yet more astonished to realize that he still clutched his umbrella.

"Now," he said, drawing a long breath, "what happens next?"

"Across the stream and up the other side. It is not so difficult, the other side."

Nor was it; merely a precipitous scramble which was by comparison easy. When they reached the top of the ravine and rejoined the road on the further side of the bridge, Jean-Alphonse hopped up upon the least loaded baggage mule and they all proceeded comfortably together.

"I suppose," said Brown, "that I shall be able to change my French francs into your currency? What is your currency?"

"Francs and centimes, monsieur. I do not use money myself, it is not necessary."

"But, if you wish to buy——"

"Monsieur, I have geese but no vineyard. My aunt's cousin Jules-Philippe has a vineyard but no geese. When I want wine I go to him and say 'how many geese for so much wine?' Then there is a little discussion and so I get my wine."

"I see. Tell me, if there are no taxes, how do you pay for your roads?"

"Pay?" said Jean-Alphonse, staring. "There is no need to pay for the roads; they have always been."

"But when they need repair?"

"Then each man does the piece which belongs to him. A load of gravel, well spread, and it is done. When it is anything important like repaving the market square—we have a market square in the town, Monsieur will see it—then we issue some more stamps. Foreigners buy stamps, does Monsieur know why? But they do. Then there is money and the square is repaved. The Six attend to all that."

They were passing along a track through extensive woods; pine trees first, giving place to chestnut as the road led gently downwards. At last the forest ended and the riders came out into the open as suddenly as a man stepping out of a doorway, and Brown pulled Perfecto to a halt.

Before them lay a green amphitheatre some seven miles across with the hills rising steeply all about it, one of the typical cirque valley heads of the Pyrenees. Away to their left, on the sunny side of the circle, grey stone houses crowded one above another up the hillside with a whitewashed church conspicuous in the middle. Higher yet, above the topmost houses, a green shelf ran across the hillside, and upon this stood a house of some importance though not of great size. It had a tower in the middle and two-storey wings upon either side; the windows glittered in the sun. Subsidiary buildings stood apart, which Brown correctly assumed to be stables and farm buildings; terraces bright with flowers and linked by stairways dropped down the face of the hill to connect with the town below. The place was at least three miles distant from where Brown sat upon his mule with his trouser legs rucked to his knees, but so radiant and clear was the air that it seemed that a flicked pebble would fall among the houses.

"Sainte-Roche, monsieur," said Jean-Alphonse. "The big house with the tower, that is the Palace where you will live."

CHAPTER II

The Six

"This afternoon," said Prince André, "I preside for the first time at a meeting of the Six. You will find my official coat in a tin box on the floor of that cupboard. It has 'S.A. le Prince Jerome' on the lid."

Brown pulled the tin box—it was a uniform case—out of the cupboard and opened it. Layers of tissue paper swathed a black jacket with gold lace on the stand-up collar, down the front, and round the cuffs.

"Any moths?" asked the Prince casually.

Brown carried out a hasty search.

"Apparently not, Your Highness, from a first hurried survey. The lace on the right cuff is a little——"

"I will try it on," said the Prince, getting to his feet. He was already in his shirt sleeves and had been sitting in the window seat playing with a tortoise-shell cat.

Brown put the coat on his master and stood back with a doubtful expression.

"It's a bit roomy," said the Prince, examining the fit in a looking glass, "is it not?"

"Your Highness," ventured Brown, "has lost weight since the coat was made?"

"Heavens, man, this thing wasn't made for me. It was my father's. Hence 'Jerome' on the lid. He died ten years ago when I was fifteen. I can't afford a new one, at least the Six say we can't, so this one will have to do. It will last a long time yet and, anyway, it's only to meet the Six."

"It could be altered to fit," said Brown, "if there is a tailor——"

"Certainly there is a tailor, but there's no time now; the meeting starts in half an hour. Black evening trousers, Robert. They at least will fit since they are my own. By the way, you are to attend the meeting."

"I, Your Highness?"

"Certainly. That is, you will attend me at the meeting, standing behind my chair. I suppose you ought to be an equerry but I haven't got an equerry in working order at the moment. Old d'Albert is my hereditary equerry and he's eighty-nine and bedridden. You'll do."

"But I am only Your Highness' personal servant."

"Don't argue, Robert. Besides, the Six want to meet you. They pay your wages, you know. They naturally want to see what they've got."

Brown opened his mouth and shut it again.

"If you are worrying about an official uniform, don't. They know you've only been here two days and one can't see to everything at once. There's the uniform of a halberdier at the Court of Louis XIV somewhere—my father wore it at a fancy-dress dance when he married. It must be practically new. You needn't wear the breastplate. Never mind that now, where are my gloves?"

"The meeting," said Brown, "is held in the Town Hall, I understand, Your——"

"Not now I am of age. It is held in the Great Hall here for the first time for ten years. Has anyone explained the position to you? Well, it is this. Princes of Sainte-Roche come of age at twenty-five; I was twenty-five last Sunday. The privileges of coming of age include, among other things, the provision of a personal manservant. Hence you. Before the age of twenty-five we are waited upon by a succession of footmen from the palace household doing a month's duty each in rotation. I think the idea is that if the Prince's attendants are continually changed there is less chance of intrigue and a palace revolt against the reigning Prince, but since I am a brotherless orphan the point does not arise. The custom, however, continues. If I were to tell you what I have suffered at the hands of some of these well-meaning yokels, Robert, large salt tears would deluge your waistcoat. It is time to go. Where is—ah, yes."

There came a thundering knock on the panels of the door; at a nod from the Prince, Brown flung it wide open. An old man in a dress practically covered with rather tarnished silver lace stood in the doorway. He supported himself with a tall black staff having a silver knob the size of an orange on the top. He bowed deeply.

"The Six hopefully await their Prince."

"Who comes gladly," said the Prince, completing what was obviously a formula.

The old man straightened up, turned about, and led the way, the Prince followed behind, and Brown fell in to bring up the rear.

He had already seen the Great Hall, a vast chamber with a high roof and ancient banners hanging upon walls which would have been improved by a fresh coat of whitewash. There was a long and heavy table in the middle, there were three heavy chairs upon either side, by which six men were standing; at the end of the table there was a larger and even heavier chair for the Prince, who stalked over to it and sat down as Brown pushed it forward.

"Be seated, gentlemen. Thank you. I believe it to be customary for each member of the Six to deliver an address of welcome upon the occasion of a Prince taking his seat for the first time at the head of this Council. In view of the fact that you all addressed me at some length only last Sunday, my birthday, I suggest that we omit a second instalment and get on with the business. Those in favour?"

No hands were raised, and the Prince's amused glance swept round the table.

"What? Every single one of you with his heart set upon reciting my problematical virtues and giving me good advice?"

A thin-faced dark man moved uneasily, and the Prince named him instantly.

"Marcel Avril, poet, author, and editor of our Sainte-Roche *Bulletin*, speak your mind."

Avril stood up, bowed, and said that, when a man had taken considerable trouble to compose an address of welcome, it was disappointing not to be able to make it, if it pleased the Prince. He sat down again to murmurs of approval from the others.

"Of course it is," said the Prince. "I appreciate that. More, I respect it. Tell me, you have your excellent speeches all written out in full, have you?"

They agreed that they had.

"I am so glad," said Prince André, "for now I can take them away with me and give them my full attention at a second or even a third reading." He jerked his head back towards Brown behind his chair. "Collect the speeches. Let the greatest care be taken of them. They are to be conveyed to my private study."

"Your Highness," murmured Brown, and went round the table collecting the speeches, which he laid reverently upon a side table.

"I look forward to a happy evening with them," said the Prince courteously, "and I thank you all. Now to business. Who has matter to unfold before this Council?"

At the Prince's right hand sat a square and solid man with thick red hair and beard just touched with grey, who had a pile of papers on the table before him. He moved forward in his seat, and Prince André called upon him.

"Gilles d'Ecosse, Chancellor of our Exchequer and instructor of our children, speak your mind."

"My Prince, it is a question of money. Sainte-Roche has certain expenses which must be met. Salaries, here is a list of them," he laid a paper before the Prince. "Repairs to public buildings; the roof of the Town Hall is, I am told, in a dangerous condition——"

"It has been possible to see daylight through it ever since I can remember," agreed the Prince.

"It is now possible to see the stars at night also," said the Chancellor dryly. "The town water supply is intermittent, the aqueduct is breaking away near its source, and this is serious. The town drainage system has given trouble ever since a rockslide fell into it when the snow thawed last spring. The school requires new benches and a new blackboard——"

"The list is formidable," said the Prince. "The reverend curé, Father Denys, speak your mind."

The curé was an old man with bright silver hair and hands so thin that the light shone through them.

"My Prince, in the laws of this state it is laid down that an annual payment shall be made for the upkeep of the church and its services. For my stipend I care little. It is not important since the people bring me food, but the robes of Our Lady are in rags and the floor of the church is so broken as to be dangerous and the organ——" He lifted his hands and dropped them again. "My Prince, the church has received no payment from the state for nearly five years."

"Why is that?" said the Prince to his red-haired Chancellor.

"There is no money," said d'Ecosse bluntly.

"I thought," said Prince André, "that there was a levy for the benefit of the church upon all wine sold in this state. Am I right?"

"In theory, yes, my Prince," said d'Ecosse.

"But there is a gap between theory and practice?" The Prince looked at a fat bullet-headed man who sat at the far end on the left. "Henri Tonnerre, winegrower and innkeeper, speak your mind."

The fat man rose, bobbed his head, and answered in a dialect so thick that Brown had difficulty in following it.

"My Prince. If I and those who follow my trade was paid in money, it would be easy to pay the reverend his tenth. But, as all know, we Sainte-Rocheans do not use money all that much. Men come to me with a pig or six fowls or a basket of eggs and say, 'Tonnerre, that is wine for me for a month, for six months,' according. That is well for me. I keep an inn—the pig goes in a sty and the fowls in my yard till I need them. But the reverend here cannot pave his church with tenths of a fowl, still less with eggs."

The curé shook his head, smiling. "My Prince, I think sometimes that if I am brought many more eggs I shall cluck instead of preaching."

"I see your difficulty. Jean Latour, farmer and stockbreeder, if you have any suggestion to make, speak your mind."

A horsy-looking man with a weather-beaten face rose to his feet.

"My Prince, I am sorry. I think my trade deals more in barter than any other. I fear I can make no useful suggestion."

"But we have a currency," said the Prince. "Where is all the money? Louis Durand, our postmaster, if you can answer this, speak your mind."

The postmaster was a tall thin man with pale blue eyes and a dreamy expression. Brown thought that he had never seen a man who looked less like the postmaster of a busy office.

"My Prince. For what my opinion is worth, the coins of this realm are in boxes under beds or other safe hiding places. For if a man can save up a little, what else can he store it in but coins? Eggs grow stale, fowls grow old, pigs——" He paused.

"We will pass over what happens to pigs when they are kept too long," said the Prince briskly. "We take your point, Durand. We have now reached the question of whether there is any means of inducing our people to produce any of their hoarded money."

There was dead silence and no one moved.

"I had, as you all know, an English tutor for part of my educational process and a French tutor for the rest. Both of them talked to me about what they called systems of taxation. May I have your views about the results of introducing some system of taxation payable only in currency?"

"Riots," said the editor.

"Murder," said the farmer.

"Revolt," said the postmaster.

"Revolution," said the innkeeper.

"Dear me," said the Prince blandly.

"It was tried," said the schoolmaster, the Chancellor, "in 1474. The result was an immediate uprising culminating in a furious attempt to burn the Town Hall. It was then that so much damage was done to the great main doors that they had to be shored up. That is why we still use the little door on the south side, because the great doors are shored up."

"And the taxation," prompted Prince André.

"Was immediately remitted, my Prince."

"Very wise too. But that is—what—four hundred and eighty-three years ago. Do you not think, Chancellor, that all that may have been forgotten by now?"

"With respect, no, my Prince."

"Father Denys?"

"In the memory of an illiterate peasantry, five hundred years are but as yesterday, my son."

"My Prince," said the innkeeper, "only last week there was a man mentioned it in my bar, saying as the front man on the battering-ram had the same name as himself and was, to his mind, one of his forbears."

"I am obliged to you all for this frank expression of your views," said the Prince briskly. "I have, of course, known this story from my childhood but I was anxious to learn if it had any bearing upon the present day. It has. Very well. By the way, before leaving this subject, how do we pay our salaries, Chancellor? In eggs?"

"In currency, my Prince. There was a large amount minted in your grandfather's time, and though it is getting low it is not yet exhausted."

"And when we pay it out, where does it go?"

"I agree with the postmaster, my Prince. Into boxes under beds."

"I see," said the Prince, and looked thoughtfully up at the great roof beams overhead while his Council looked steadily down at their hands—all except the curé, who merely looked amused.

"Well, now," said Prince André, "since we cannot raise money within the country, we must get it in from outside. Any suggestions?"

There was a short pause till the innkeeper looked round. "Henri Tonnerre, speak your mind."

"My Prince, I don't myself understand these things, but we have always done very well out of stamps."

The postmaster and the Chancellor shook their heads simultaneously.

"Postmaster Louis Durand, speak your mind."

"My Prince, it is true that we have done well in the past, but the last issue brought in hardly enough to pay the printers."

"Why is that, do you think?"

"We have put out four issues a year for the last nine years, and I suppose people outside are tired of them."

"Chancellor?"

"I agree with Durand, my Prince. We did very well last year over a mistake in the printing of that very charming picture of the main drain outfall. It came out upside down if Your Highness remembers."

"I do. I thought it rather an improvement."

The curé drew his hand over his mouth and chin, but the Prince's expression did not alter.

"We noticed the mistake and kept back the faulty sheets——"

"Thirty in all," broke in the postmaster. "My Prince, I counted them, to make a complaint. But one went out along with the correct printings by mistake—my mistake, I admit it—and for some reason the faulty sheet sold again and again for the most fantastic prices."

"Your foreign clients agreed with my artistic preference, you think?" asked the Prince dryly.

"So naturally I sent off the other twenty-nine sheets," continued the postmaster, "but to my disappointment they did not sell at all well."

"My Prince," said the Chancellor, "in my poor opinion the one faulty sheet had scarcity value which was destroyed when twenty-nine more followed it."

"But what was worse, my Prince," said the postmaster, "two subsequent issues, showing a young goat and an old goat respectively, hardly sold at all."

"You surprise me," said Prince André. "Still, one must bow to economic fact. Stamps are out. What else?"

There was dead silence which the Prince eventually broke.

"Father Denys, our revered curé. You are from the outside world and you have visited it frequently since you came here to bless us with your presence." Father Denys looked affectionately at the young man. "Can you, of your wider knowledge, advise us in this matter? What can we export that the outside world would wish to buy?"

"I wish I could help you, my son. I have not visited the outside world since the bridge fell down fourteen years ago—that goat's road out is not for an infirm old man. But I have correspondents and I sometimes see a newspaper. I do not think that in day-to-day matters the world has changed much. I cannot think of anything you can supply which the outside world cannot provide as well or better for themselves. Your riches are in your marvellous scenery, your peaceful lives, and your own contented hearts. Such things are not exportable."

"Thank you, Father——"

"But I have one suggestion to make, my son. You ask me for news of the outside world; why me, when there stands behind your chair one who, I understand, has not only just come from thence but has actually lived in the great cities of London and Paris. Am I right?"

Brown hesitated but the Prince said: "Speak, Robert."

"It is true, Father," said Brown. "I was born in London and have also lived in Paris."

"I was born in Paris eighty-one years ago," said the curé quietly. "You and I will talk together of Paris at some convenient time, if you please."

Brown bowed.

"It is no part of my duty," said Prince André, "to dictate to this Council whom they should hear, but it is in your statutes that the Six may call upon any man of good repute to give expert advice upon any matter which is not within the Council's personal knowledge. Is it your wish that Robert should be asked if he has any suggestion to make?" He looked round the Council. "Those in favour?"

Six hands went up.

CHAPTER III

Robert Lights a Bonfire

Robert Brown took two paces forward, bowed deeply to the Prince and generally to the Six, folded his hands before him, and paused for a moment to collect his thoughts.

"Your Highness, gentlemen. I am not sure—I have no idea at all—how much is known in Sainte-Roche of the struggle between communism and Western democracy."

The Prince's eyebrows went up; whatever he had expected it was not this. He exchanged glances with the curé, looked at his Chancellor and then at Brown.

"It will be better to assume that none of us knows anything, but condense your remarks as much as possible."

"Certainly, Your Highness. Put as briefly as possible, the tyrannical principles of Russian communism have spread across half the Northern Hemisphere and are being contained within bounds, with difficulty, by the great democracies of the British Commonwealth, the United States of America, and what might be described as the more civilized countries of Europe. The difficulty I mentioned is occasioned by the tendency of communism to leak out, if I may so put it, of the containing bounds I have just mentioned."

Brown paused and looked round the table. The curé and d'Ecosse, the Chancellor, nodded, and the Prince said: "Very well put," in a faintly surprised voice, but the expressions upon the other four faces were those of men who see themselves being led into alarming mysteries.

"Do you mean," asked the innkeeper, "as there is a war on? I do not believe it; we should have heard about it."

"There is no war," said Brown. "The struggle is political, not military, as yet," and the curé bent his head and made the sign of the cross. "The Communist method is to encourage discontent and disloyalty in one country after another. There are strikes and revolts, elections in which Communists come to power and—and so on. The Western democracies respond by encouraging by every possible means the side of law and established order in the countries which are being attacked in this way. The principal means they employ is that of supplying money."

Brown stopped again, but no one said anything. After a moment he went on.

"The money is supplied, mainly by the United States of America, to improve the conditions under which the people live. To make roads, build bridges, improve agriculture, repair and increase housing accommodation and preserve ancient buildings, advance education, all these things. This prevents the spread of communism, because happy and contented people do not turn Communist—only those who are poor and in misery."

He paused—for longer this time, and the Prince spoke.

"It is true that we are poor but I believe that we are happy."

"My Prince," said the Chancellor, "I cannot believe that we are being urged to introduce communism in order to induce intervention by the Western powers," and there was a stir all round the table.

"Robert?"

"Your Highness, heaven forbid that we should ever do such a thing. No, no. But we might make a good show of it. If news were sent to the outside world that there was Communist trouble in Sainte-Roche, newspaper reporters would come hurrying from all directions to see for themselves and send back news to their——"

"My Prince——"

"Marcel Avril, editor of the Sainte-Roche *Bulletin*, speak your mind."

"My Prince, of course they would come rushing, but, when they were here, what would they see? A placid and industrious peasantry——"

The Prince lifted his hand. "I have a feeling that Robert has more to say, though I have no idea what it is."

"I thank Your Highness, I have. They would be taken to see a confused battle in progress with much noise of gunfire and shouting and clouds of smoke drifting through the trees. Of course there would be no bullets in the guns, but men would fall, screaming, and be carried off by their comrades. The Prince's Army would advance; after fighting had continued throughout the day, night would fall," said Brown, who had a pictorial imagination, "upon fires in the distance, yells in the dark, dimly seen figures appearing and vanishing in clouds of smoke, and, in the cold light of dawn, strings of disarmed and dejected prisoners being led into captivity. This, Your Highness, is what the newspaper men would report."

Brown paused for breath, and the Prince said that it was an exciting picture, certainly, but what would follow after that?

"Your Highness would receive the congratulations of the whole civilized world and an American mission would be sent to help Your Highness to put this country upon a sound financial basis."

"Suppose they don't," said Latour, the farmer, bluntly.

"We have only to suggest that we must reluctantly accept help offered by the Communists if none other is forthcoming, and it will be," said Brown confidently. "It always is."

"I see one small obstacle," said the Prince with a laugh. "We have no Army. The last of our Army died, as the Council will remember, in 1898, aged ninety. We have never replaced him. Yes, postmaster?"

"Your Highness, we still have the uniforms."

"Indeed? But are you sure, postmaster, that moth and decay

38

have not robbed us of them in secret during the last—how long is it since they were worn?"

"In 1898 they were last worn, my Prince."

"In 1898? But we had only one soldier then and we have—how many complete uniforms?"

"Fifty-two, my Prince. But the illustrious Private Aristide Le Blanc used to wear them in rotation, week about, since he was all the Army there was for the last ten years of his blameless life."

"Commendable," said the Prince. "Even so, fifty-nine years have elapsed since then."

"Aristide Le Blanc's daughter took charge of them when the old man laid down his musket; since her death her daughter has cared for the uniforms with loving solicitude, Your Highness. They are in excellent condition."

"We are decidedly in debt to Aristide Le Blanc's grand-daughter—who is she?"

"My wife, Your Highness."

"Oh? Oh, indeed. In that case, gentlemen, we may take it that we have uniforms for an army of fifty-two, if we decide to enrol one. But are we not descending upon detail before we have decided upon a general scheme? The suggestion laid before the Council was, if I have it rightly, to stage a sham fight to astonish the Press of various foreign powers. Am I right, Robert?"

"Your Highness has put the whole scheme in a nutshell with, if I may be permitted to say so, unequalled clarity."

The Prince leaned back in his chair and looked from one to another of his Council.

"I do not expect a decision here and now upon so novel a suggestion. I do not desire one. I would suggest that for the moment we should confine ourselves to asking any questions which occur to us as necessary, and thereafter adjourn this meeting for sufficient time to enable us to think it over quietly. Would that be your wish?"

Six hands went up.

"Good," said the Prince. "I will start by asking the first question myself. Louis Durand, postmaster, is our telephone working?"

"My Prince, we spoke to our post town of Py as usual upon the second Thursday in the month, which was Thursday in last week, and it was working perfectly."

Brown's lower jaw dropped and the Prince noticed it.

"Our link with the outside world," he explained kindly, "is a telephone installed in our post office. It is connected to the town of Py and from there to the whole of civilization. An inspiring thought."

Brown called his facial muscles to order.

"Yes, indeed, Your Highness."

"Any more questions?"

A prolonged pause for thought was broken by Jean Latour, representing the farming interest.

"Where would this battle take place?"

The Prince said that that was yet another of those details which would come up for discussion after the question of holding a battle had been decided. First things first.

"By permission, my Prince, but if there's to be armies galumphing about over our crops and guns being fired off to frighten our livestock, we should know about it before we decide to hold a battle. It'll be too late after."

"The choice of a suitable spot for holding battles will naturally be a matter for your decision alone, gentlemen. It will be for you to decide," said the Prince. "I think that before we consider this matter further, Father Denys should tell us whether this scheme is morally permissible."

The curé sat perfectly still for a few moments, looking down at his hands; when he lifted his head there was a flush on his face which suggested mild amusement.

"It would appear, surely, to be a question of giving good value for money. The modern world craves entertainment and is willing to pay well for it. If the entertainment provided by

Sainte-Roche is of a sufficiently high standard, I can see nothing dishonest in the state taking rewards for its efforts."

"The father means," said Chancellor d'Ecosse, "that if the battle is sufficiently—er——"

"Well performed," suggested the Prince.

"I thank Your Highness. Well performed, there will be no ethical objection to it?"

The curé bowed his head and the corners of his mouth were twitching.

"Rehearsals," said the postmaster thoughtfully.

"A script," murmured Marcel Avril, poet and author as well as editor. "A fully detailed script."

The Prince sat up abruptly and the Six all came as it were to attention.

"It is my pleasure," said the Prince, "to thank you for your invaluable counsel."

"Which is no more than our duty," the Six responded as one man, and stood like statues while the Prince rose from his great chair and walked slowly towards the door preceded by the old seneschal with his wand of office and followed by Brown with his hands full of the speeches of welcome.

When once more the Prince and his valet were in the Prince's study and the old seneschal had closed the door behind him, the Prince sank into a deep armchair and looked at Brown.

"Well, now you have started something!"

Brown clasped his hands lightly together before him.

"Your Highness, with deep respect I trust that my few remarks did not in any way exceed Your Highness' wishes. With respect, I did not wish to speak——"

"Robert——"

Brown waited in silence. A wood fire had been lighted in the open hearth and the Prince turned his face towards the flames which threw a warm light upon his comely features. Brown had thought him old for his age, but in that soft light he looked like a boy.

"Robert, I am twenty-five and I have never left this country.

41

I shall, heaven helping me, do my duty in this place but hitherto I have looked forward with some dread to long years of boredom. There, already I am saying to you what I could not say to any Sainte-Rochean."

"Your Highness——"

"Yes, I know. I have met other foreigners but they were my tutors who taught me what I ought to do. You are the first man to whom I have been able to disclose what I should like to do." The Prince rose to his feet and stood, with a spark of pure mischief in his eyes, looking down upon the square figure of his servant. "I have always wanted to—to enliven things a little, but there was no money and there is my position. You, however, in a short ten minutes before the Six, have inaugurated a reign of inspired lunacy such as Sainte-Roche has never seen in all its generations. Avril has gone off to compose a script of which none of the others will approve and, since there will certainly be long speeches in blank verse, I shall side with the others. Latour, being a farmer, will find fault with whatever is suggested. Tonnerre, who keeps The Goat, will consult his wife, and our postmaster will make indeterminate noises. D'Ecosse with the red beard will be all for it, and Father Denys will drift about in the background and be gently amused by all of us. I don't know whether you realize, Robert, that not a single man in this country has ever been a soldier. Have you?"

"Why, yes, your Highness. That is, I served during the last war in various places."

"You look like being commander in chief."

"Your Highness, heaven forbid if I may make so bold as to suggest it. Surely there must be someone who has had some experience——"

"One. Father Denys, who, whether you believe it or not, was a smart young officer of cuirassiers before he entered religion. Now do you see what you've done?"

"Your Highness can always disown my suggestion, which has, indeed, many objections which could be——"

"But I don't want to! No, Robert, you have started the bonfire, and I shall spend happy days adding fuel to it. Tomorrow I will personally conduct you round the castle armoury. How much do you know about flintlock muskets?"

"N–nothing, Your Highness."

"You will, Robert, you will."

In the meantime the Six were walking slowly down the steps from terrace to terrace on their way home.

"If the uniforms are worn," said the postmaster, "they will be soiled and even, possibly, torn. My wife will not like it."

"What is needed," said Avril, "are some heart-stirring and inspiring speeches such as leaders of old were accustomed to address to their troops before battle. Henri Quatre, before Ivry——"

"I agree the necessity for action," said d'Ecosse, "but not for speeches."

"Great care," said Latour, "must be exercised in delimiting the area of conflict so as to obviate any risk of damage to property or livestock."

"I am not sure whether I like this idea at all," said Louis Durand, postmaster. "I am a man of peace and so is my wife."

"The project is not yet finally decided," the curé reminded them.

"That is true," said the postmaster gratefully.

"Then will you kindly suggest a better?" said d'Ecosse. "For money we must have."

"What is needed is a touch of poetic imagination——"

"Of course, an army will need food and drink."

"The uniforms——"

CHAPTER IV

Tell the World

It was precisely four months to the day from Brown's arrival in Sainte-Roche when the preparations for holding the battle could be called complete; of these four months it is fair to say that two were spent in argument. At last the rehearsals, always held on Sunday afternoons after Mass, were running fairly smoothly. Every repeat performance had its variations as different participants worked off their bright ideas; the only occasion to prove a complete failure being when farmer Grosgrain's cowherd released a frisky young bull against the Communist menace. This brought one rehearsal to an abrupt end as Communists and Loyalists alike fled and left the stricken field to the bull.

At last the gunpowder factory, run as a side line by the village cobbler because his father and grandfather had run it before him, had accumulated a sufficient store of gunpowder to supply both the opposing forces throughout twenty-four hours of hotly contested conflict.

"It cannot go on for twenty-four hours," said farmer Latour crossly. "Who will milk the cows—feed the pigs—shut up the hens——"

"If I may venture to put in a word," said Brown, "it is not necessary to assume that the battle will last for twenty-four hours. The emergency which His Highness had in mind in giving that as the duration was, if I understood him correctly, the probability of twenty-four hours' ammunition being fired off in less than half that time. Even well-trained troops have been known to transgress in that manner under the influence of excitement, Monsieur Latour; how much more our well-intentioned but scarcely disciplined levies."

"How you do talk," said Latour. "I've got work to do." But it was noticeable that Latour never missed a rehearsal in his part as captain of Loyal Irregulars, the Sainte-Rochean Home Guard, with armbands. D'Ecosse commanded the Army, all fifty-one of them. He needed the fifty-second uniform himself.

The Communists were distinguishable by a studied negligence in dress, a particular grubbiness of face and hands, and strips of red rag tied round their arms. When the rehearsals ended and the combatants strolled home to Sunday supper in amicable groups, a casual visitor would have deduced a recent smallpox scare.

At last the muskets in the Palace Armoury were all cleaned up, de-rusted, and put into working order. The Sainte-Roche gunsmith, with two assistants, had done the work, but Brown had found it advisable to carry out inspections.

"But they aren't but for to be carried for show, like, are they?"

"His Highness," said Brown sternly, "particularly desires that they shall all be capable of being fired."

"But there's no bullets being cast."

"No bullets are to be used. Blanks only will be fired."

"Blanks?"

"Balls of hay well rammed in."

"You want wads, not hay. A couple wads, that's what. What's the idea of hay?"

"It makes a bigger bang," said the expert.

The Sainte-Roche doctor, who normally dealt almost exclusively with accident and midwifery cases—the Sainte-Rocheans were disgustingly healthy, he said—entered into the spirit of the affair and commandeered the curé's tithe barn for a hospital. Not much could be done to it except to sweep the cobwebs down and wash the cobbled floor, since nobody had

beds to spare or would lend them if they had; but the red crosses
on the outside walls were both colourful and impressive.

The Prince, upon one of his tours of inspection, put his head
in at the hospital door and said: "What, no straw?"

"Straw, my Prince?"

"To lay the wounded on. The wounded are always laid upon
straw in Napoleonic battles. We are fighting with the weapons
of that date, Doctor. Let us at all cost be consistent."

"There shall be straw. It will at least serve to twine into my
hair if the battle becomes too complicated."

"I do not anticipate a heavy casualty list," said the Prince
solemnly. "My Army will be speedily victorious. At least, I hope
so. What happens if those grubby mountebanks, the Communists, chase my Army off the field?"

"I suggest that Tonnerre at The Goat and Gobain at The
Hunter emerge and ring dinner bells loudly. That will stop the
battle. As for the casualties, I should think there would be
quite a lot. Your Highness, if I may disagree. A couple of hundred men rushing about in the dark will at least fall over
things."

"No doubt you are right. But you have not many facilities
here, have you?"

"I shall treat them at my surgery as usual and then they can
walk up here and lie down in the straw. It's less than a kilometre
from my surgery, and the correspondents will want something
to look at."

"I suggest a few bloodstained bandages," said the Prince, and
the doctor nodded.

"When the time comes, my Prince, I will tell Dupont the
butcher to kill a pig."

Finally, the day came when Brown walked up to the excessively tidy post office and spoke to the postmaster.

"It is time, His Highness says, that a preliminary message is
sent hinting at internal trouble in Sainte-Roche. Here is the
message which His Highness wishes to have despatched."

"But——" said the postmaster.

"But?"

"I do not myself send the messages. His Highness knows that."

"But a postmaster with a telephone in his office——"

"—is not necessarily a telephonic engineer. I am not. A postmaster sells stamps. I sell stamps."

"No doubt," said Brown, "Monsieur also collects and delivers the mails?"

"Me? Certainly not. The schoolmaster collects them at a suitable interval after the doctor has delivered them."

Brown put his hand to his head. "The doctor——"

"Monsieur is a stranger; he does not know our ways."

"Too right, I don't," said Brown in English.

"*Pardon?* No doubt things are different in foreign lands. And the little girls, too, of course."

"The little girls deliver the letters?"

"Letters? We do not have letters in Sainte-Roche—not by post that is. Too many of our people cannot read and, between people who can, it is quicker to send a messenger."

"Then what do you do with the stamps?"

"Sell them to foreign countries, of course. Monsieur heard a reference to that at the first meeting of the Six which he attended."

"Very true. Now, if we may return to the subject of this telephone message. May I know who is the telephonic engineer?"

"Marcel Avril, naturally, in his capacity as journalist."

"Naturally," said Brown, a little breathlessly. "I should have thought of that. Where, at this time of day, may I hope to find Monsieur Avril?"

"In his office at this time of day," said Durand, courteously accompanying Brown to the door. "Three houses down on the left there is a narrow passage. At the far end of the passage, the editorial office of Monsieur Avril."

"A thousand thanks," said Brown, turning away.

"One would be more than enough for so small a service," said the postmaster courteously.

Brown walked down the passage and found that it emerged in a small paved yard with high walls upon either hand and, facing him, a wooden building with a row of large windows and a door. Above the windows there was a board inscribed "Sainte-Roche *Bulletin*"; upon the door a printed card in a wide variety of fancy types announced the Editorial Office, Editor Marcel Avril, Associate of the Havas Agency, Paris. Below the announcement there appeared a small halftone picture of a cherub with wings.

"Mercury when young," said Brown to himself, and knocked upon the door; a voice called him to come in. He opened the door and entered. Marcel Avril sat at a wildly littered desk near the door with a pen in his hand; behind him dust sheets covered large and unshapely lumps presumably the printing machines. There was a smell of oil, dust, and printer's ink.

"What a pleasure," said Avril, rising. "Do come in and tell me in what manner I can serve our visitor from the outside world. Do sit down."

He cleared a chair by merely dropping a pile of dusty paper on the floor.

"Thank you so much," said Brown. "Please forgive me if I am in error in applying to you, but the postmaster directed me here. His Highness wants a message sent out by telephone."

"I am the man to whom it should be entrusted; I work the telephone. Yes, yes, you have come to the right man."

"Here is the message."

Avril rose to his feet to take the paper since it was in the Prince's bold angular handwriting, and sat down again to read it aloud.

"Communist Unrest in Sainte-Roche. Rumours of a Communist rising in the peaceful Principality of Sainte-Roche may confidently be disregarded. The noisy but ineffectual demonstrations of a few hotheads have been put down by the arrest of the ringleaders, and order has now been completely restored."

Avril put down the paper, cocked up one dark eyebrow till it nearly touched his hair, and looked at Brown, who explained.

"A preliminary notice only, of course. A *ballon d'essai*, if I may so put it. Merely the opening shot, Monsieur Avril, of the press campaign."

"Very good," said Avril slowly. "Very clever. Our young Prince has a surprising grasp of the essentials of publicity."

"His Highness," said Brown, "has a brilliant brain and an astonishing perception of affairs."

"Yes, yes indeed. We are singularly fortunate. This message will be followed——"

"With others at proper intervals, conveying——"

"—an increasingly alarming view——" said Avril.

"—culminating, in three or four days' time, in a rousing story of treachery and bloodshed manfully resisted by a gallant young Prince and his faithful adherents."

"A tale to stir the blood," said Avril eagerly. "A subject for sagas, for epics. Ballads shall be sung about it."

"No doubt. Well, there is the first, Monsieur Avril. His Highness desires that it shall go today."

"At once," said Avril, rising so impetuously that he knocked his chair over and did not wait to pick it up. "My hat—here it is. Shall we go?"

"This telephone," said Brown, "is it then so complicated to work?"

"Not at all, but our good Durand at his first attempt gave himself an electric shock and refused to touch it again. Besides, after all, it is usually I who wish to use it. After you, my dear monsieur, after you."

Brown left Avril earnestly calling up the Havas Agency in Paris and walked back to the Palace. On the topmost terrace he found Prince André sitting on the balustrade watching six men who were loading into a waggon the two brass cannon which guarded the head of the stairway.

"Ah, Robert."

"Your Highness?"

49

"My Army has just found itself without artillery. I am, therefore, lending them mine. I suppose it was the right thing to do? All the best armies have artillery."

"Undoubtedly, Your Highness."

"Men! Load the guns' carriages also and be very careful not to lose the wedges. . . . I have also sent a message to the cobbler and his sons to make some more gunpowder. We cannot be short of gunpowder."

"On no account, Your Highness."

"General d'Ecosse had some idea of firing off the guns *in situ*, here, on the terrace, but I dissuaded him."

"If I may presume to say so, a wise decision, Your Highness."

"Window glass is scarce and expensive in Sainte-Roche. Has the telephone message been sent?"

"Monsieur Avril was in the act of transmitting it when I left him, Your Highness."

"Very good. Now to my study and we will draft another for tomorrow."

The Havas Agency sent out the first report, and most European newspapers found half an inch at the bottom of a column which would just take it comfortably without comment. The next day's message said merely that the situation in Sainte-Roche was well in hand and that energetic measures were being taken to prevent a recurrence of the trouble. This news advanced halfway up the page and was followed by a short factual paragraph about the Principality; its geographical position; its form of government—a democratic monarchy; its industries, agriculture, forestry, woollen cloth manufacture, and on a small scale the mining of iron, silver, and lead. Tobacco was grown and processed and there were vineyards. Communication with both France and Spain was difficult and even dangerous.

The next day's bulletin said that firm measures were being taken to deal with the Communist insurrection in Sainte-Roche, that the Parliament (called the Six from the number of its members) was in constant session and that the Prince André had signed a decree calling out the Army Reserve. This news reached the headlines and was supported by such details as haggard sub-editors could dig out of encyclopaedias. Prince André Amadeus Joseph Theodore, aged 25, whose family was descended from a cadet branch of the House of Savoy. . . .

The British Press took it up, the Commonwealth discussed it over breakfast, in all the Americas the news broke, and the telephone bell in the postmaster's office in Sainte-Roche rang and rang again. Marcel Avril moved a truckle bed into the office and slept there.

"My Prince, the bell now rings at all hours. They are beginning to ask if they are permitted to enter the country."

"What happens if you take off the receiver?"

"They cannot communicate, my Prince."

"Good. Take it off—what is the time? Just on noon—and leave it off until six this evening. I will, by that time, have some more news ready for you. D'Ecosse!"

"My Prince?"

"Warn the Gallienne family, the frontier guide fellows, that two or three visitors to Sainte-Roche may be expected at any time. A watch must be kept for them; they are to be welcomed and treated with courtesy. Send the message at once."

"Very good, my Prince."

At six that evening the Prince himself returned to the post office; the town noticed with surprise that he who normally walked about among them unescorted, like one of themselves, had on this occasion a guard of six of his hunters with guns over their shoulders. Avril opened the door as the Prince approached and entered. The escort waited outside.

"Here is the message, Avril. Read it through to yourself, and then I will tell you how it is to be delivered."

"As the Prince commands," answered Avril, and read the message in silence.

"Now listen," said the Prince, and gave him detailed directions. Avril nodded eagerly with an occasional glance through the open door at the men outside who were looking carefully to the priming of their muskets. Then he lifted the receiver.

51

"Py? Sainte-Roche calling Py. Get me Paris, please. Yes, Paris. . . ."

At the Havas agency in Paris a young man took a telephone message, noting it down in shorthand as it came.

"Sainte-Roche, yes. Yes, this is Havas, carry on please. 'The situation as regards the Communist insurrection is serious but by no means critical. The Loyalist forces, acting with most admirable energy and initiative, have thrown back the enemy from the small and unimportant foothold on the outskirts of the town of which they obtained'—yes, go on, I've got that, 'which they obtained'—'temporary possession during the night. They are now'—*Mon Dieu*, what was that? Sounded like a shot fired. Monsieur Avril, are you all right? What was—there's another!"

There was a short interval of silence.

"Sainte-Roche! Monsieur Avril, what is happening? Nothing important, only a few shots? Yes, go on with the story. 'The insurgents are now being driven back to their hide-out in the hills with the Loyalist forces in pursuit. It is not expected——' "

There followed a crash of breaking glass and a shot so close behind Avril that he started nervously and dropped the receiver, producing a clatter in the Havas man's ear which made him flinch. However, the voice of Sainte-Roche continued at once, breathless and hesitant but determined.

"It is not expected—that the insurgent resistance can last—longer than another twenty-four hours. Already their efforts have the character of the last throes of desperation. The prince bears a charmed life." There came two more shots a little further away. "The battle is moving further away." Sounds of running feet were superimposed upon Avril's voice. "Did you hear that, Havas? That was our Army hastening in pursuit. The surrender of the remaining insurgents is expected within the next few hours. Message ends."

One final shot was heard and the sound of the receiver being replaced.

"Well done," said the Prince. "Men, you can go home now. Avril, my English tutor made me learn a poem beginning: 'The

boy stood on the burning deck, Whence all but he had fled.'
Your performance brought him vividly back to mind."

"When Your Highness smashed the bottle just behind
me——"

"I thought it came in quite well, myself. If that performance
doesn't fetch them, nothing will."

CHAPTER V

Seven Thirsty Men

Soon after midday upon the following afternoon a small boy of the Gallienne family arrived in the town of Sainte-Roche, riding upon a pony which belonged to another family who had not been consulted. The small boy had been sent with a message, "go and tell them in the town." He had not been told to address himself to any particular person, so he drew up the pony with a clatter of hoofs upon the paving stones of the market square and shouted: "News! News! I bear news," in a high shrill voice which brought everyone running out of the houses.

"News? What news? Who is the brat? What news? What about? Speak, you limb of Satan!"

D'Ecosse came with long strides from the school and recognized one of his pupils who should have been in class.

"Jean-Louis Gallienne, what are you doing stuck up on that pony like a sparrow on a pig's back when you ought to be in school?"

"News! I bear news!"

"Get off that pony which, in any case, belongs to the family Tarri and not to yours, and come with me."

D'Ecosse took his pupil by the ear, led him into the post office, and shut the door behind them.

"This urchin says he has news."

"News!" said Marcel Avril, abandoning a half-finished poem to become a journalist once more. "Out with it, imp."

"G–good news?" said the postmaster nervously.

"My father sent me, saying go, tell them in the town that the travellers arrive."

"Who are they?" asked Avril.

"Foreigners—how should I know?"

"How many?" barked d'Ecosse.

"We do not know. We did but look across the broken bridge at them and they were all about, at the end of the bridge and among the bushes. They are without number, like bees."

"Nonsense. You always exaggerate, Jean-Louis."

"But, monsieur! How can one count people dodging about behind bushes?"

"One cannot, of course," said the postmaster. "There are always more than one sees. Are there fifty, boy? Oh, what shall we do?"

"Nonsense," said d'Ecosse again. "This boy is the biggest liar in my school, and that is saying something."

"They demand that the bridge be instantly repaired."

D'Ecosse, Avril, and the postmaster replied in exact chorus with the Sainte-Rochean equivalent of "what a hope!" What they actually said, being half Spanish, was: "This bone to another dog."

"My father, my two uncles, and three of my cousins have gone across to reason with them."

"To bargain with them," corrected d'Ecosse. "Go back at once to your family, Jean-Louis, and tell them that these strangers are to be courteously treated and not robbed. I speak as Chancellor. As your headmaster, put that pony back where you found him and apologize to the family Tarri. Go!"

Jean-Louis went, but not so fast as to prevent his telling the news to the townspeople as he mounted.

"Fifty strangers!" lamented the postmaster. "It is an army! What shall we do?"

"We shall not lose our heads, for a start, postmaster," said d'Ecosse severely. "For another, we need not believe what that little liar says. I shall be very much surprised if there are a dozen of them. Avril, you are busy with the telephone?"

55

"Not if I can help you in any way," said Avril. "This telephone, *je m'en fiche*. It can ring. For me, I have no message to give as yet today."

"The novelty has worn off, eh?" suggested d'Ecosse.

"For me, I do not touch the machine," said the postmaster firmly.

"If you would be so good as to tell Tonnerre at The Goat, Avril, that visitors are expected," said d'Ecosse, "I will go and inform His Highness."

"Certainly," said Avril, "though I have no doubt that they have heard already. Your young friend is still addressing an audience." He pointed out of the window at the tousled black head of Jean-Louis on his pony above the heads of a ring of listeners.

D'Ecosse flung the door open and bellowed: "Jean-Louis!" in so menacing a tone that the pony took fright and bolted with the boy clinging round its neck. "It will be a hundred strangers by now."

"I was always against this wildcat scheme," said the postmaster bitterly.

Avril pointed out that he had provided the uniforms, but Durand merely walked through the inner door of the post office and locked it after him.

"He is feeling a draught," said Avril, coming out upon the street.

"Strongly non-collaborationist," agreed d'Ecosse, and they went their separate ways.

Halfway up the terrace stairway to the Palace, d'Ecosse met Prince André coming down.

"Good day, Chancellor. What is this I hear about a compact horde of several hundred foreigners besieging our frontier?"

"Blast that boy! My Prince, I beg Your Highness' pardon."

"Not at all. Pray don't apologize. I did not believe it. I also know the Gallienne family. How many journalists are there do you think? Half a dozen?"

"There might be ten," said d'Ecosse cautiously.

"Five francs my guess is nearer than yours."

"Done, my Prince."

Towards evening, as the shadows were lengthening, the distant sound of a hunting horn came faintly to the ears of those who were listening for it. It signalled the arrival at the edge of the forest three miles away of a procession of mules. They paused, as Brown had paused when he first arrived, at the point where the track through the forest came out into the open valley, because it is quite impossible to come suddenly upon that scene and not stop to feast the eyes upon it. The company stared, wide-eyed, till a few minutes later their absorption was rudely broken by the sound of a horn.

"What is that?"

"We go on," said Jean-Alphonse Gallienne. "Forward, messieurs, please."

"Was that a signal?"

"Certainly, messieurs. A signal that it is safe for us to proceed. Forward, then."

The string of mules ambled on its way.

In the market place of Sainte-Roche three of the Six were waiting to receive their visitors. Jean Latour, farmer, was not there, because it was milking time; Father Denys was not present, because it was the hour of vespers; the postmaster was also absent from public view, though present behind his bedroom curtains, peering out. There were, therefore, d'Ecosse, Avril, and Henri Tonnerre, landlord of The Goat. To them there came from the Palace the dignified form of Robert Brown in a neat blue serge suit and polished black shoes, wearing a bowler hat and carrying a neatly rolled umbrella.

"His Highness," said Brown, "directed me to offer my services as interpreter in the event of any of our visitors not being conversant with the French language, if agreeable to you, messieurs. The decision whether or not to make use of my services rests, of course, entirely with you, and I will retire at once should you so desire."

"I am glad to see you," said d'Ecosse. "Some such difficulty had occurred to me."

"Stay by me," begged Tonnerre, "for if I'm to put up these people it'll be a fine thing if they can't understand a word I say. Or me them, either."

"I will support you," promised Brown, "for as long as my duties at the Palace will permit."

The sun went down behind the encircling hills and at once the twilight rushed in as it does in mountain valleys, but no lights appeared in any of the houses, because all the townspeople were out lining the sides of the square, among them some tall men in the blue uniform with red facings of the Army of Sainte-Roche. These men had their kepis tilted over their left eyebrows and leaned casually upon their muskets.

"They come," said someone, and the word went round the square, "they come," and all faces turned towards the corner of the road from France.

A mule, ridden by Jean-Alphonse Gallienne, turned the corner and advanced into the middle of the square. It was closely followed by another and another and yet more, ridden by strangers. They came to the group by the central fountain and pulled up, one after another.

"The visitors," said Jean-Alphonse with a spacious gesture, and d'Ecosse stepped forward with the first sentence of a speech of welcome ready upon his lips. It was not destined to be uttered, for a tall man at the head of the party leaned from his saddle and spoke first, in a carrying voice audible all over the square.

"Good evening," he said. "Am I right in assuming that we have now arrived at the capital city of this interesting Principality?"

Since he spoke in English, d'Ecosse beckoned Brown forward.

"Yes, sir," he said. "This is the town of Sainte-Roche. The townspeople——"

The rider turned in his saddle and addressed his company.

"It's all right. We're here." Then, to Brown, "Would you kindly direct us to the best hotel?"

"How many," said Tonnerre, digging Brown hard in the ribs, for he recognized the word hotel, "how many are there? Ask him!"

Brown translated.

"Seven," said the rider. "Seven thirsty, hungry, weary travellers, some with blisters and some without. Where is the nearest bar?"

"What is all this?" demanded d'Ecosse. "I have a speech of welcome——"

"They are travel-worn and exhausted," explained Brown. "They are asking for instant refreshment. I think the speech——"

"Look," said the tall rider, "can we do without the formalities and find a bar? Don't, now don't say there isn't a hotel in this wonderful old-world place?"

"Hotel," said Tonnerre, pointing across the square, "hotel, hotel." He seized the mule's bridle and led the procession towards The Goat. The others fell in behind.

"Cannot any of them speak French?" said Avril, and repeated it more loudly. "Can any of you gentlemen speak French? I am accredited correspondent of Havas Agency."

"Monsieur," said the fourth rider in the cavalcade, "permit that I salute a brother journalist. I represent *Paris-Soir*, monsieur. One moment while I alight from this uncivilized form of transport. Ah, what a relief! Come, monsieur, of your charity, with me wherever I am being led, for I am far from home."

They linked arms and disappeared after the others into the wide innyard of The Goat.

The concourse in the square drifted away and lights sprang up in all the little houses. Brown had vanished into the inn with the travellers, and in five minutes the market place was empty but for one solitary figure leaning against the central fountain in the gathering shadows.

"It is, in any case, a waste of time making speeches of wel-

come in a tongue incomprehensible to those to whom they are
addressed," said d'Ecosse. He folded a paper which he was
holding in his hand, put it carefully into his pocket, and
walked home alone.

Prince André was breakfasting in the morning sunshine on
the terrace outside the Palace, and Brown was attending to his
needs.

"Now tell me, Robert, exactly what happened last night."

"They came——"

"How many of them?"

"Seven, Your——"

"Five francs," said the Prince firmly, "and it will be in the
currency of the country. I have eggs of my own."

"Your Highness' pardon?"

"Nothing. Go on."

"The gentlemen were conducted to The Goat tavern, which
in some respects appeared to surprise them, if I may so put it,
Your Highness. They——"

"Were struck dumb?"

"On the contrary. They were misled by the hens pecking
about the kitchen floor into thinking that they were in the
stables, but Monsieur Avril and I were able to dissuade them
from vacating the premises. This success was largely due, Your
Highness, to Monsieur Tonnerre's picturesque description of
conditions at The Hunter, the only alternative open to them.
They would, he said, only be exchanging hens for small piglets,
if I have the agricultural term correctly. It would appear, Your
Highness, that Gobain's sow died in childbed and Madame
Gobain is rearing the offspring by hand."

"Very creditable of her. The journalists might have helped
with the feeding bottles."

"They decided to remain where they were, and we led them
into the dining room——"

"Where, I trust, there were no hens."

"No, indeed, Your Highness. Tonnerre brought liquid

refreshment of which they were pleased to approve. The meal, when it was served, surpassed my expectations to a remarkable degree, if I may be permitted to say so. There was a ragout of veal which——"

"I take it that you tested the food in the only practical way?"

"I considered it my duty, Your Highness, to partake of a small quantity, and found it delicious."

"Madame Tonnerre was once the cook here, in the Palace, until that rogue Tonnerre induced her to marry him. I have never been so well served since."

"Indeed, Your Highness. Most unfortunate."

"Go on, Robert."

"The journalists were pleased with both food and wine, but their transports were considerably moderated when they were introduced to the sanitary arrangements. They asked to be shown the bathroom also. I would not venture to repeat to Your Highness what they said when Tonnerre showed them the pump in the yard."

"I will not embarrass you by insisting upon it."

"I thank Your Highness." Brown refilled the Prince's coffee cup. "By the time they saw the sleeping accommodation their critical faculties were, if I may so express it, at once mellowed and blunted by their previous buffeting by the winds of circumstance, if I may be permitted a poetic metaphor for a somewhat unpoetic predicament, Your Highness."

"I hope the beds were clean," said the Prince a little anxiously. "We do not want them to find us quite revolting."

"The rooms appeared reasonably clean, and Madame Tonnerre assured the guests that the hens were never allowed upstairs."

"Splendid."

"It was after that," said Brown a little diffidently, "that certain problems began to arise. They wanted to go out and see the town. We—Monsieur Avril and I—endeavoured to dissuade them, Your Highness, and fortunately at that point Monsieur d'Ecosse came in, in army uniform, to add the weight of his

61

military authority to our entreaties. He said that they must realize that if they were shot it would embroil us in an international incident of a most serious nature, and that if his orders were not obeyed he would consider it his duty, as commander, to put them under arrest. If it is not a liberty, Your Highness, I should like to be allowed to add how much I admired his authoritative bearing."

"I am sure you did, but did they?"

"Not without argument, Your Highness, in the course of which three of them slipped out before we could prevent it. The night was almost excessively dark," said Brown reminiscently. "That, if I may hazard a guess, was the only reason why they did not all go."

"And the daring three?"

"One wandered into the graveyard and the sexton heard him asking, with perfect politeness, a lady to direct him to The Goat."

"A lady——"

"The angel upon the enclosure reserved, I am given to understand, for the family Tarri. He discerned her dimly by starlight, Your Highness. The second gave up the venture and returned safely. The third was less fortunate; he fell into the main sewer outfall and was assisted out by one of the Army. The journalist was unhurt, Your Highness, but when he returned to The Goat his companions objected to his presence upon the grounds of olfactory inconvenience. He retired to bed, Your Highness, while one of the serving wenches washed his trousers."

"What is happening this morning? It all," said the Prince, turning from the table to light the first cigarette of the day, "looks extremely peaceful. Too peaceful, Robert, surely. I see men loading sacks at the mill, Latour's cows are entering their pasture, Durand's wife is feeding her hens, and Father Denys is returning from the church to his house for breakfast." The Prince sat down upon the balustrade. "Would anyone believe, Robert, that we have a war in progress?"

"It is all arranged, Your Highness. Monsieur d'Ecosse and I

discussed plans for the day after putting the journalists to bed."

"Putting the——"

"With Your Highness' approval, as we hoped. It is not to be expected that they will rise early today. As soon as they do, a signal will be given from an upper window at The Goat and a demonstration, if I quote Monsieur d'Ecosse correctly, will be audible from the woods. Gunfire and also the cannon, if I understand his intentions."

"You'll never keep those fellows within doors when they hear that, Robert."

"No such attempt will be made, Your Highness. The Army are surrounding the town. It was suggested that, if Your Highness would kindly excuse my attendance for a couple of hours this morning, I should conduct the party round the town and show them the church, the Town Hall, the wool spinners behind the mill, and other objects of interest, if Your Highness approves?"

"Certainly, but you'll never keep those fellows quiet for two solid hours in a place this size. Bring them up here, Robert, and I'll hold a—what do they call it?"

"A press conference, perhaps——"

"A press conference. This afternoon, what will happen?"

"If Your Highness approves, Monsieur d'Ecosse proposes to hold the battle. It cannot be long delayed, he says, because the—the participants are becoming dissatisfied at being kept from their own work. The harvest, it would appear, is imminent, Your Highness."

CHAPTER VI

The Battle

The journalists came down to breakfast, and a sheet was hung from an attic window of The Goat. Since they did not appear to require much beyond several strong cups of coffee each, they were taking turns at the pump in the yard or at Tonnerre's six square inches of shaving mirror above the kitchen sink before they were disturbed.

"You boys hear anything in the night?" asked the tall American. He turned to an English colleague. "Be a good scout and work that pump handle for me while I put my head under, and I'll do it for you. This is the primitive life all right."

"Close to the bosom of Mother Nature and all that," said the Englishman, laying hold of the pump handle.

"Ouch! Not so darned hard. I want to be washed, not washed away——"

"Sorry. No, I didn't hear anything. This is, without exception, the quietest war I have ever been in."

"It is," said the Belgian, who was waiting to fill a basin, "the sound of aircraft which is so oddly absent from——"

"What's that?" said the Englishman, and stopped pumping. "I heard a shot—there's another——"

Boom!

"Artillery of a sort," said the American, abandoning the pursuit of cleanliness to hurl himself into his shirt, "though I never heard quite that sort of noise come out of a gun in battle before. It reminds me—what does it remind you of?"

"Here, don't run off, you're going to operate my bath," said the Englishman. "It reminds me of the starting guns at Cowes Castle in regatta week. Pump a bit harder."

"Brass cannon starting off yacht races?" said the American, bending to his task. "You might have something there. That's enough, certainly. Come on."

Boom!

The inn was full of voices protesting in six languages because Avril was trying to explain that a visit to the battle would be personally conducted that afternoon, after lunch. Not yet, on no account yet. A battle must be allowed to settle down, to locate itself, to develop into a well-defined combat——

"Oh, nuts," said the American, removing Avril bodily from the doorway and rushing out, followed by the other six. They ran across the square and disappeared down various alleys.

Avril wrung his hands. "I was to stop them, but they would not hear me. Alas, I have failed——"

"If I might suggest," said Brown's voice just behind him, "a small glass of wine is known to have beneficial effects at moments of crisis. Let us go in. Madame, two glasses, if you please, of that golden wine we were enjoying last night. Monsieur Avril, let me beg you to calm yourself. The Army will bring them all back here in a short time; it is all arranged. Quite a fusillade appears to be in progress at the moment, does it not? A cigarette, Monsieur Avril? Ah, thank you, madame. Monsieur Avril, your very good health. We are singularly fortunate, if I may say so, in the weather today, are we not?"

Avril gasped, drank some of his wine, drew on his cigarette, and relaxed perceptibly.

"Are—are you sure it is all right? They won't escape?"

"They will all be back here in ten minutes," said Brown with calm authority.

He was right; they were. Ruffled and protesting, they came in one by one under army escort. A few minutes later d'Ecosse looked in, he had added lustre to his military appearance with a long sword at his side.

"Tell them," he said abruptly to Brown, "that if I have any more trouble with them I will put them in the cells under the Town Hall. Is not one enemy at a time enough?"

He slammed the door; through the window they saw him beckon to someone and stalk away with long strides. From left to right across the square there passed a half company of soldiers in uniform, running after him, and once more the market square was empty in the sunshine.

"This is absolutely unendurable——"

"Gentlemen, gentlemen," said Brown, "if I may put in a word—gentlemen, please——"

"Well?"

"War correspondents are invariably kept to the rear by all of the best commanders," urged Brown.

"He's right, you know," said the Englishman.

"In a real war, maybe, but not in a ten-cent fancy-dress ploughboys' outing like this! Call this a war! I haven't seen one guy yet who can shoulder arms if you call those museum antiquities——"

"Gentlemen! May I be permitted to point out that the commander meant exactly what he said and, if I may make myself clear, then some. Arrangements have been made to conduct you to the scene of conflict this afternoon when you will be able to—er—tour the battlefields. Lunch will be served here at a little after midday. In the meantime I shall be happy to show you round this interesting and historic town until eleven o'clock, at which hour His Highness Prince André has graciously promised to receive you all in audience. Thank you, gentlemen."

"That's a promise, that we go out to the battle this afternoon and no kidding or stalling?"

"It is, gentlemen."

"In that case——"

"Thank you, gentlemen. This way, please. We shall first visit the church where the Reverend Father Denys awaits us. Built in the eleventh century——"

The morning passed off fairly well, though it is possible that both Brown and his conducted party found it rather long. One of the places visited was the newspaper office and printing works, Marcel Avril receiving them in person. This was really the most successful moment of the tour; the visitors were so deeply impressed as to be practically speechless. Avril cast off the dust sheets from his machines and displayed them with a simple pride which it would have been inhuman to undermine.

"Well, well!"

"*Epatant! Magnifique!*"

"*Unglaublich! Fabelhaft!*"

"*Maravilloso!*"

"Ask him, will you," said the American to Brown, "does he actually print and produce his newspaper on these machines which we see before us?"

Avril proudly replied that he did.

"What, not daily? Don't tell me he goes through all that suffering every day. Weekly, I assume?"

"The Sainte-Roche *Bulletin* does not come out at regular intervals but only when there is some news to put in it."

"What?" said the Englishman weakly.

"It is of no use publishing a paper with no news in it. No one would wish to buy it."

"You know," said the American darkly, "he's got something there."

After this, even the visit to the Palace to meet one of the few crowned heads in Europe was almost an anti-climax. The Prince received them with all the charm which Nature had so generously bestowed on him and offered a variety of drinks which went down even better than the charm. He glanced at the clock and then at Brown and proceeded "at the risk of boring you, gentlemen, pray forgive me," to address them on the subject of Sainte-Roche's economic difficulties, which were, of course, the reason for the unrest in the land. "My people are not wicked, gentlemen, or greedy, or savage, but they are desperately poor. In such soil evil seeds grow apace, but we shall root them

67

out." When the press conference began to fidget the Prince invited questions, when these came to an end he glanced at the clock again and took the party for a tour of the reception rooms, the Great Hall and the Armoury, with many bare spaces on its walls which he did not attempt to explain. When the clock struck twelve he took leave of them at the head of the terrace steps.

"You are due for lunch now, I believe? I wish you a good appetite, gentlemen. After lunch I understand you are to be taken to see the battle. Be careful, gentlemen, no accidents, please. Write kindly, I beg, about my poor country. Good-bye, gentlemen, good-bye."

At two o'clock there came a small party to the door of The Goat, the Prince's six hunters in their picturesque green uniforms with silver buckles on their belts and the badge, in silver, of the Prince's house on their left breasts. They carried rifles under their arms and were led by Marcel Avril with a dagger in his belt. He opened the inn door, stepped inside, and nodded to Brown.

"If you are ready, gentlemen," said Brown.

The journalists sprang to their feet as one man and only delayed to sling cameras about their persons.

"Where's the transport?"

"Your feet, messieurs. It is not far and, in any case, there are no roads where we go," said Avril.

"Lead on," said the American cheerfully. He came out of the doorway and was faced with the six hunters. "Well, now, see who's here. Who are they, anyway?"

"The Prince," said Brown, "anxious for the safety of those who are in a sense, if I may so put it, the guests of his country, has sent these men of his personal bodyguard to ensure that no harm should befall any sojourner within his realm."

"You," said the Englishman with conviction, "should draft public announcements for politicians."

"Thank you, sir."

The party moved off with the hunters leading. Avril and Brown brought up the rear.

"May I take it," said Brown in a low voice, "that those men have their orders?"

"Oh yes. It is all arranged. Besides, Nature is going to lend a helping hand—look."

Avril nodded towards the mountaintops ahead of them, and Brown saw that they had disappeared from sight.

"Mist?"

"Low cloud. It rolls down. Most helpful."

The party began to climb, first through steep meadows and then among trees; as they entered them the battle broke out ahead with most imposing fury. Gunfire roared just out of sight, the cannon boomed again and again, and the mountain echoes multiplied the sound. Smoke drifted through the trees and quite a lot of it smelt strongly of gunpowder; there were also shouts, yells, and a few quite convincing screams. The hillside was seamed with gullies up which the guides led the party at a merciless pace while the smoke grew thicker between the tree trunks and among the tangled undergrowth.

There was a burst of confused firing on the slope just above them, the thud of running feet, crashing noises, and furious yells. Avril bellowed "Down! Down on your faces!" and the hunters threw themselves into defensive attitudes as a wild charge of men, fighting furiously, swept across the gully over and through the correspondents and vanished up the other side. They had scarcely picked themselves up when a further charge burst through them; this time the men were in army uniforms.

"Which way?" they yelled, and the hunters pointed after the fugitives. One of the soldiers paused, lifted his musket, and fired it off within a foot of the American's ear. Since the gun was loaded with black powder, the detonation was startling. The American slipped on the loose stones and sat down heavily.

D'Ecosse appeared on the bank in a swirl of smoke and peered down at them.

"You here? Get out of this at once. Avril, are you mad?"

Someone shouted, d'Ecosse turned and vanished from sight in a bedlam of sound and fury.

"We seem," said the Englishman to Brown, "to be in the middle of it."

"His Highness," said Brown earnestly, "will be most upset, sir, I do assure you. His Highness' orders would appear, sir, to have been grossly contravened." He looked severely at the hunters, who talked hurriedly together, pointed in different directions, and suddenly urged the party on again.

The rest of the afternoon was passed in violent physical exercise alternated by brief periods of cowering under rhododendrons while the battle rolled by. The uproar was unceasing, and Brown found time to marvel at the industry of the cobbler and his two sons, hereditary gunpowder makers to His Highness. Surely, at this rate, the battle could not go on much longer.

"Could we not," said the Englishman in one of these moments of respite, "go to Command Headquarters for an appreciation of the situation?"

Brown consulted Avril, who consulted the chief hunter—or appeared to do so. The word was passed back that Command Headquarters was mobile, as the Army was advancing.

"Fine," said the American, "fine. I suppose they know which way they're going. I haven't seen more than twenty yards in any direction for two hours and"—in the Englishman's ear—"some of our party are dying on their feet."

"One can't wonder, really," said the Englishman.

"Well, there's something in what you say. I'd be glad if—oh Lord, here we go, again."

It is not to be supposed that the small boys of Sainte-Roche had stayed quietly at home. They had been pressed into service to carry things earlier in the day; later on they armed themselves with any weapon which a tired warrior might have laid down for a moment, and retired into the smoke with a pilfered ration of powder to ginger up the battle.

"Silly," said Jean-Louis Gallienne, "only firing off powder. Silly."

"But there's no bullets," said Gaston Latour, the farmer's youngest.

Pierre Gobain, whose father kept The Hunter, knitted his brows.

"What's the matter with little pebbles?" he said.

So the horrifying sound of small projectiles ripping through the undergrowth added a touch of realism to the scene. Quite genuine yells of pain and anger rang through the smoky air.

The war correspondents were led into a shallow ditch and encouraged to walk along it, stooping.

"*Les têtes en bas, tous*," said the hunters, pushing the heads down one after another while Brown unnecessarily translated. "Keep your heads down, gentlemen, please. Keep your heads down."

They had proceeded about twenty yards when from somewhere just above them among the bushes a voice suddenly bellowed an order and there followed a bright flash and a bang which shook the ground and sent the echoes flying. The journalists went down flat on their faces and so did their entire escort.

Brown raised himself cautiously and brushed mud and leaves off his face; Avril, close beside him, was disentangling a spray of bramble from round his neck.

"I trust I may be permitted," said Brown in a fierce whisper, "to offer the suggestion that there is such a thing as excess of zeal."

"May I remind Monsieur," murmured Avril, "that he started all this?"

One of the hunters dashed up the bank and returned with news. The guns had been moved up. It would be wiser to return the way they had come.

"For myself," said the German loudly, "I have more than sufficient seen. I demand that a guide to lead me back to the town provided is. At once. I must a despatch to my office instantly write and by telephone transmit. At once."

Since it was, of course, unendurable that one correspondent should scoop the news while the others went on barking their shins on rocks in a forest full of smoke, he was backed up by the rest of the company. They emerged from the ditch, and the American seized Brown by the arm.

"Listen, friend. Will you tell one of these Prince's bodyguard boys that if he can get me to a telephone before the rest of this outfit, there's five dollars for him?"

"I will endeavour, sir, to make some such arrangement with the men," said Brown.

"One man," said the American, detaining him, "for me alone."

"We'll share the tip—and the guide—and the telephone," said the Englishman, rising up behind his shoulder, "for you won't lose me, you know. Anglo-American solidarity and all that, what?"

"You would pop up," said the American, grinning, "but at least let's beat the United Nations to it."

Brown drew Avril aside and said: "They want to go back to the town. Will it be all right now?"

"They have lasted longer than we thought they would," answered Avril. "The battle is running out of gunpowder; they cannot fire the cannons again."

"The American and the Englishman will pay well to get there first," said Brown.

"Get where?"

"To the telephone, to make their——"

"I am the agent of Havas in this country," said Avril angrily. "When I have finished with the telephone, we shall see. I will speak to the guides about taking them down, then I will go on ahead myself. There are some preparations to be made for their reception in the town. You will come with them, will you?"

"If I might be permitted to accompany you, Monsieur Avril,"

said Brown politely, "it has occurred to me that I might then have not so far to walk."

Avril grinned suddenly and said: "Did you, then, also hear the vespers bell? Yes, yes, come with me. I will instruct the guides and do you tell the party they will be taken home by the shortest route—the very shortest route. Impress that upon them."

"I will inform the gentlemen, monsieur."

"And as for those two getting there first——"

"The risk would be far too great," said Brown gravely. "The party must not separate."

"On no account."

Brown conveyed this decision to the seven war correspondents. "All together, gentlemen, please. The bodyguard will escort you by the very shortest route so that nothing will be gained by splitting up the party. Happily, the distance is not great," said Brown with a sensation of faint surprise at speaking the truth for the first time that day. "You will be at your hotel in an hour or so. *Au revoir*, gentlemen."

"And you—what about you? Where are you going?"

"Even now," said Brown with noble self-sacrifice, "it is not too late for my comrade and myself to snatch up a musket in our Prince's cause. *Au revoir*."

He stepped back, gave them a semi-military salute, and disappeared round a clump of rhododendrons.

CHAPTER VII

By Telephone

The doctor dived out of his improvised hospital and detained Brown and Avril as they were passing.

"Those infernal journalists," he said; "where are they?"

"On their way home," said Avril. "They should arrive in—ah —three quarters of an hour or so. Why?"

"Because if they want to see the casualties in hospital they must do so within the next hour. My so-called patients will want to go home to supper."

"Naturally——"

"I have arranged a melancholy party to parade past them at the mill and trail miserably to the hospital. Our guests may visit them after that. Tomorrow morning will be no good, the casualties will all be back at work, and our visitors may think such complete recoveries a little suspicious, eh?"

"If I might presume to suggest," said Brown, "Monsieur le Docteur could perhaps attribute the miracle to your superb mountain air?"

"Get out," said the doctor. "Or rather, get those seven busybodies out. Right out, over the frontier. Excuse me. I have to see the butcher about a bucketful of blood."

He went away with long strides. Brown and Avril looked at each other.

"I foresee certain possible difficulties," said Brown, "in the event of the gentlemen not wishing to depart so promptly."

"Yes," said Avril, tapping his teeth with a pencil, "yes. So do I. One moment. Yes, I have it. Leave it all to me; I will arrange their affairs." He departed at a run in the direction of the post office; Brown looked after him for a moment and then turned into the welcoming door of The Goat. There, at least, one could sit down.

Avril had a long telephone conversation with the Havas Agency in Paris and then hung up the receiver. The tall thin form of the postmaster was drifting vaguely about behind the counter, duster in hand.

"Durand," said Avril, "in about half an hour or less seven excited newspapermen will rush in here demanding to use the telephone."

"You, no doubt, will be here to attend to the machine."

"Certainly not. You have only to point it out to them and let them work it themselves. Or try to."

"Try to——"

"If they should complain that they cannot get a connection, you have only to tell them that there must be a fault in the line as sometimes happens, postmaster. A fallen branch in the woods, probably."

"Twice only in the last twenty years, to my knowledge."

"Hush! It might have been broken in the battle."

Durand turned his curiously pale blue eyes upon Avril.

"I assume you are up to some devilment. I am not sure whether His Highness the Prince will approve."

"I have consulted His Highness," said Avril, and it was perfectly true. He had found the Prince sitting upon the church-yard wall waiting for his Army to march in. "He approves. He thinks that your dignity will be better served tonight if you put on your uniform."

"As the Prince commands," said the postmaster, turning towards his private door, "though shirt sleeves are much more comfortable within doors."

Avril ran off to the Sainte-Roche *Bulletin* office but only remained there long enough to take a pair of wire-cutting pliers from a drawer. He paused in the doorway to make certain that no one saw him and slipped quietly away into the woods.

When the war correspondents tramped wearily into the town, the evening shadows were falling and lights were lit in all the windows. The party were halted just below the mill while a procession went slowly past. Ragged bandages with blood soaking through, improvised crutches and arms in slings impressed the onlookers deeply; when these were followed by stretchers in the hands of weary bearers and a farm cart with still forms among the straw, even the hardened journalists removed their hats.

They were held up again as they reached the square. This time the procession was of dejected men who shuffled along with their heads low. On either side of this column marched the Army in their picturesque blue uniforms with red facings, bringing in the prisoners.

The battle of Sainte-Roche was over.

"Now," said the war correspondents with one voice, "to the telephones. Where are they? At the post office? Good."

But their rush was halted by the sight of a square, solid man with a red beard who wore a sword with his army uniform. He was standing in a beam of light from a doorway and looking away to his left. The correspondents swirled round him, babbling like hounds.

"Commander d'Ecosse! May we offer our congratulations, sir? This must be a proud day, sir. Awfully sorry to trouble you, sir, but may we please have a few words from you about the battle?"

D'Ecosse awoke as from a deep reverie.

"Ah yes. The gentlemen who wanted to see everything. I have one more duty to perform this evening before I rest. Come with me and you shall see that too. This way."

They entered a long barn with straw on the floor and men in the straw moving uneasily or lying very still. The place was poorly lighted, but the correspondents could see kindly, anxious women bending over the wounded and the doctor passing, calm and reassuring, from one moaning patient to another.

"My men," murmured d'Ecosse, "my men." Then, remembering the journalists, "Excuse me, gentlemen, please. I must speak to these poor fellows." He moved off; the American stared for a few moments and turned away.

"This is Europe, can you believe it? I'm going to telephone."

He plunged out of the doorway and went off towards the post office, with the other six journalists crowding upon his heels. The post office was lighted by four spherical candles in shallow hammered-iron bowls, the door was ajar, and behind the counter stood a tall thin man in a blue uniform with a strip of silver braid upon collar and cuffs and a silver badge upon the left breast engraved with the words "Sainte-Roche. *Postes et télégraphes.*" Durand had a duster in his hand with which he was slowly polishing the top of an already speckless counter.

The war correspondents charged in together and came to a stop. Durand turned his eyes vaguely in their direction and bowed.

"I wish you a good evening, messieurs."

The English-speaking correspondents summoned up their best French.

"Good evening. Monsieur the Postmaster? Is it permitted that we use the telephone?"

Durand waved his hand towards the instrument which stood upon the counter at the far end against the wall.

"Certainly, messieurs. It is there."

The Spaniard made a rush at it, but the American reached it first.

"America," he said severely, "begins with A."

He lifted the receiver, placed it to his ear, and added without a pause: "For whom does one enquire, Monsieur the Postmaster? For Paris?"

"If one desires to speak with Paris, certainly, monsieur."

The American, hearing nothing in the receiver, joggled the hooks upon which it had rested.

"I can't hear anything."

"For effective use," said Durand, "it is advisable to wind the little handle on the right." He pointed, not to the handle, but to a small typewritten notice framed above the instrument. "Instructions for Use," it said. "Lift the Receiver, Rotate the Handle, and Listen."

While the American obeyed these simple instructions, Durand turned his back upon the company and went on dusting the empty shelves behind the counter.

"I still don't hear a thing," said the journalist. "Don't you have to drop a coin in someplace or say a charm over it?"

"Let me try," said the Englishman.

"But no, but no, but no," said the Belgian rapidly. "Belgium is for B." He took over from the American, and some member of the party suggested that they were winding the handle the wrong way, possibly?

"It only winds one way," said the American gloomily.

"There would be," said the German, "some device of the nature of a ratchet provided, in which some sort of not-reversible wind has incorporated been."

"BR for Britain," said the Englishman, and took the receiver from the baffled hands of Belgium. "You don't switch on anywhere, do you, or plug in?"

"No, monsieur," said the postmaster, continuing to dust.

"Monsieur the Postmaster," said the American, "listen."

Durand turned round politely.

"One would almost imagine," continued the Voice of America, "that something has gone wrong with this machine."

"It seldom happens," said Durand, "but it is, of course, possible."

"In that case, couldn't you stop dusting for a minute and see if you can't fix it for us?"

Durand drew himself up.

"I am, monsieur, the postmaster of Sainte-Roche, not a telephonic engineer."

"No, no. Of course not. We all realize that. I was just thinking that maybe there was some little thing——"

"No," said the postmaster.

"It's kaput," said the Englishman, yielding the instrument to France, Germany, and Spain in that order.

"It sometimes happens," said the postmaster, "that a branch from a tree in the forest falls upon the line and breaks it."

"Such things will happen," agreed the Englishman. "Tell us, where is the——"

"Alternatively," said the postmaster, remembering his instructions, "it might be the battle."

"—where is the telephonic engineer?" said the Englishman, finishing his sentence. Durand turned a dreamy stare more or less in his direction.

"I could not say at all, monsieur. I regret."

"He is not in the town?"

"I believe not, monsieur."

"No idea at all where he is?"

"He may be in the woods. Or, possibly, fighting in the battle. He may even have gone to Spain."

"To Spain? Do you go to Spain from here?"

"Oh no, monsieur. Never."

"One of us," said the Englishman, taking his head in his hands, "is crackers."

"Relax, brother," said the American, laying a kindly hand on his arm. "The salient point is the telephonic engineer is not here. Where he's gone doesn't matter."

"It would," said Great Britain mulishly, "if it was somewhere he could be fetched back from."

"I've got a better idea," said the American. "We can't have the telephone fixed. Right? Very well. But we can hire mules."

"Mules?"

"To get on and ride out of this darn country. Let's go back to the inn, order mules, pack up, pay bills, ride away. Right?"

"I'm with you," said the Englishman.

"We will dine first," said the Belgian, "for the wife of the innkeeper is a cook of the most surpassing." He turned his eyes to heaven, presumably for corroboration.

"Certainly, certainly," they all said together, and moved towards the door. "*Au revoir*, Monsieur the Postmaster. *Auf wiedersehen. A rivederci.* Good-bye, and thank you."

"A pleasure," said the postmaster ambiguously, and came round the counter to shut the door after them. From the dark street outside there floated back the Voice of France complaining in its native tongue.

"Mules, mules! Again of mules?"

The war correspondents dined so well that they did not start until very early the following morning. Jean-Alphonse Gallienne, together with a couple of nephews and a string of mules, came to the door of The Goat before the sun was above the eastern mountains; when the cavalcade reached the point where the trail to the broken bridge turned off into the woods the first rays of sunlight were filtering between peaks to gild the sombre forests and scatter with diamonds the new-drenched meadows. Below them in the valley thin spires of smoke rose from cottage chimneys, white water foamed from the mill wheel, and small boys conducted cows to pasture. The mules stopped from habit and the travellers turned in their saddles.

"It certainly is a very lovely land," said the American. "No place for war."

"Quite good, actually," said the Englishman.

"The cooking," said the Belgian.

"The wines," said the German.

The cavalcade resumed its journey.

When at last they had made the awkward transit by the broken bridge and stood once more by the vestigial Frontier Post, Jean-Alphonse collected payment for his services, off-loaded the mules, and piled baggage and equipment at the side of the road.

"It has been an honour," he said politely, and bowed to each

of the seven separately. "A good journey, messieurs. Come
again to Sainte-Roche, come again."

"But," said the Englishman, "how do we go on from here?
I say, Yank, we ought to hang on to those mules."

"What? Oh, Lord, yes. Here, come back!"

But the tails of the last mules were already vanishing behind
bushes. Jean-Alphonse, hearing the shout, turned round, swept
off his hat, and bowed deeply. He then spun round on his heels
like a dancer, stepped behind a juniper bush, and vanished as
completely as the mules.

"Someone will come," said the Frenchman calmly. "For me,
I do not regret the mules."

"You like walking, yes?" said the German acidly.

"Gentlemen, gentlemen," said the Englishman.

"You know," said the American, "I thought we were just
off-saddling for a little refreshment——"

"Listen," said the representative of Spain.

They fell silent, and there came to their ears the sound of
motor transport labouring under adverse conditions. A few
minutes later two large ancient cars came over the brow of the
hill, drove down to the waiting company, and stopped.

"I suppose they are real," said the Englishman, "or do they
have mirages in these mountains?"

"Mirages don't rattle," said the American, and strode
forward. The first driver raised his hat.

"Bonjour, messieurs. The party desiring conveyance to Py?"

"That is so, indeed, but how did you know?"

"But by telephone, monsieur. One rang from Sainte-Roche
early this morning."

"Oh. Oh, did one."

The luggage, cameras, and other gear were loaded into the
cars, and the journalists began to climb in. The Englishman
went up to the American, who was gazing absently into the
blue distance.

"Are you staying on?"

The American awoke.

"They telephoned from Sainte-Roche this morning, did you hear that? Do you know something? We've been had. We are a nice bright go-ahead-and-get-it bunch of reporters, we are. We know our way around, we're smart guys; look at us." He shook his fists in the air. "That hatchet-faced skinny little weasel Avril has done us in. That innocent polite child of Nature, that guileless hillbilly—" He choked.

"The telephone," said the Englishman. "Of course, he is a correspondent of Havas; he said so. Positively no deception, ladies and gentlemen. He put his account through last night and then disconnected the phone. Simple."

"Okay, simple, and that goes for us, too. That dreamy-eyed guy with the duster, the postmaster, he was in it too, of course. If we get to Py and find the morning papers full of a long Havas despatch from Our Special Correspondent——"

"Come," said the Englishman, urging him towards the cars, "come on. At least he had the common decency to whistle up transport for us."

"That wasn't common decency, that was just to get us the hell out. I've a good mind," said the American, taking his foot off the running board again, "to go back and knock his block off and——"

The Englishman, who had played Rugby in his time, heaved the American headfirst into the car, slammed the door upon him, and shouted: "Drive on!" He himself travelled in the second car; it was less explosive.

When they reached Py, they leapt out and bought papers. The Revolt in Sainte-Roche Quelled. Resistance Collapses. Loyal Forces Triumphant. Havas Agency Special Correspondent (by telephone).

CHAPTER VIII

Crisis

It was inevitable that reaction should settle upon Sainte-Roche when the excitement was all over, when the woods had been cleared of the debris of battle, when the two brass cannon had been replaced upon the highest terrace, when the muskets were once more hanging upon the armoury walls of the Palace, and the blue-and-red uniforms had been returned to Madame Durand for cleaning, repair, and storage.

Marcel Avril arranged by telephone for copies of papers containing the war correspondents' eyewitness reports to be sent to Sainte-Roche by post. This was a complicated process involving an arrangement with the herdsman who lived nearest to the Frontier post on the French side, who met the postman from Py by appointment and was himself met at the broken bridge by some member of the Gallienne family who brought on the mails if it was not raining. The mails must not get wet.

The only paper which was really popular in Sainte-Roche was the French *Paris-Soir*; naturally, since that was the only language they could read if, of course, they could read at all. The French correspondent's dramatic account of the battle had been heavily pruned by his sub-editor, but his last paragraph had been left untouched. This pointed out that Sainte-Roche would be a wonderful centre for travellers who had tired of the usual tourist resorts, if only it could be provided with a few good hotels fitted with modern amenities. The scenery was marvellous, the air pure, the standard of cooking surprisingly high—this correspondent had only eaten at The Goat—and the country wines—ah!

Henri Tonnerre retailed all this to his less literate customers. He did not repeat the Frenchman's comments upon The Goat's toilet inconveniences; he thought them almost rude. He was right, they were.

Those who could read English—the Prince, the curé, Marcel Avril and, of course, Brown—studied the English and American papers with enthralled interest, especially the American.

"This," said the Prince, tapping the sheet, "is the sort of thing we need. A most sympathetic report. Considering the man was only here for some thirty-six hours, it is an astonishingly complete account of conditions here."

"Yes indeed, Your Highness."

"No doubt these men are all trained observers."

"Indubitably, Your Highness."

"The only trace of acidity occurs in his references to our local Press and, particularly, to our Editor."

After this, time passed on and nothing happened except that the Sainte-Rochean harvest was gathered in. Five weeks after the battle, an emergency meeting of the Six was held at the Palace.

"You will again attend me at this meeting, Robert," said the Prince.

"As Your Highness commands."

"It is fortunate that my official chair has a tall and solid back," added the Prince thoughtfully.

"May I presume to ask why?"

"Because if they throw things at you, you can dodge behind it."

There came a knock at the door and, as before, the old seneschal entered.

"The Six hopefully await their Prince."

"Who comes gladly."

The meeting started in the usual way with the Prince seating himself in the great chair and looking round at his standing Council.

"Be seated, gentlemen. Thank you. Who has matter to open before this Council?"

D'Ecosse moved forward in his chair.

"Gilles d'Ecosse, Chancellor and instructor of our children, speak of your mind."

"My Prince. It is, as always, a question of money, and I regret to say that the matter is now become even more pressing than before. The necessary repairs to our buildings have become increasingly urgent and will be even more so when the coming winter is fully upon us. There are also salaries and, for the first time, an actual debt. I refer, my Prince, to the bill for gunpowder. It has been sent in to me and I regret I have not the funds to pay it. I should be grateful for advice in the matter."

He sat down, and the Prince looked round the table.

"Louis Durand, postmaster, speak your m——"

"With pleasure, my Prince," said Durand, bouncing in his chair with impatience. "This bill for gunpowder ought plainly never to have been incurred. We were told"—his pale eyes rested pointedly upon the impassive face of Brown behind his master's chair—"we were assured that if we were to put on that indefensible sham fight we should have the world at our doors offering us help. Has any help arrived? Has it? I ask for a reply." He sat down abruptly.

"Not yet," said the Prince. "Father Denys?"

"It is many years, my son, since I was in touch with the outside world. It was, I think, a simpler and quieter place then, where men were not so busy over many things. Yet, even then, results were slow to follow upon action. It is now only five weeks since our visitors left us. I would suggest that it is early days to despair."

"Thank you, Father. Er—Jean Latour, farmer, speak your mind."

"My Prince, it may be early days to despair, but it is already time and past to consider where we are to get the money to pay our bills. There are certain charges for damage to property and livestock, let alone the loss of many hours of labour due by the farmhands to the farming community."

"A consideration, certainly," said the Prince gravely. "I understood, however, that apart from the actual day of the battle, rehearsals were held after working hours and on Sundays after Mass. We decided unanimously at a Council here that the actual day of the battle was to be regarded as a public holiday with the usual arrangements about pay. Am I right, Chancellor?"

"Your Highness is perfectly correct."

"Damage to livestock—— Yes, Chancellor?"

"My Prince, all this was discussed earlier and it was agreed that all the farming community would keep their animals shut up on that day for the express purpose of avoiding any harm to livestock and consequent claims arising."

"You can——" began Latour.

"Jean Latour, farmer, speak your mind."

"I beg Your Highness' pardon. My Prince, we did shut the beasts up, but the noise, particularly the cannon, scared them so they was unmanageable for days. My Prince, unmanageable pigs is bad enough but hysterical cows is a menace."

"Do I understand," said the Prince, "that you are requesting compensation for the extra trouble involved?"

"My Prince, if all that tomfoolery had brought in some good results we farmers would have thought the extra trouble was worth it. As it is, we don't."

"Tomfoolery?" said the Prince. "I must remind the Council that, after due consideration at several meetings, this scheme was unanimously approved at your own free choice. Unanimously."

"My Prince," stormed Latour, scarlet in the face, "we were all misled by the silver tongue and—and misleading advice given of us by a stranger in our midst, a stranger who is a paid servant of us all. Now look at the mess we're in."

"My Prince——"

"Yes, postmaster?"

"By permission, I support that."

"You need no permission from anyone to say whatever you please in this Council, postmaster, as you all know perfectly well."

"Anyway, my Prince, I support it."

"Noted," said the Prince. "There are two Councillors who, I notice, have said nothing since this meeting started. May we have your views? Henri Tonnerre, innkeeper, speak your mind."

"My Prince, I don't hardly know what to say about paying the bills, but I must say we didn't do so bad out of the visitors we did have, though they was here only so short a time. Full of money they seemed to be, pretty funny stuff some of it was, but it's all money. They paid for their board and their rooms, they paid the hunters who took them to see the battle, they paid the Galliennes for the mules three times what they need have done, they paid the children to have their photos took and the women drawing water at the fountain. They bought silly little things that took their fancy. My Prince, what I say is, can't we fix up to have some more visitors like that?"

"Thank you, Tonnerre, for a really constructive suggestion, the first this Council has heard."

"And, my Prince, as for our stranger, I'd like to say as no one could have been more helpful."

"Thank you for your views. Marcel Avril, if you have any suggestion to make, speak your mind."

"My Prince——"

He was interrupted by a thunderous knocking on the panels of the door; it was in fact produced by the solid-silver knob upon the head of the seneschal's staff. There was, of course, an official formula for use when anyone dared to interrupt the proceedings of the Council. The Prince looked round the table.

"I hear a sound of knocking," he said. "Does the Council also hear the sound?"

If they had not wished to be interrupted they would have

replied: "We hear nothing but our voices in Council," and no further notice would have been taken. However, since no one had dared to interrupt the proceedings of the Council since the mill had caught fire in 1885, curiosity was too much for them.

"We do," they said.

"Marcel Avril, as our youngest Councillor, pray ascertain who knocks."

Avril walked to the door and opened it. Outside stood the venerable figure of the seneschal. He bowed.

"May I receive pardon," he began. "There is a message which—*get back, wretched urchin!*"

But he was not quick enough to stop a grubby black-haired boy from slipping under his arm into the Council Chamber and seizing Marcel Avril by the sleeve.

"Come quickly—run, monsieur, run! The telephone, it rings and rings and drives Madame Durand beside herself and she listens and it says it is Paris, urgent, urgent!"

"Messieurs——" began Avril.

"Go," they said with one voice.

"Run," said the boy, and disappeared with Avril after him. The seneschal, wearing an expression of extreme outrage, stood like a statue.

"Thank you, seneschal," said the Prince.

The old man bowed and backed out and the heavy door thudded into place.

"Let us resume," said Prince André. "The problem before the Council is that of increasing our revenue. Henri Tonnerre has advised the encouragement of visitors. Has anyone else any further suggestion? Jean Latour."

"My Prince, the visitors talked freely among themselves, and when it was in French most of it was understood by them as heard it. The things they said about the hotels here were not such as I should think it fitting to repeat in Your Highness' presence."

"Dear me. Yes, innkeeper?"

"My Prince, it was only what they called modern plumbing as was wanted and could no doubt be provided—plumbing and bathrooms."

"D'Ecosse?"

"These things cost money, my Prince, and where is that to come from?"

"Out of the pockets——"

"Latour!" said the Prince.

"I beg Your Highness' pardon. Out of the pockets of those who did make money out of the visitors, of course. Where else?"

"My Prince——"

"Go on, Tonnerre."

"My Prince, if that remark was aimed at me, I want to say as I can't remember asking anybody's charity to help me pay for it. I didn't make no fortune out of them visitors and I don't believe I could pay all myself, but I'm no beggar." He sat back, scowling.

"I think we are more likely to solve our problems if we do not lose our tempers. Let us avoid provocation," said the Prince. "Yes, postmaster?"

"My Prince, judging by the number of catalogues of sanitary fittings which came in with those newspapers, Monsieur Tonnerre should be able by now to give us some idea of the cost of such things."

Tonnerre bounced in his chair, but the Prince waved him down.

"I asked for further suggestions for raising money. I have not heard any. Am I, therefore, to conclude that this Council approves Tonnerre's suggestion and is prepared to discuss it? D'Ecosse, our Chancellor."

"My Prince, it is a sound suggestion and we may come to it someday, but it will take time to mature. It will not solve our immediate difficulties—the repairs and the bill for gunpowder, for example."

"A qualified approval. Postmaster, your views. Do you approve?"

"No, my Prince."

"Father Denys?"

"I agree with the Chancellor, my son. I regret I have no suggestion for our immediate needs."

"Jean Latour, farmer."

"Well, I have, my Prince. I suggest that those who let us in for this madcap scheme should be asked to pay," and Latour looked pointedly behind the Prince's chair. Brown did not move a muscle.

"My son——"

"Father Denys, our beloved curé, speak your mind."

"If I remember correctly the order of events at that first Council meeting of your happy reign, it was I who suggested that advice should be asked from the stranger in our midst. I assume, therefore, that it is I who should be expected to pay for the expenses incurred thereby." The curé smiled benignly round the table.

"My father," began the Prince. "Yes, Chancellor?"

"My Prince, in view of the fact that our curé's salary has not been paid for five years, however savage we may feel we cannot do more than set one off against the other."

"And still be no better off," smiled the Prince. "I agree, Chancellor. Yes, farmer Latour?"

"I never meant Monsieur le Curé at all. Everyone knows about him. I meant your manservant, my Prince, as must have been quite plain."

"Are you recommending——"

"He led us into this, didn't he? And gets a good salary for doing it."

"I agree," said the postmaster.

"I don't," said Tonnerre.

"Gentlemen," said the Prince in a tone of sudden thunder which rang to the rafters, "you will behave yourselves and address me only, or I dissolve this Council!"

There was silence.

"Do I gather," said the Prince in a tone of ominous calm,

"that you are proposing to deprive me of the services of a personal attendant? If so, I will remind you that under our customs you cannot do so."

"My Prince——"

"Jean Latour."

"My Prince, I never meant any personal discourtesy to Your Highness. I only meant that perhaps you might have someone as didn't talk so much."

"Even when authorized by a vote of the Council?" said the Prince silkily, and Tonnerre sat forward. "Yes, innkeeper?"

"Far be it from me to suggest anything which—which——"

"Go on, Tonnerre."

"I wouldn't wish to be taken as—as—er——"

"I am sure you would not. What is it, then?"

"I had an idea, my Prince. No, it might sound as if I was suggesting something. I don't think I'll say it if Your Highness will let me off."

"Henri Tonnerre, the only sensible suggestion hitherto made at this meeting was made by you. If you have another idea pray let us hear it."

"But," said Tonnerre, and dried up again.

"Besides," said the Prince persuasively, "you are killing me with curiosity, and that is very unkind."

"My Prince, with the deepest respect, it was only it just crossed my mind that if things was to fall out so it would be very convenient for all concerned and be a good thing in several ways especially for the future——"

"For heaven's sake, Tonnerre!"

"Since the Prince commands. It was only if Your Highness was to meet a nice young lady of good family with plenty of money, if Your Highness will forgive—we only want you to be happy. Nothing else matters, Monsieur le Curé, does it?"

The curé smiled but said nothing; the Prince leaned back in his chair and the Six looked steadily at him.

"I will admit to the Council," said the Prince slowly, "that at the present time I feel no inclination towards matrimony. Besides, though I know little of the outside world beyond what I have read, I believe that charming and unattached young women of good family and possessed of large fortunes"—he smiled—"are not found sitting behind every bush. However, to quote our Chancellor, we may come to it someday, though once again it is no immediate remedy. Innkeeper, I thank you for your concern for my happiness which comes, I know, from the heart." Tonnerre nodded violently. "In the meantime——"

The door opened and Avril came in, a little out of breath with running violently up four flights of terrace steps.

"Marcel Avril," said the Prince.

"My Prince, I have news. The telephone message was from an American agency in Paris. They had written to Your Highness and received no answer. They wish, with your approval, to send a small Commission to Sainte-Roche to ascertain if anything can be done to"—he paused to draw a long breath—"to put this country's economy upon a sound financial basis."

No one spoke for a moment.

"Before we consider this very helpful offer," said Prince André, "I should like to have it explained to me how a letter addressed to me personally could fail to be delivered. Postmaster?"

"My Prince, we—that is—no doubt it was at Py and we did not know it was there."

"Is it not customary for Py to inform us by telephone when there is mail for us, in order that we may instruct the herdsman to meet the postman?"

"That is so, my Prince," said Durand, whose normally pale and sheep-like face was red with embarrassment.

"And the telephone is in order? Can it be that it rang and no one responded?"

"It might be that it rang," stammered the postmaster, "and no one heard it."

"I see." The Prince looked round his Council. "Since it seems likely that in future we may have more communication with the outside world than formerly, gentlemen, do you consider it advisable that steps should be taken to avoid such delay in the future? Yes, d'Ecosse?"

"My Prince, I propose that, in future, whenever the telephone rings it should be answered immediately. Promptly. Without delay."

The postmaster looked imploringly at Avril, whose eyes were steadily upon the rafters of the roof.

"Since it seems that Madame Durand handled this dangerous mechanism without mishap, it cannot be so difficult," said the Prince. "Those in favour of the Chancellor's suggestion?"

Five hands went up, and the postmaster's followed more slowly.

"That is unanimous. Postmaster," said the Prince blandly, "you will no doubt charge yourself with the matter. Now, Marcel Avril, if you have recovered your breath, did this message give any details about the Commission and its visit?"

"My Prince, I said that their letter had no doubt been delayed by the somewhat primitive postal service between here and Py but that we would send for the letter tomorrow. They said that in that case—I beg pardon, they asked first if it was Your Highness himself speaking. When I said that I was merely a junior member of your Council, they said that as their letter was highly confidential and addressed to Your Highness in person, it would be most improper to disclose its contents to anyone else. The letter would explain everything. They rang off. I took the responsibility, my Prince, of ringing up Py, and they said that an important letter was, indeed, there. I told them to send it out with the postman tomorrow. I also sent off a messenger to the Galliennes, telling them to instruct the herdsman to collect it. I hope, my Prince, that the Council will approve."

Six heads nodded solemnly.

"In that case," said the Prince, "the letter should reach me tomorrow. I shall then call you together again to consider its

93

contents. Agreed? Good." He sat up abruptly and the Six did the same. "It is my pleasure to thank you for your invaluable counsel."

"Which is no more than our duty."

CHAPTER IX

Horn of Plenty

The Commission consisted of seven men. It was led by Morris M. Mathews, a middle-aged but fortunately active business-man, the Economic Adviser. He was accompanied by two younger men, ex-army officers; Edward K. Spenlow, the expert on Roads, Bridges, and all forms of Postal and Telegraphic Communication, and Donald S. Farson, Housing and Educa-tion specialist. Each of them had a secretary complete with files and a portable typewriter. They wasted no time; ten days after the official letter to Prince André had been received and answered, they arrived at the broken bridge in two large cars hired in Py. The seventh man was an interpreter.

By the remains of the frontier post a French gendarme was waiting to usher them courteously out of France. The party stopped the cars and called him over.

"Are we, please, on the right road for Sainte-Roche?"

The interpreter stepped into the linguistic breach and the gendarme saluted smartly. This was, indeed, the road to Sainte-Roche.

"Seems a pretty poor road. Does it improve beyond the frontier?"

"On the contrary, messieurs."

"What? Not passable for cars? Maybe these cars are too big for country roads, eh?"

The gendarme smiled pityingly. If the messieurs would give themselves the trouble of walking on for fifty yards, they would

95

see for themselves. He pointed out the gaunt masonry of the bridge towers showing through the trees.

"Oh? Is that the frontier?"

"The frontier is here," said the gendarme, and indicated the stump by which he had been standing. "All beyond this is Sainte-Roche."

"Better get your notebook out, Ed," said Mathews to the roads expert. "Item, one new frontier post."

"That's right," said Edward Spenlow. "Should we walk down as far as that interesting structure? I have a feeling there's a lot more to come."

The three men climbed out of the cars and walked on together, taking the interpreter with them. They passed under the archway between the stumpy towers and came to a stop. There was a short silence.

"Item two," said Mathews softly. "One bridge, Ed."

"That's right."

"Have either of you," asked Donald Farson, "ever been in the Balkans?"

They shook their heads.

"You get used to it," said Farson.

They turned and walked back to the cars with the interpreter following in a semi-detached manner behind.

"Where's that gendarme?" asked Mathews.

"He went away," said the secretaries.

"Well, well."

There was another silence which lasted until Farson put two fingers in his mouth and produced an ear-splitting whistle which rent the astonished air.

"Someone answered," said Spenlow, bending his ear.

"Remember a song about Little Sir Echo years ago?" said Mathews.

"Yes, why?"

"I think he lives here."

The bushes parted and there stepped out the rustic figure of Jean-Alphonse Gallienne.

After this, proceedings followed closely upon the pattern of Robert Brown's entry into Sainte-Roche, the only difference being that, since there were more visitors to convey, there were more mules and, of course, more Galliennes. When the party had descended intact the side of the gorge, crossed the stream, and scaled the further side, they gathered in a group by the other side of the broken bridge and looked at it.

"First priority," said Mathews. "One new bridge."

"One detachment of Pioneers and necessary materials," said Spenlow.

Since the Galliennes could not understand what was being said and nobody translated, they were not pained, but stood about grinning cheerfully.

Mathews turned away. "Tell them we are ready to proceed," he said to the interpreter. "What comes next, farm carts?"

When they were undeceived they remounted the mules.

"Columbus," said Spenlow, "here we come."

They were ceremoniously received by the entire Six in the market square of Sainte-Roche and conducted to The Goat, where they settled in with some surprise but without audible comment. Prince André invited Mathews, Spenlow, and Farson to dinner at the Palace, where, if the cooking was less superb than it was at The Goat, at least the Commission ate off solid silver for the first time in their lives. Mathews, a man entirely without false pride, said so frankly, and the Prince laughed.

"We do not make china in Sainte-Roche," he said. "Only a rough country pottery, but we do mine a little silver. There is this about a silver plate, gentlemen. If the servants drop it it does not break."

The Commission were shown round Sainte-Roche by d'Ecosse and Avril and had pointed out to them the roof of the Town Hall, the condition of the church, the defective aqueduct which wasted more water than it conveyed to the town, and the impeded main drainage outfall, which was a wide deep ditch paved with flagstones. The Commission stood in a group and regarded the last item with interest.

"You know, boys," said Mathews, "the expression 'main drainage' certainly means something quite different here from what it does back home. I thought I'd had reason to believe there was no main drainage in this town."

"Surface water, mainly," said Spenlow.

"Mainly, but not entirely," said Farson, peering at it.

"Well, no. Shall we move on?"

The Commission spent a week in Sainte-Roche examining everything with a thoroughness which pained and even exasperated the Sainte-Rocheans. Why should they not have their pigsties alongside the well? Yes, of course they used the well; it never hurt anybody. Flies, there were always flies—who could tell where they came from? Yes, they got in the milk; everyone knew that flies like milk. It never hurt anyone.

"It is quite true," said the doctor when Farson tackled him. "It doesn't hurt them. When I first came here I had a lot of prejudiced ideas about hygiene, but it was less than useless trying to teach them; the people just thought I was silly, and it is a mistake to let people think their doctor is silly. Bad for them and very bad for the doctor. He might even come to believe it himself. No, these people have acquired an immunity, that's all. People do, you know."

"Yes. I guess they do. But suppose visitors came here?"

"Then the milk must be boiled or avoided. The water here is quite good if you get it straight from the town supply, but even so I don't recommend your drinking it. Not till you've lived here at least ten years."

The Commission also had a long interview with d'Ecosse on the subject of finance and a short session with the Six, Prince André being in the chair. This turned into a sort of fencing match with the Commission trying to find out something definite about the inroads of communism and the Six trying to find out how much money America was likely to send them. This match was drawn, no points being scored by either side, and after a farewell dinner at the Palace the Commission remounted its mules and rode away.

"Come back soon," said the Prince, who had delighted in the company of his travelled visitors.

"If this goes through," said Mathews, "we'll be back soon. Yes, sir, and glad to come. Sainte-Roche only needs a few little things to be a very pleasant place."

"Yes, sir, that's right," said Spenlow.

Farson agreed rather absent-mindedly. He was watching a woman who came out of a cottage to empty the contents of a bucket into the "main drainage."

After all this excitement there was another pause of some weeks, during which Sainte-Roche suffered the tedium of hope deferred.

"They will not come again," said Jean Latour. "For me, I am not disappointed, since this is what I expected."

"They will inform us one way or the other," said Avril. "These things take time."

"We must be humble and patient," said the curé. "We must remember that we are very unimportant indeed in the eyes of men who are dealing with the destinies of half the world."

"Patience patches no roofs," said d'Ecosse. "Postmaster, are you sure your telephone has not rung?"

The postmaster merely looked angrily at him and walked away, and Avril laughed.

"D'Ecosse, my son," said Father Denys, "I think that you are goading our poor postmaster."

"I am helping our poor postmaster, Father," said d'Ecosse. "A rota of my more intelligent pupils keeps watch outside the post office for the sound of the telephone bell."

"And when it rings?"

"They rush inside the office and tell him," said Avril, "crying out in loud voices to be heard above the shrilling of the bell. Then he sends one of them to tell me and so the telephone is answered."

"Is there anything the matter with the installation," asked the curé, "which makes it dangerous to use?"

"Nothing whatever," said d'Ecosse. "Saving your presence,

Father, Durand is a complete mule like his father and grand-father before him."

The curé hesitated momentarily and a twinkle came into his eyes.

"That were impossible," he said mildly, and turned away.

But a day or two later the telephone did ring. A Mr. Elihu J. Morgan, representing the United States Foreign Aid Council, would be arriving at the broken bridge at noon on the following day with proposals to lay before His Highness Prince André and his Council. It would be appreciated if transport within the Sainte-Rochean boundary could be provided. Avril, in a voice vibrant with cordiality, promised that it should.

Mr. Morgan was so exactly like a caricature of a government civil servant that it was hard to believe that that was what he actually was. He had a thin dry face, a thin figure in formal clothes, and a dry precise manner. He spoke fluent French and carried a brief case from which he was not parted for a moment, not even while descending the ravine. He was given lunch at The Goat and thereafter conducted to the Palace for an emergency meeting of the Six.

Mr. Morgan addressed the meeting, beginning: "Your Highness. Gentlemen." He said that his business there was merely to inform them of what the Foreign Aid Council proposed and to answer any questions necessary to clear up any obscure point. The FAC proposed to finance Sainte-Rochean development under the following headings:

Roads, bridges, postal and telephonic communications.

Buildings, including repair and modernization of ancient structures and also the provision and equipment of modern hotel accommodation.

Improvement of agricultural processes, including forestry and stockbreeding.

Provision of adequate water of a high standard of purity and the installation of a proper system of drainage and sewage disposal for the town. Adequate health services.

School accommodation and modern equipment.

"For the FAC," said Mr. Morgan, "sees a future for Sainte-
Roche as a resort, possibly a health resort, and a centre for
tourism."

He then sat down, having spoken for exactly two minutes,
and the Six looked at each other.

"Thank you, Mr. Morgan," said the Prince. "Has any
member of the Council any question they wish to—yes, Henri
Tonnerre?"

"My Prince. Might we have that list again a bit more slow
and gradual so as we can write them down? Speaking for myself
as a man known to be slow-witted, I feel quite swept away as
it might be."

"I think we all do," said the Prince. "Mr. Morgan?"

"I will read the headings again," said the emissary, "at
dictation speed," and he did so while all the Council scribbled
furiously.

"I have, of course, official details in writing, which I now
lay before Your Highness," he added, and laid a thick wad of
quarto sheets on the table in front of Prince André.

After a pause the Prince looked round the table.

"Has anyone—d'Ecosse, our Chancellor."

"My Prince. Do I understand correctly that the FAC are
really prepared to pay for all this?"

"That is so," said Mr. Morgan.

"My Prince," pursued d'Ecosse, "to pay outright or is this—
this very munificent offer—a loan and, if so, upon what terms?"

"Mr. Morgan?"

"The original outlay as detailed in the schedules now before
Your Highness is a gift, not a loan, nor will any reimbursement
of it or interest upon it be expected at any time."

"I suppose we are awake," said Marcel Avril, plainly unaware
that he had spoken his thoughts aloud.

"I am sure that Mr. Morgan will know how to appreciate
our delighted bewilderment," said the Prince, smiling, but Mr.
Morgan's face showed no change at all.

"May I ask," said Father Denys, "who will be employed upon these works?"

"Local labour entirely, except for technicians and, of course, expert advisers in the various branches."

"My Prince——"

"Jean Latour, farmer."

"Do I take it that people will come and tell us how to run our farms and all that?"

Perhaps Mr. Morgan had met farmers before.

"The agricultural experts sent will be advisers only, able to give any information desired upon modern improvements in farming machinery, new fertilizers, and so on. They advise, not give orders."

"Not bosses," said Latour, anxious that there should be no mistake.

"Definitely not bosses," said Morgan, with the faintest possible flicker of amusement.

There was another pause.

"Henri Tonnerre, innkeeper."

"My Prince, how soon can all this begin?"

"Mr. Morgan?"

"If Your Highness and your Council decide to accept the proposals of the FAC, the next step will be for Your Highness and your Foreign Secretary to come to Paris to sign the necessary agreements. Your Highness will find examples of these agreements among the papers before you. As soon as these have been signed, matters will be put in train at once."

"Myself and my Foreign Secretary," said the Prince slowly. "Those are all the signatures required?"

"The minimum signatures required, Your Highness, and all that are, in fact, necessary, though it is of course open to Your Highness to bring a staff of any size which you may consider desirable."

"Thank you. I understand."

"It may be your wish," said Mr. Morgan, "that I should now withdraw. If any further points should arise, I am entirely at your disposal until noon tomorrow when I return to Paris. Your final decision and any action arising therefrom can most conveniently be discussed by correspondence."

Mr. Morgan then rose and the Prince himself accompanied him to the door, making much of him and sending grateful messages to the Paris branch of the Foreign Aid Council, that embodiment of humanitarian principles in action, that en-sample of international brotherhood which——

"I, sir," said Mr. Morgan, turning upon the threshold, "am merely a clerk entrusted with the conveyance of documents. I am as it were a phonograph record to reproduce the words of the Council to whom your most admirable sentiments should be conveyed direct. I have the honour to wish you a good after-noon."

He bowed and turned away.

"Seneschal!"

"Your Highness?"

"Escort this gentleman forth of the Palace with all possible courtesy."

"As the Prince commands."

CHAPTER X

Foreign Secretary

The great door closed heavily behind Mr. Morgan, and the Prince returned to the chair.

"Well, gentlemen?"

The Six sat round the table and beamed at him. So radiant were these beams that they even overflowed the chair and irradiated the imperturbable figure of Brown, standing behind it.

"Has no one," continued the Prince, "anything to say or are we all struck dumb? It would not be surprising if we were. Yes, Henri Tonnerre?"

"My Prince, it seems we must find somebody for—for Foreign Secretary was it he said?"

"That was it, but—yes, Postmaster?"

"My Prince, has Sainte-Roche ever had a Foreign Secretary? If not, does our Constitution permit of one being appointed? If not, how can we appoint one?"

"D'Ecosse, our Chancellor, speak your mind."

"My Prince, I propose we should first accept this offer from the United States Foreign Aid Council."

"That is the first step. Does anyone support——"

There was a surge round the table and the Prince said firmly that the Reverend Father Denys was the seconder. "Those in favour? That is unanimous, thank you. Since the invitation was addressed to me in the first place I suppose it is for me to accept it. I will write tonight and Monsieur Morgan can convey the letter. Agreed? Good. Now we can return to the question of a Foreign Secretary. Yes, d'Ecosse?"

"My Prince, there have been Foreign Secretaries before but not, I think, continuously."

"You are right, Chancellor. Since the foreign policy of Sainte-Roche has always been one of isolation, we have only appointed a Foreign Secretary temporarily to deal with any matter as it arose. The last appointment was made to deal with the insolent demands of the French usurper Napoleon Bonaparte at the time of the Peninsular War. Henri Tonnerre?"

"My Prince, who was appointed?"

"One of the Six. The Chancellor of that date, in fact."

"The Chancellor——"

"My son."

"Father Denys, our beloved curé."

"My son, before proceeding to the choice of a Foreign Secretary, should we not first ask ourselves what quality will be required of him?"

The Prince looked steadily at the curé.

"Many qualities, Father, are expected from a man in such a position, are they not?"

"Doubtless, my son, doubtless, but I said 'quality' in the singular. Perhaps I should have said 'accomplishment.' It would seem that on this occasion the Foreign Secretary of Sainte-Roche should speak fluent English."

"Ah yes," said the Prince. "That suggests to me that it should again be our Chancellor, Gilles d'Ecosse, and very suitable too. Yes, d'Ecosse?"

"But, my Prince, I cannot speak English or I should not have required an interpreter when those journalists came. I can read English, yes, but to speak it is a very different matter indeed. One would say, another tongue. It is the pronunciation, as Your Highness knows, which is quite beyond all reason. It has neither sense nor logic, it is—it is not to be borne!"

"Marcel Avril?"

"Our Chancellor is right," said Avril gloomily. "I myself

addressed the Americans in what I thought was their tongue, and even their interpreter did not recognize it."

"My Prince——"

"Jean Latour."

"I think we'd best appoint Your Highness to be our Foreign Secretary as well as our Prince, since it seems Your Highness is the only Sainte-Rochean to speak English well."

"I do not speak it well; I speak it very badly. Still, I do understand it and can make myself understood—usually. But that will not meet the difficulty. There must be two men and, even more important, two signatures. Yes, postmaster?"

"My Prince, could you not sign twice, once as Prince and again as Foreign Secretary?"

"And have a mirror carried round behind me to fool the Americans into thinking there are two of me? Gilles d'Ecosse, speak your mind."

"My Prince, what will the world think of a country which cannot produce even one Foreign Secretary?"

"I can't imagine. Marcel Avril, speak your mind."

"My Prince, it isn't so bad as all that. What we cannot produce is a second man who can speak English, and why should we?"

There was a murmur of approval, but the innkeeper signified disagreement.

"Henri Tonnerre."

"My Prince, saving your presence, that's not true. I hereby propose we appoint Robert Brown Foreign Secretary, since he speaks English, it being his own tongue. He done us very well before."

Brown started as though he had been stung, but the Prince, who appeared to have eyes in the back of his head, held up his finger and the manservant did not speak.

"It has been proposed that Robert Brown be appointed Foreign Secretary, on account of his exceptional qualifications. I should like the Council's views on this. Chancellor."

"I should like to support this, but Monsieur Brown is not of Sainte-Rochean nationality."

Tonnerre bounced in his seat.

"Henri Tonnerre?"

"My Prince, can't we adopt him? There's a word for it——"

"I think 'naturalize' is the word you want, innkeeper. Let us continue round the table. Postmaster?"

"My Prince, as I asked before, would it be legal?"

"I think the Chancellor and I must look carefully into that. I have an idea that there is a precedent, but I cannot be precise about it. Chancellor, do you know?"

"There's something," said the Chancellor, rubbing his brow, "but what it is——"

"We will find out. Father Denys?"

"An excellent suggestion."

"Marcel Avril?"

"I support it."

"Jean Latour?"

"I don't quite like it. It should be one of us, but as the man must speak English and Monsieur Brown is the only one who does, it seems there's no choice."

The Prince summed up. The first move would be to bestow Sainte-Rochean nationality upon Robert Brown, the second to find out whether one not a member of the Six could be appointed Foreign Secretary. After that—yes, Marcel Avril?

"My Prince, with respect, need we go into all that? As farmer Latour has rightly said, Monsieur Brown is the only possible choice and the matter is urgent. Let us, with Your Highness' concurrence, appoint him at once and naturalize him at the same time."

The Prince looked slowly round the table from one face to another.

"This is, in effect, the proposal originally made by Henri Tonnerre, and I take it that Marcel Avril seconds it. Those in favour, please? That is unanimous." The Prince paused and then glanced over his shoulder. "Robert Brown, is there any-thing you wish to say to the Council?"

Brown walked slowly forward to stand at the end of the table beside the Prince's chair. He bowed to the Prince and then to the Council, and there was a curious little pause. The old curé leaned forward in his chair and rested his elbow on the table, covering his mouth with his hand, to look intently at the Englishman, who looked at the curé with an odd expression which might almost have been fear or entreaty. Suddenly the curé dropped his hand and smiled faintly; Brown threw his head back and looked round the table.

"Your Highness, gentlemen. I am very sensible of the great honour you propose to do me. I am completely unworthy"—his eyes met the curé's again—"of that honour and of the trust in me which—of your trust in me. But it is plain that——" He came to a stop and looked down. "I am—that is, I can serve you in this matter and I ought not to refuse. I will do my best." He stopped abruptly, bowed again, and stepped back.

"Thank you, Robert," said Prince André. "Has anyone any further matter to bring before this Council? Then it only remains for me to thank you for your invaluable counsel."

"Which is no more than our duty," they answered, and stood in their places while the Prince left the room, with Brown following closely at his heels.

Prince André turned in the doorway. "D'Ecosse."

"My Prince?"

"If you will attend me we will write that letter of acceptance for Monsieur Morgan to take to Paris tomorrow."

"As the Prince commands," said d'Ecosse cheerfully, and Brown stood back to let the Chancellor precede him.

"I think you should go before me," smiled d'Ecosse.

"Not yet," said Brown hastily, "not tonight. Let it pass for tonight."

"Brown's right, you know," said the Prince over his shoulder. "He hasn't signed on yet."

D'Ecosse laughed and went on; when they reached the door

of the Prince's study Brown turned away and entered the dressing room. Since Prince André was even more untidy than most young men of his age there was a trail of clothes thrown on chairs and shoes kicked off at random.

"I am the Prince's personal man still," murmured Brown, and reduced confusion to order. While he was tidying the dressing table he saw himself in the glass and stopped to look.

"You, of all people," he said, and laughed shortly.

Presently one of the Palace footmen came to the door.

"Monsieur, the Prince desires you to go to his study."

It may have been because Brown's emotions had recently been so unexpectedly stirred, but at the words "go to his study" a vivid picture flashed up in his mind of himself at sixteen, a short broad-shouldered boy at school lounging in a doorway. One of the masters had come up to him and said abruptly: "The headmaster wants to see you in his study," and it was to Brown as though someone had hit him in the wind. It was a serious matter; in fact, an Awful Row, but he had talked himself out of trouble that time. He had been less successful when he got into trouble again at Oxford; no amount of talking had availed him and he had been sent down. His father——

The footman shuffled his feet, and Brown returned in one leap from the past to the present.

When he entered the study d'Ecosse was still there.

"Ah, Robert," said the Prince. "Here is your naturalization certificate. If you will sign in the right place—d'Ecosse will show you—he will witness your signature."

The two men signed the paper while the Prince strolled restlessly about the room.

"You will have to sign the Burgher's Roll also," said d'Ecosse, "but that will do tomorrow. Your appointment as Foreign Secretary will take a few days to prepare, but there is no immediate hurry."

"We have to search among our archives," said the Prince gravely, "to remind ourselves what an appointment as Foreign Secretary looks like. After all, we have not made one since

1808—was it? We are not to blame for being a little rusty." He grinned suddenly, that impish grin which was part of his charm. "Chancellor, we were talking about raising money for this visit to Paris. To Paris! I can't keep my voice down when I say that. It goes up to a squeak of its own accord; I must be excited. Let us be serious about money. I was going to say, Chancellor, that there are all those simply hideous crown jewels. We might sell something, don't you agree?"

"The Six will have to agree also," said d'Ecosse.

"Of course they must and I'm sure they will."

"Not, of course, the Great Diamond," went on d'Ecosse.

"Of course not. Robert and I are only going to visit Paris, we are not proposing to buy the place. I was really thinking of that frightful baroque breastplate thing stuck all over with rubies. You must see it, Robert—it will make you feel sick. But it's fabulously valuable."

Brown looked from one man to the other and his eyebrows went up.

"You are wondering," babbled the Prince, who did, indeed, seem incapable of keeping still, "why we should talk of selling jewels when we are about to receive unlimited largesse from the United States, may the good Lord take a liking to them. It is a matter of prestige, Robert. D'Ecosse has said, and I agree with him, that it is not consonant with the dignity of a sovereign state to ask for a dollop in advance with which to pay our hotel bills. We may be poor but not disgustingly poor. Eh, d'Ecosse?"

The Chancellor laughed.

"If I might venture a suggestion——" began Brown.

"Continue."

"I thank Your Highness. In order to raise a sum of money for a temporary embarrassment, it is by no means invariably necessary to part with valuables outright. One may obtain a proportion of their value upon loan by depositing the said valuables, Your Highness, as security for repayment of the loan, if I make myself clear."

The Prince wrinkled his nose.

"Robert. Do gentlemen do this kind of thing?"

"Indeed, yes, Your Highness. It is, if I may say so, done in the best circles, Your Highness. Charles II of England did it frequently, or so I have been given to understand."

"I also have read English history, Robert, and I am not sure that the example of your Charles II is one which a high-minded young Prince would be well advised to follow. Eh? I am, no doubt, painfully ignorant of the ways of the world and pathetically ingenuous as well, but I do not quite like this scheme, for some reason. It seems to me to be a little—what—unpleasantly clever, perhaps?"

"I humbly beg Your Highness' pardon for having suggested——"

"Not at all. You were perfectly right to offer the idea, and I am probably being merely foolish. I just feel that I would rather sell something outright than be under an obligation to anybody. Eh, d'Ecosse?"

"The lenders probably charge interest," said d'Ecosse. "Do they, Brown? Yes, I thought they would. Still, I respect Your Highness' scruples and should prefer to indulge them."

"Thank you, d'Ecosse. Don't look downcast, Robert. You shall sell the breastplate for me and ensure that I am not cheated; that is, if you know of anyone who will buy crown jewels. Do you?"

"Any of the great jewellers of Paris, Your Highness, can be trusted to give a fair price for what they buy," said Brown smoothly.

"I suppose so. We need not trouble about it till we reach Paris, need we, d'Ecosse? I take it that there is enough in the privy purse to pay our railway fares."

"I think so, indeed," answered d'Ecosse. "Now, if Your Highness has no more commands to give me, I will take that letter to Monsieur Morgan at The Goat and he can pack it safely in his brief case with the two brass locks upon it."

"Do so," said the Prince. "Good evening, d'Ecosse. Robert,

I want you."

D'Ecosse went out of the room. The Prince lifted down a rapier from the wall, drew the weapon from its sheath, and, sword in hand, called Brown to come to him.

"And now, kneel down," said Prince André. "On one knee is considered more graceful; that's right. How difficult it is to kneel gracefully in trousers, is it not? Robert the Englishman, I hereby appoint you Chevalier of the most exalted Order of St. Simeon Stylites of the Holy Rock." He tapped Brown upon the shoulder with the naked sword. "I hereby appoint you Chevalier of the most noble Order of the Star of the Pyrenees." Another tap on the shoulder. "I hereby appoint you Chevalier of the most excellent Order of the Golden Wheel." Another tap with the sword. "Arise," said the Prince magnificently, "Chevalier Robert of Sainte-Roche. Stand up, man, the ceremony is now over. It is, however, quite genuine, and when you go to England your friends and relations must call you Sir Robert. What's the matter? You have turned bright pink."

"Your Highness, these honours, I have done nothing to deserve——"

"Oh, I wouldn't say that," said the Prince, sheathing the sword and hanging it again upon the wall. "You have tapped for us the limitless wealth of the Golden West, haven't you? Surely that deserves some acknowledgment. Besides, when we go to Paris—ah!—my Foreign Secretary must have some Orders to wear. I will get the insignia out for you tomorrow; they are locked up with the crown jewels. I will show you that ruby affair at the same time. If that doesn't make you blink, nothing will. That is all, Robert, for the present."

Brown backed out of the room, hesitated for a moment, and then made his way out upon the terrace. He leaned his hands upon the balustrade and looked down upon the town and the valley below where the evening shadows were sliding across the fields.

"When we go to Paris," he murmured, and showed his teeth.

CHAPTER XI

Paris

The days before the Prince and his Foreign Secretary left for Paris seemed alternately to drag and rush. Letters were exchanged with the American authorities in Paris. The Prince's wardrobe came under careful review.

"What about those shirts, Robert?"

"Although made of the most exquisitely fine material, Your Highness, the cut is not such as to commend itself to the Paris of today, if I may say so without offence."

"You don't surprise me. They were made for my father; I believe he bought shirts by the gross. Interesting man, my father. Kept goldfish in his bath."

"Indeed, Your Highness? Presumably they could be evacuated when his late Highness wished to perform his ablutions."

"Not at all. He used to swim in the fountain pool on the terrace. Where the goldfish are now. Great man for the open air, my father. We'll buy some more shirts in Paris, Robert."

Brown received the insignia of his various Orders from the strong room in which they were kept. The Order of St. Simeon Stylites, encircled by rather dubious brilliants, showed the saint kneeling dramatically upon the top of a spiky natural pillar apparently about ten feet high.

"That's the Holy Rock. They started to build the church round it but somebody leaned a ladder against it and it fell down, so they made it into the chancel step. Apparently that was the pillar upon which St. Simeon started his pillar-sitting career. He moved on to higher ones as the years went by. I think he was an exhibitionist myself, and even Father Denys doesn't think much of him."

"I have sometimes wondered," ventured Brown, "what gave the saint that idea to start with, Your Highness."

"Wolves, I should think. Or ants. Look, Robert, here are the crown jewels."

Brown looked and blinked. He had heard of these jewels before he came to Sainte-Roche.

"Magnificent," he breathed, and it was true.

"Yes, but a bit lumpish, I always think. One shouldn't stick gems close together like fruit in a plum cake; you can't enjoy any of them. Except, of course, this one. This is what they call the Great Diamond. My mother had it reset."

It glittered alone in a plain and strong claw setting upon a plain gold chain, a very big diamond, though by no means one of the largest known. It was, however, of extraordinary purity of colour, so white as to be almost blue, and Brown caught his breath at the sight of it.

"And this is the ruby breastplate."

It was not, of course, a breastplate at all but a very large and unpleasantly elaborate pendant, thickly encrusted with rubies set closely together. The Prince looked at Brown with one eyebrow cocked.

"It conveys the impression, Your Highness, of extreme costliness."

"I must congratulate you, Robert, upon your unerring choice of words."

"I thank Your Highness."

The Six met once more to deal with various matters and to approve the sale of the ruby ornament.

"You may not remember it, gentlemen," said the Prince. "The Great Diamond you all know, but this thing has not been out of its case for years. Her Highness my mother could not stand it at any price and never wore it. I think you ought to see it. Robert, here are my keys. Will you go and get it?"

"As the Prince commands," said Brown, and went.

When he reached the strong-room door his hands were shaking so much that he could scarcely put the key in the lock. He opened the door, stepped inside, and looked about him; his face was grey, and a little trickle of perspiration ran down his temple. He took the case containing the rubies and came out; in the act of relocking the door he hesitated and looked round; there was no one in sight, and at the end of the passage the terrace door stood wide.

He straightened his knees with an effort, relocked the door, drew out the key, and returned to the Council meeting in the Great Hall to lay the keys and the case on the table before Prince André.

"Well, here it is," said the Prince, opening the case. "Pass it round, gentlemen. Isn't it a horror?"

Jean Latour was rather disposed to admire it and asked if they were not very beautiful rubies.

"I understand that, in fact, they are not of the best," said the Prince. "Father Denys, do you know?" The old priest shook his head and said that he had long forgotten what little he ever knew about such vanities.

"Robert," said the Prince, "do you know about rubies?"

Brown took up the pendant.

"I think Your Highness is right. These stones, if my judgement is correct, are too dark. The really valuable stones are of the colour called pigeon's blood."

"But, happily, there are a great number of them," said the Prince. "And quite a lot of surprisingly solid gold. Well, shall I sell it?"

The Six agreed.

While the Prince was talking to Avril after the meeting, Father Denys spoke to Brown.

"You are knowledgeable about precious stones, my son, are you not?"

"I have had the privilege of seeing some valuable jewels, Father, in the course of my employment."

"I suppose so, I suppose so. When do you start for Paris? Upon the day after tomorrow? My son, you are well aware that our young Prince is a child in the ways of this world. You will stand between him and trouble."

Their eyes met.

"I will do so," said Brown.

The Prince came across to them.

"Are you telling my Foreign Secretary to keep an eye on me in Paris, Father?"

"I am confident, my son, that the Chevalier Robert will be a most excellent travelling companion."

The old man patted Brown vaguely upon the arm and drifted away.

Prince André of Sainte-Roche and his Foreign Secretary arrived in Paris and went straight to the suite which had been reserved for them at the Hotel Georges V. Since the Prince was not the guest of the French Government there was no official reception, but there was a considerable amount of polite fuss. There was a representative of the French Foreign Office to announce that a car, with driver, had been placed at the Prince's disposal during his stay. There was an emissary of the French police to say that a police escort would consider it an honour to attend His Highness at any time, a suggestion which horrified the Prince, who, at home, went about with no more ceremony than any landed gentleman might receive from his tenants. He thanked the emissary politely, having been well brought up, but said that he would not wish to trouble them.

"No trouble at all," said the French police. "A pleasure. It is only to save Your Highness from possibly embarrassing attentions from the crowds."

"Crowds? What crowds? Why?"

The French police smiled charmingly.

"Your Highness does not realize that a reigning monarch who has actually led his troops into battle is a hero."

"Oh," said the Prince blankly. "But that was nothing; they

were only Communists, you know, and my commander in chief did all the work."

"Delightful modesty——"

"Besides, how should anyone know who I am, since I have never been here before?"

"The car," explained the emissary, "with a pennon on the bonnet and a motorcycle escort will inform the onlookers that here is a distinguished visitor. There are, also, the photographs in the Press."

"I see, yes. Please convey to your commander of police my deep sense of his unexampled courtesy."

"I will not fail of it," said the emissary, and took himself off.

"How interesting it is, Robert, to observe the workings of men's minds. They inform the world that here is a distinguished visitor by providing an escort which would not be needed if it were not there in the first place. Never mind. If we wish to be private we can just walk out on our feet. Is there anybody else to see?"

"There is a large gathering of the Press. Would Your Highness desire me to deal with them or would Your——"

"Oh no, I like newspaper men. Send them in."

But it is one thing to talk to a few journalists anxious to get away to watch a battle and quite another to face a horde of men of all types all asking questions, some of which the Prince considered impertinent. He retired to his bedroom and left Brown to deal with the emergency.

When the journalists had gone away Brown found the Prince looking at a half-empty wardrobe.

"Have we any money, Robert?"

"I regret, Your Highness. Very little now remains. With Your High——"

"I want some shirts. There is a shop along the street off which we turned to come here—I saw it when we arrived. It is full of most beautiful shirts, and now I cannot endure these of mine."

"No, Your Highness. I will count the money," said Brown, and did so with the Prince leaning over his shoulder. "Forty thousand seven hundred francs. That is all, Your Highness."

"It looks like a lot of money to me."

"It is much less than it looks, if I may so put it. Only about forty pounds in English money——"

"I don't know anything about English money."

"And Paris is a very expensive city, if Your Highness will forgive my pointing it out, and this is an expensive hotel. Your Highness may have to wait a few days before you actually receive the purchase price for the ruby——"

"Then I'll buy one shirt," said the Prince, gathering up a handful of notes. "About that ruby thing, what are you doing?"

"I was about to suggest, with Your Highness' permission, that I should go out and——"

"Go at once, Robert. Just a moment and I'll give it to you. Here it is. Good-bye, hideosity. Robert, are you sure anyone will wish to buy this? For the gems and the gold, of course. You can explain that I have no objection to its being broken up. In the meantime I will go and look at shirts." The Prince picked up his hat and looked at it. "I don't think I like this, either. Go and see your jewellers, and if they want to know why we are selling rubies you can explain that I want to buy a hat. Have those journalists gone? Then I'm going too. We will meet here, Robert, presently."

Prince André put on his hat, looked at it in the glass, made a face at it, threw it across the room, grinned at Brown, and dashed out bareheaded.

Brown, still smiling, went into the sitting room, taking with him the pendant in its case. He was not anxious about the Prince, since he knew, though the Prince did not, that two alert but inconspicuous men in plain clothes would never be far from the royal elbow. Brown telephoned to a famous jeweller in the Rue de la Paix to introduce himself and make an appointment and then looked round for a piece of paper in which to wrap the case, since it was too large to go into his pocket. He opened the case and looked at the pendant, estimating its value. Something between three hundred and fifty and four hundred pounds probably, since, though the rubies were not of the most desirable colour, some of them were agreeably large. Certainly it should provide the Prince with a new outfit besides paying their hotel bills. Without the slightest warning, a voice spoke behind him.

"What cheer, Bish?"

Brown swung round. The door of his own bedroom stood open and there was a man in the doorway, an undersized weaselly man with a thin face and uneven teeth. He was dressed in a blue serge suit which had never been well cut and he looked like a second-rate clerk, which was what he had been.

"Hullo, Fishy," said Brown casually. "I thought I should see you as soon as I got to Paris."

Fishy Pike advanced into the room with his eyes on the pendant.

"So you managed it. You are a one, aren't you?" he said admiringly. "I said to old George, trust the Bish, I said. He'll get away with it."

"George here with you?"

"Oh yes. We've been following your doings in the papers. Not half been some didos in that little one-horse place, have there? So when we saw in the papers that your Lord High-Muck-a-Muck was coming to Paris we thought we'd better take a run over. That's some of the stuff, is it? Where's the rest of it?"

"Where this came from," said Brown shortly. He closed the case, put it in the table drawer, shut the drawer, and sat upon the edge of the table. Fishy Pike's brows drew together.

"Well, you might let's have a look at it."

"No," said Brown.

"Look here," said Pike angrily, "I tell you straight I don't like your manner. Yes, I heard you ringing up that jeweller with a tale about selling it for the Prince of Sainte-Roche and you was his secretary, huh! You was going to sell it for yourself, that's what, and if me and George hadn't had a bit of forethought, that's the last we'd have seen of you, you double-cross-ing twister! Hand it over."

"Listen——" said Brown.

Fishy moved sharply and there was a pistol in his hand, but Brown sprang at him and twisted it out of his grip. The next moment it was aimed at Pike, who backed away, nursing his wrist.

"You can think yourself lucky I didn't break it," said Brown grimly. "Now you will listen. Tell George from me I'm through with all that business, I've got a good position, and I'm going to keep it. I am selling this thing for the Prince André and not for myself and certainly not for you. I am going straight now and if you pester me I'll break your neck next time. I am the Foreign Secretary of Sainte-Roche and I'll put that country on its feet if it's the last thing I do. Tell George that. And now, get out!"

Fishy whined.

"Look here, Bish. This is a dirty trick after all me and George did to get you in there. All those lovely references you had—who wrote them? Me. Who got the crested paper to write them on? We did. Who arranged to intercept the letters if they wrote back?"

"I did," said Brown.

"Well, so you did, but they didn't write so that came to nothing, and if they had I'd have written the answers, wouldn't I? Can you write six different hands? Not you, for all your col-lege education. Now you've got the doings and you won't divvy up. Foreign Secretary my foot! You're the Prince's flunkey, that's all, and you're so mean you'd make a snake throw up."

"That'll do," said Brown sharply. "You pull a gun on me and then whine because I won't make your fortune? You rat. Still, it's true you and George helped me to get the job. I'll send you some money to London——"

"Huh!"

"—provided you clear out and don't pester me or you won't get a penny. Tell George that too. Now," said Brown, backing across the room until his hand was on the bell, "get out before I ring for the servants and have you thrown out!"

"After all the times we've worked together," said Fishy disgustedly. "I wonder you aren't ashamed. Well, I call your bluff. Go on, ring."

Brown pressed the bell push and there was a short pause.

As the door opened the pistol disappeared into Brown's pocket and a manservant came in.

"I have no idea," said Brown, "upon what pretext this man introduced himself here, but he is an imposter. Be good enough to remove him and make sure that he is not admitted again. The Prince is not to be troubled by persons of this description."

The manservant began to apologize but Brown waved him away.

"Come out instantly," said the servant, addressing Pike.

He went without another word.

CHAPTER XII

Fishy Goes Home

Pike walked out of the hotel in such a state of fury that he scarcely knew where he was going, but when he emerged upon the Boulevard des Italiens a short stocky man turned away from a shopwindow and took him by the elbow. Pike shook him off without glancing at him and walked on, but the short man hurried after him.

"What's the matter, Fishy? You look as though you were sleepwalking."

"What—oh, it's you, George."

"What's the matter?" said George again. "Wasn't he there?"

Pike drew a long breath and told him that Brown was, indeed, there and that he had a plaque thing of rubies about eight inches square——

"Rubies eight inches square? There's no such thing."

Pike explained. Brown had got it and was going to sell it at a shop, which he named, in the Rue de la Paix and was going to hog the whole proceeds himself. "He did say as he'd send us some money to London on condition we left him alone. Very haughty his lordship was—'don't pester me,' he says." Pike went on to say what, in his opinion, Brown was in addition to being haughty.

"That's funny," said George. "That doesn't sound like the Bish."

Pike admitted that the Bishop had, indeed, changed. "Says he likes his job and means to keep it. Princes and such," said Fishy bitterly, "have gone to his head, that's what."

"He admitted he was going to sell it?"

"Had to! I overheard him phoning the shop. Then, of course, he said he was selling it for the Prince. I don't know what sort of a mug he thinks I am to swallow that. I tried appealing to his better feelings but what does my lord do but ring the bell and have me chucked out."

They walked on in companionable gloom till suddenly Pike threw up his head and said: "I got an idea."

"What's that?"

"Say we go down to the Rue de la Paix and wait about till we see him go in the shop. Then I'll ring up the police and tell them there's a well-known jewel thief in there trying to flog some rubies the property of the Prince of Sainte-Roche. Then we'll stand back and watch the fun."

"'Larceny as a bailee by a servant while in charge of his master's property,'" said George gleefully.

"That's right. Very serious. Get a packet for that!"

So they hung about in the Rue de la Paix until they saw Brown enter those discreetly opulent portals and then hurried to a telephone, for, though George knew no language but his own, Pike could speak French fluently. All this having been done, they entered a café upon the opposite side of the street to the jeweller's, ordered coffee, and awaited events. While they sat there Pike told George, with hoots of scornful laughter, what Brown had said about being Foreign Secretary of Sainte-Roche and putting the country on its feet. "All so solemn about it you'd never believe. Ought to tell fairy stories in Children's Hour."

But George, who had known Brown for longer than Fishy had and was also a better judge of men, was not amused.

"It could be true, at that."

"Wha—at? You're mad."

"Oh no, I'm not. I always thought he'd turn honest one of these days. Had it about him, if you get me."

"You're kidding."

"I'm not, then. He was brought up——"

"Look," said Fishy, staring across the street. "*Flics.*"

"Flicks?"

"French detectives."

Two men in raincoats and wearing soft felt hats turned into the shop opposite, and once again the conspirators waited.

Presently two policemen on motorcycles came roaring up the road in perfect alignment and stopped outside the jeweller's shop.

"There," said Fishy, "what did I tell you?"

The motorcycles were closely followed by a very smart car, chauffeur-driven, with a little pennon on the bonnet. This also drew up outside the jeweller's, and a tall handsome young man leapt out and entered the shop. George and Fishy scarcely looked at it; expensive cars holding decorative young men just naturally drive up to jewellers' shops. The only odd thing about it was that there was not a decorative girl there too.

Almost at once a crowd began to gather round the car and in front of the shop, and more policemen arrived to shepherd them.

"And now we can't see a damn thing," said Pike. "Let's go across and gawp like the rest."

They paid for their coffees and went across to join the crowd.

"But he is so handsome," said a woman. "So romantic."

"And so brave," said another. "Figure to yourself that he actually led his soldiers in battle."

There was some time to wait until at last the shop door opened and the distinguished proprietors came outside, bowing nearly double, to escort to his car His Highness Prince André of Sainte-Roche and his Foreign Secretary, who had come to Paris to negotiate for an American loan. The Prince was laughing; even as George and Pike watched with bolting eyes, he slipped his hand through the other's arm and murmured something in his ear.

("And to think," said the Prince, "that Father Denys sent *you* to Paris to keep *me* out of trouble!")

"Stand back, please," said the police, pushing. "Make way there, please."

"Excuse me, monsieur," said Fishy politely to a gendarme who was leaning heavily against him. "Have the goodness, monsieur, to tell me who those two gentlemen are?"

"The Prince of Sainte-Roche," said the gendarme civilly, "and his Foreign Minister, the Chevalier Robert. Move along now, please—ah! Make room here quickly. A gentleman has fainted."

When Fishy Pike had recovered—it was not so much a faint as that his legs gave way—he and George returned to their rooms in one of the innumerable hotels near the Gare du Nord. Here they ordered much needed restoratives and sat down to talk things over.

"That's it, then," said George. "He's turned honest. I'm not altogether surprised; I said so just now. His heart wasn't in the business, as you might say."

"Huh!"

"A man doesn't get called the Bishop for nothing."

"That was just his soapy manner and the long words he thinks up."

"More than that. Well, I'm going to pack."

"Where for?"

"Back home to London of course. Where else?"

"So you're a quitter," said Fishy angrily. "Run away, then. No, listen, George. I'll admit I was wrong and he wasn't stealing the rubies, but he's been a jewel thief, hasn't he? He got that job on forged testimonials, didn't he? Reckon he'll pay a bit to keep that story from being told."

"That's blackmail."

"So what?"

"Several things. One, it's a foul game I've never played and I don't intend to start. Two, it's a dangerous game, and if you're caught you go down for a long long time. Three, suppose he says, like the Duke of Wellington or whoever it was, 'Publish and be damned'—what do you do? You don't suppose anybody'd take your word against his, do you? No. I know when I'm beat and that's now, so I'm going home; and if you've got any sense you'll come too."

"So you're quitting," began Pike, but was interrupted by a knock at the door, for they were sitting in George's bedroom. He called out, "Come in," the door opened, and two men in raincoats, carrying soft felt hats in their hands, came in.

"Bonjour, messieurs."

Pike, the linguist, grunted a reply.

"May we see your passports, please," said one detective.

"But certainly," said Pike. "George, they want our passports."

"Always wanting passports," said George cheerfully, for he had nothing on his conscience in France. "Couldn't we lend the gentlemen a nice Edgar Wallace if they want something to read? Tell 'em that, Fishy." He handed up his passport, and Pike did the same.

The detectives took them over to an adjacent table, looked through the pages, and finally stamped both of them.

"Here," said Pike, who knew perfectly well that this was unusual, "what is it that you do there?" He snatched back his passport and looked at the stamp, which read *Rentrée Prohibée*. "Re-entry prohibited! But this is an outrage!"

"Calm yourself, monsieur, I beg," said the detective with the most exasperating politeness. George asked what was the matter and Pike told him in emphatic terms. George shrugged his shoulders.

"Suits me," he said. "I was going, anyway." He nodded at the detective and said slowly, "O.K. O.K. I go."

The detective bowed amiably as to another reasonable man and added in French to Pike: "There is a train from the Nord in forty-five minutes. The messieurs will wish to pack."

"But I'm not going to be——"

"Monsieur, we shall have the honour of attending the messieurs to that train."

Pike scowled but translated, adding in English: "It's only as far as the first stop outside Paris and we can hop off and come back."

But the second detective, who had been standing by the door saying nothing, chimed in here.

"Eet is all ze no-good, zat. We go wiz you to Calais, messieurs."

George broke into a wide grin at this, for he had a sense of humour, and the detective smiled back.

"Come on, Fishy," said George. "We've had it."

"Let us go out," said the Prince, flattening his nose against the windows of his sitting room. "We now have some money, which, in itself, is a novelty to me, and the evening shadows of the tint of the pale wood violet expand themselves across the city of lights. I read that in a poem, and the peculiar thing about it is that it's quite true—look at them. This is Paris and I have never been here before. Come, Robert."

"As the Prince commands."

"Not so much of the Prince, if you please. In fact, no Prince at all tonight. I had enough of being stared at this afternoon. Tonight I will be plain Monsieur if I must be Prince again tomorrow. Where does one buy uniforms?"

"Uniforms, Your——"

"Of the Corps Diplomatique. Father Denys said that we must get some at once."

But a uniform of the Corps Diplomatique had never been among the things Brown had wanted in Paris. He said he would find out at once.

"You go on counting that beautiful money," said the Prince. "I will go down and ask the hall porter. I remember my father saying that hall porters not only know everything but far too much." He danced out of the room leaving Brown to follow.

Monsieur and Madame Dubois had just arrived in Paris and Monsieur was booking in. He gave the hall porter one of his cards for details of his name and address. The porter looked at it a little disdainfully and dropped it face downwards on the counter. Monsieur and Madame Dubois, complete with luggage, were whirled up to the fifth floor just as the Prince came down.

Porters are not disdainful with princes, and there was a serious discussion before a tailor's name and address were supplied. Brown reached the hall to find the Prince saying, "No, that little square of paper is no good; I shall only lose it. Here, what is this card? I will write on this—it is better for the pocket. Much better. Boulevard des Italiens Number what?"

The Prince showed this to Brown and said that they would go there tomorrow. What was on the other side? Ah, André Dubois from Périgueux in the Dordogne, whoever he was. "There we are, Robert. My *nom de guerre* for tonight. I shall remember André—it is my own name—and Dubois is easy."

"Happily," said Brown, "for Your Highness' purpose, Dubois is perhaps the commonest name in France, as common as Smith in England."

"Excellent. Tonight, then, I am Dubois and you are my friend Brown from England, eh, Brown?"

"As you wish, Dubois."

"And don't bow when you speak to me! One might as well have a fanfare of trumpets at once. Come on."

So they strolled about the streets of Paris as the lights came up, stared into shopwindows, and leaned over the parapet of the Pont du Carrousel to look down upon the Seine. To the Prince, who could vaguely remember having seen a car or two before the bridge of Sainte-Roche was destroyed and had never seen electric light, everything was a marvel.

"What is that tall square vehicle with all the people in it?"

"An autobus, Your—h'm—Dubois. Public transport."

"Public? Can anyone travel on them? Oh, come on!"

The Prince galloped after and sprang on one of them, only to be sternly repulsed by the conductor.

"It is absolutely forbidden to mount upon a vehicle of the

Public Service other than at a recognized stopping place. Hop it, you!"

Brown, running madly, fielded the Prince from under the bonnet of a taxi, the driver of which advised him (Brown) to buy a collar and chain for his escaped lunatic (the Prince).

"There seem to be a great number of rules of conduct in Paris," said the Prince ruefully. "More than you would expect, to look at it."

They had dinner at the Tour d'Argent, where the view from the windows, the decoration of the rooms, the marvellous food, and the smooth excellence of the service delighted the Prince beyond measure.

"This is the way to live," he said rapturously. "Isn't it, Robert?"

When he saw the bill he turned quite pale, but Brown reassured him.

"To dine at the Tour d'Argent," he said, "is an essential part of every young man's education, if I may say so, er, Dubois."

"Never mind," said the Prince bravely. "It was worth it."

But he was seized with a fit of nervous economy and refused to enter an expensive night club. They went instead into two or three small cafés to watch a floor show and drink a glass of wine and finally descended many steps to a *caveau* where French traditional songs were sung and there was some quite unbelievable juggling. The place was not crowded, and they sat in chairs three or four rows back.

In the second row, sitting alone, was an extremely pretty girl with bright smooth hair; in the row behind her there was a young man of a flashy type who was leaning upon the back of the chair next to the girl and trying to engage her in conversation. She ignored him in silence for some time and then suddenly lost patience and turned on him.

"Will you go away and let me alone?" she said in a clear carrying voice and in English. "I don't know you and I don't want to know you."

"This cannot be allowed," said the Prince abruptly.

He rose from his seat, walked forward to where the girl was sitting, made her a low bow, and sat down beside her.

"Please forgive that I leave you alone so long," he said in his careful English. "I was so much delay, I am sorry." He turned round and directed a hard cold stare upon the young man in the row behind; Brown, thinking that there might be trouble, also came forward to stand at the Prince's elbow.

The young man looked from one to the other, sat back in his chair, fidgeted, and finally got up and went out.

"Oh, thank you so much," said the girl. "I think you've just about saved my life or something. That nasty man's been pestering me for a quarter of an hour, and though I didn't understand one word he said, I didn't like what it sounded as though he meant."

"He was not a nice person, no, mademoiselle."

"My father would say it served me right, going around by myself in Paris," she went on.

"It was perhaps not wise for so beautiful a lady to come to such a place as this unescorted," smiled the Prince.

"You may be right," she said. "But my father had to go out to meet some men about business and I got so bored I had to do something, didn't I?"

"Naturally, mademoiselle, but as things are, may I please to offer myself for escort? I will promise, no pestering, indeed. If you wish, I go." He half rose in his seat.

"No, sit down, please. I do need an escort, and it seems that I've found one." She gave him a dazzling smile. "Tell me, you are French, are you?"

"My name is André Dubois, mademoiselle, and this is my friend Monsieur Brown of England."

Brown, who was sitting just behind them, stood up, bowed, and sat down again, murmuring that he was honoured.

"And I'm Betty Hopkins of New York, so we're an international group."

"Mademoiselle pays a visit to Paris?"

"Yes. My father, Adam K. Hopkins of the Hopkins chain, came over here on business and I got him to bring me along for the trip. But you, you live in Paris, Mr. Dubois, do you?"

"Alas no, mademoiselle, I come from—from the very far South of France. This is Mademoiselle's first visit?"

And so on, while Brown sat in the chair behind them, wondering whether the blond Betty Hopkins was one of the troubles he had promised Father Denys to ward off.

She was innocently willing to talk about herself, their penthouse apartment in New York, and their summer home in the Adirondacks; her mother, who was an enthusiastic socialite and loved giving parties; and her father, who didn't like them at all.

"Your father, he is perhaps," said the Prince, struggling to express himself, "a man most serious? The party, it is too—too light for him?"

"Well, in a way. It's the people. Dad likes men who do something, and what he means by that is make money. No, that's not quite right. It isn't the money itself so much as the fun of getting it. Do you understand?"

To the Prince André, money had always been merely embarrassing when it was not there and of no interest whatever when there was enough of it. This revelation of so different an outlook merely sent his eyebrows climbing, but the end of the story made all things plain.

"Ah, now I see. Your father, he is the hunter, tireless after his quarry. Since he must live in a city where there is no ibex he must hunt the money. The man who climbs and stalks all day and at last he comes home with the dead beast, he is King for the time, no? So is your father among his friends when he shoot down the most money. Simple. I shall like your father, the King of money."

Betty opened her mouth, shut it again, and then said that Monsieur Dubois had better not use that word to her father. "He doesn't like titles, not inherited ones, you know."

"Oh," said the Prince, deflated, "doesn't he?"

CHAPTER XIII

The Hopkins Chain

The Chevalier Robert, Foreign Secretary of Sainte-Roche, was exceedingly busy in the days that followed. He and the Prince had gone to Paris under the impression that they had only to sign some large important documents with massive red seals attached, after which they could return home, the money would begin to roll in, and they could spend happy months supervising repairs and restorations.

They were soon undeceived, for the Foreign Secretary found himself spending busy mornings going through schedules which had been prepared by the American Commission of Enquiry, Messrs. Mathews, Spenlow, and Farson. He was humiliated to find that they had learned more—far more—about Sainte-Roche in a week than he had discovered in six months. They asked questions about land tenure, about rights of way, about forestry laws, about overriding interests, about custom and wont, ecclesiastical rights, and governmental authority until his head went round, and he appealed to the Prince.

"Your Highness should have brought Monsieur d'Ecosse, if I may take the liberty of suggesting it. He——"

"What? Bring one of the Six to Paris? Heaven forbid."

"I hope I know my place better than to suggest that Your Highness should be burdened with a share in these negotiations——"

"Then don't suggest it, Robert."

"But," wailed Brown, "I do not know the answer to one in ten of the questions they ask me."

"You can always refer to me. I probably do."

"If I may be allowed to say so, that is why I suggested that Your Highness should occasionally deign to throw light upon some of these problems."

"But I do, Robert, don't I? Only last night I spent nearly an hour explaining to you our system of farm tenure. Don't tell me you weren't listening."

"Every word Your Highness does me the honour to address to me is ineradicably engraved upon my——"

"Then that's all right. Don't fuss, Robert, you are doing extremely well and I am pleased with you."

Brown practically wrung his hands.

"I am most deeply gratified by Your Highness' approval, but it is the delay caused by my continually having to refer to Your Highness which weighs upon me."

"Don't let it. Am I complaining about the delay? Answer: No, I am not. It suits me very well. I have fallen in love with Paris, and heaven knows when I shall be able to come here again. You carry on."

Brown tried once more.

"If Your Highness would but come to even one of these conferences——"

"I am far too busy," said the Prince firmly, and Brown gave it up.

The fact was, and the Prince knew it perfectly well, that Brown was not only worried about these conferences but also about what the Prince was doing all by himself with no escort except a couple of practically imperceptible detectives who would certainly guard but could not guide. However, some days later the Prince himself threw a certain light upon his doings, probably because he was fast arriving at the stage where he had to talk to somebody.

"She is wonderful," he said. "Completely undazzled by rank and wealth."

"Er—Miss Hopkins, Your Highness?"

"Certainly Miss Hopkins. She actually came to Paris to get away from an Italian count whose pretensions had her mother's support."

"Indeed, Your Highness."

"Indeed yes. He is a 'no-good twerp from Twerpville.' She says that that is what her father says. She says that he is a great big oily brute with oily manners and she can't stand him."

"The young lady disapproves of her father?"

"Don't be inane, Robert. The young lady disapproves of the count and her father concurs. Her mother likes titles and her father does not. The situation is a little awkward."

"It would appear so, Your Highness. The young lady's mother is not in Europe?"

"No. What a good thing that I am Monsieur Dubois."

"Yes, indeed, Your Highness."

"So she appealed to her papa about the count and the good Hopkins brought her away to Europe with him. Thus," said the Prince, gazing dreamily out of the window, "we met."

"Your Highness has also met Mr. Hopkins?"

"Oh yes," said the Prince, returning abruptly to this hard world, "yes, I have. Robert, he wants to know what I do for a living. I said that I was managing an estate—that is reasonably near the truth, is it not? He asked me to whom the estate belonged, how many men I had under me, where the estate was, how much I was paid, what prospects of advancement I had, how long I had 'held down the job' and how much longer I proposed to go on holding it."

"Most embarrassing, Your Highness."

"I found it so. He told me that it was a mistake to stay in one job too long. He said that by the time he was my age he had washed dishes in a restaurant, sold newspapers, broken into the film business, started a chain of laundries, owned a fleet of motor launches at Miami, and now he is the Hopkins chain. Robert, what is this Hopkins chain?"

"I will endeavour to ascertain, Your Highness."

"Do so, Robert. Some association with machinery, possibly? He says he could use me in the business if I were prepared to start at the bottom and work up. He has, he says, no use for a man who expects to step into a managerial post without having gone through all the stages." The Prince sighed. "It is all very awkward."

"Yes, indeed, Your Highness."

"And when I didn't jump at the offer he says he's got no use for lazy bums who think the world owes them a living. When I evade his questions he asks why I am hedging and the next minute he is saying what he thinks about effete European minor royalties, in which category he includes anyone with a title. Robert, what will happen when he finds out who I am?"

"I could not take it upon myself to say, Your Highness."

"No. How are the negotiations getting on?"

"I was about to inform Your Highness that they are all but complete and the official signing is now expected to take place in the morning of the day after tomorrow."

"Oh, is it? I have to do that in person, don't I? Yes. Tomorrow evening, then, Robert, I will have copies of the agreements here for me to read through and you will explain to me anything which I do not understand."

"It shall be done, Your Highness."

"For I may be a complete booby in the affairs of this world, but I recall that the last thing my father told me before he died was never to sign anything without reading it first."

"Most excellent advice, Your——"

"Robert. I have not seen her for three days."

"Indeed, Your Highness?"

"Robert, as my Foreign Secretary you should be told that I intend to marry this lady if it be possible, but I am not sure that it is. I have accordingly written to the Six to direct them to search through our archives to find out whether it is lawful for me to marry a commoner."

Brown looked at the Prince, who was walking up and down the room with his eyes on the carpet.

"I have kept away from her," went on the Prince, "because I could not bear to see her again without telling her what is in my mind, and if the marriage is impossible according to our laws, the sooner I go home the better."

"Your Highness——"

"My Highness. That's the trouble. I wrote nearly ten days ago and no answer yet from the Six. I suppose they had to call a meeting to authorize a search of the archives and then search through them and then call another meeting to draft the reply." The Prince laughed shortly. "Robert, how wonderful it must be to be plain Monsieur Dubois and free to marry whoever you like and take a post in the Hopkins chain—did you find out what that was?"

"Not yet, Your Highness. I asked one or two and they did not know of anything called the Hopkins chain."

"Never mind. Try to find out. I shall go to bed, I think. It is late and perhaps there will be a letter tomorrow."

On the following morning the Prince had just begun breakfast when one of the hotel staff came to the door with letters on a tray, and one of them was from Sainte-Roche. The Prince took it up and looked at it, set his jaw, and tore it open while Brown tactfully retreated across the room. The next moment there was a yell of joy.

"Now God reward the enterprising soul of my great-great-great-grandfather Theodore! Read that!"

The Prince threw the letter in the general direction of his Foreign Secretary and rushed out of the room.

Two hundred years earlier, Prince Theodore II had married a Scots lady, the daughter of a General Kennedy, and thereby thrown open the palace doors to Miss Betty Hopkins of New York.

"I wonder if she had money," thought Brown. "That would be not long after the Jacobite risings, so probably she hadn't. I expect General Kennedy was an *émigré* and all the money he had would be the price on his head. Come to that, we don't know that Miss Hopkins has, either. What the devil is a Hopkins chain?"

The Foreign Secretary found it more difficult than usual to keep his mind upon the business which fell to be transacted that morning, but fortunately negotiations were so nearly complete that it was mainly a matter of checking details already agreed, and by lunchtime it was done.

"We will get fair copies typed out this afternoon," said the American negotiator. "Will ten tomorrow morning be a convenient hour for your principal to sign for Sainte-Roche? And you too, of course. Come and have a drink."

Brown had the drink, agreed to the time for the signing, "subject to His Highness' concurrence, but I do not anticipate any difficulty," and worked the conversation round to the Hopkins chain. What was it?

"Chain?" said the American. "What sort of chain? There are all sorts, aren't there? Mooring, ships for the use of, bicycle and motorcycle transmission, anchoring for dogs? There's quite a selection, isn't there?"

"There's that Hopkins who owns a chain of hotels," said another American in the group. "Adam K. Hopkins. They say he's quite a fellow. Started as a bellhop, he says himself, and he should know. Now he owns a chain of hotels half round the world and is a millionaire several times over. I stayed at one someplace—Rome was it? Lucerne? I can't recall just where it was."

Brown thanked his informant and said to himself that the young lady seemed to have at least one of the requirements of a bride for the Prince, the well-filled purse. He took a copy of the agreement to show to the Prince and went back to the hotel.

He found Prince André sitting in a chair by the window and looking absently at nothing in particular; his mouth was a straight line and he appeared to have a headache. He looked up when Brown came in.

"Ah, Robert. Is that the copy of the agreement? Give it to me and I'll go through it."

"It is complete, Your Highness. There will be fresh copies made for the signatures tomorrow."

"I suppose so," said the Prince. He took the folder and began to turn over the pages at random. "It all looks rather dull, doesn't it?"

"The literary style is indeed somewhat turgid, Your Highness, but the ultimate results should be gratifying."

"I suppose so," said the Prince again. He turned another page or two and then dropped the folder on the floor. "Robert, they have gone away."

"Gone away——"

"And nobody knows where."

"But was there no message for Your Highness?"

"No. I gave my name as usual—Dubois—and asked the porter to ring up to ask if they would receive me, and the fellow looked at me with a sort of grin and said they had left the day before. He regretted infinitely that Monsieur had not been informed. I told him not to take that tone with me and asked where they had gone. He said that he was desolated but that he was not empowered to give Monsieur any information. I then told him who I was and, Robert, he did not believe me. I think that that is the first time in all my life," said the Prince angrily, "that I have not been believed."

Brown made a shocked noise.

"So I sent for the manager, who kept me waiting, but when he at last came, he recognized me and exhausted himself in apologies. He took me to his room and said that Monsieur and Mademoiselle Hopkins had suddenly given up their rooms and departed for, he understood, Switzerland. When he asked them for a forwarding address he was given the American Express Office in the Rue Scribe here, in Paris. I asked him—I actually brought myself to ask him, Robert—if he knew why they had gone, was it some bad news. I thought that perhaps her mother—— He said he had no information but perhaps the chambermaid might know; he would send her in if I wished it. So I interviewed the chambermaid, yes, I cross-questioned a serving wench about the lady I intended to marry."

"Your Highness should have summoned me."

The Prince took no notice. "I asked her whether she could tell me why they had gone so suddenly and where to. She was most sympathetic. I had, I believe, seen her before." Brown guessed at a handsome *douceur* now and again. "She said that upon the night before last she was summoned to their suite and Monsieur told her to pack Mademoiselle's things as they were leaving early in the morning. She began at once to do so and, since Mademoiselle's room opened from the sitting room, she heard most of what was said. In short, Robert, she was eavesdropping, and I paid her to tell me what she had heard. I did that." The Prince kicked a footstool across the room.

"Your Highness——"

"What?"

"If extreme privacy were really desired, Mr. and Miss Hopkins had only to see to it that the door was shut. It even occurs to me to wonder, if I may make so bold as to suggest it to Your Highness, whether Miss Hopkins allowed the conversation to be overheard with a view to its being repeated if Your Highness should make enquiries."

"Nonsense. She would know I should never do a thing like that."

"But——"

"But I did. Yes, but she would not expect me to do so. At least, she ought not to have—— Where was I?"

"I have been given to understand, Your Highness, that the ladies are the more practical sex and do not conduct their affairs by the same rules as those which gentlemen impose upon themselves."

"Oh, do they not? Then they ought to. But, Robert, if you are right, that would mean——"

The Prince retired into a private dream, and Brown waited

with all the patience he could muster. If the Hopkins millions came to Sainte-Roche . . .

"Have I told you what the woman said?"

"Not yet, Your Highness."

"Oh. Apparently Miss Hopkins and her father were quarrelling over me. The chambermaid says that though she cannot speak English well, she can understand most of what is said. Monsieur disapproved of Monsieur Dubois because he did not work, and if Mademoiselle was getting soft over him they were going to move on. I asked where, and she said 'someplace else.' He said he wasn't going to have any idle loungers who could not account for themselves making eyes at his daughter. He said this several times in different words. Miss Hopkins, it seems, did not say much. She was angry with Monsieur but when he asked her who and what was this Dubois she had not much to say. He said he did not wish to be hard on his little girl, but where did Dubois come from? Who were his people? What was his profession? His prospects? His salary? Monsieur said that he himself had offered this Dubois a job but he had not fancied it, apparently. Then he said that there was this man he had to see in Switzerland, and then they would think what they would do next. So at last she agreed to go. That is all. Robert, the papers have published photographs of me several times of late. Why has he not seen them? Plainly, he still does not know who I am. Nor does she."

"Because, Your Highness, they are unrecognizable," said Brown firmly. "Photographs reproduced in continental newspapers—I did not recognize them myself. Did not Your Highness look at them?"

"No. Why should I?"

"Why, indeed. Your Highness wished me to find out about the Hopkins chain. It is a metaphorical chain composed of hotels in various parts of the world."

"Oh, is it," said the Prince, plainly not interested. "Not machinery. Robert, why did she not write to me or leave a message?"

"I could not hazard a——"

"Could it be because I have not called for the past three days?"

"The departure would appear to have been precipitate," said Brown. "It is conceivable, Your Highness, that the young lady prefers to wait until she can, without interruption, compose a letter to Your Highness."

"You do your best, Robert, don't you? I wish I were at home. Robert, we can go tomorrow, can we not? If I sign those papers in the morning we can leave directly. Robert, where is that agreement? Ah, thank you. Now, while I go through it paragraph by paragraph, do you pack our things so that we may leave in the morning, and before this time on the day after tomorrow I shall be at home."

"As the Prince commands."

"Robert! I am an idiot. She would, of course, address a letter for me to Monsieur Dubois at this hotel." The Prince sprang to his feet. "I am going down to the hall porter——"

"With respect," said Brown, hastily intervening between the Prince and the door handle, "it would not be fitting for Your Highness in person—— I will go at once to obviate the undesirable possibility of the porter getting—er—ideas."

"Porters always get ideas," said the Prince, "even in Sainte-Roche. I am coming too."

"But——"

"I will lurk in the background," said the Prince, pushing his Foreign Secretary before him like a wheelbarrow, "but come I will. Would you have me burst with impatience? I hear the lift. Run!"

CHAPTER XIV

Parker Hooks a Fish

The Prince stood back and impersonated a young man interested in theatrical announcements while Brown addressed the hall porter.

"Good afternoon. Would you tell me, please, whether there is any letter for Monsieur Dubois?"

The porter bowed low to the Foreign Secretary of a Sovereign Power, but allowed some surprise to appear in his voice when he said that but certainly there had been. Monsieur Dubois' letters had been claimed regularly either by Monsieur in person or by Madame his wife. Monsieur Dubois had a profuse correspondence which was always punctually collected.

"Oh," said Brown. "I gather, do I, that there is indeed a Monsieur Dubois staying in this hotel?"

"But certainly, Excellency. A provincial gentleman from Périgueux in the Dordogne. Monsieur may have seen him, a stout gentleman with a pointed beard."

"Oh, very possibly."

"If it is a question of a letter having gone astray——"

The Prince, in the background, shook his head and drifted dispiritedly towards the lift.

"Thank you," said Brown. "It does not matter."

"I was about to say, Your Excellency, that it would be difficult to enquire of Monsieur Dubois since he and Madame left the hotel this morning."

"It is of no consequence. Thank you," said Brown.

He went away to join his master by the lift, which was some-where aloft.

"Monsieur Dubois——" began Brown.

"I know. I heard," said the Prince, irritably prodding the lift button. "There still remains the agreement with the Ameri-can authorities to soothe my mind and fill my idle moments with useful employment while you pack. The call of duty, Rob-ert."

"Unquestionably, Your Highness."

"And tomorrow we go home."

The lift came and bore them away.

The agreement was formally signed upon the following morn-ing by the Prince and his Foreign Minister in their new uni-forms of midnight blue encrusted with silver lace and further embellished with the insignia of all the Orders they possessed. The Americans who also signed the agreement were dressed in lounge suits of decorous grey; when the two parties first came in sight of each other there was a momentary pause instantly broken. No one, of course, made any comment, but there were flowers in the room. The Americans, idly circling about the centre table, one by one achieved roses in their buttonholes. A nice gesture.

The Prince made a graceful speech, and the leading Ameri-can made a suitable response. "My country," he ended, "has gained a new and, believe me, a valued ally."

"A grateful and faithful ally," smiled the Prince.

After which the party broke up into less formal groups.

"And what are your immediate plans, Prince? Do you plan to make a tour of Europe before you return to Sainte-Roche?"

"No, indeed. We are needed at home to prepare my people for the arrival of Progress. I have to meet my funny little Parliament and tell them all about this," said the Prince, lifting his copy of the agreement and immediately handing it to Brown. "That is, the Chevalier Robert will tell them all about it and I shall sit at the head of the table and try to look as though I had done it all myself." He smiled deprecatingly. "My part will be to open their minds to the receipt of new ideas before your people arrive to put them into practice. You will excuse us if we rush away? We have, I am told, a train to catch. Good-bye, monsieur. I hope that someday you will come and visit Sainte-Roche. I shall be so happy to see you."

He shook hands with the leader of the American party and thereafter with all the other members in the exact order of their seniority, and drifted gracefully out of the room with his Foreign Secretary at his heels.

"And that," said one of the Americans as the door closed, "is the head of a little country a quarter the size of the state of New York. Well, I suppose they're trained that way."

The Prince and Brown arrived at Py during the morning of the next day, since it is a long way from Paris to Perpignan and the connections beyond that are slow and inconvenient. At Py they summoned a car from the garage which always provided transport to Sainte-Roche.

"To the broken bridge," said the Prince, at which the driver looked mildly surprised but made no comment, merely murmuring "*Altesse*" in a polite voice.

"You telephoned Sainte-Roche," said the Prince as the car moved off, "did you, Robert? To order the mules."

"Certainly, Your Highness."

"And who answered?"

"I believe it to have been Madame Durand, Your Highness. She did not give her name."

"She made no comment?"

"None, Your Highness, except to repeat the estimated time of arrival."

"She is a shy woman," said the Prince, leaning back comfortably, "she would not know what to say." He yawned. "I did not sleep in the train."

When Brown looked at the Prince five minutes later, he was fast asleep. The car drove on and up, mile after mountain mile, and Brown noticed with surprise that there were tracks on the road where heavy vehicles had passed that way.

The car mounted the last rise and came down to the place where the stump of the old frontier post still awaited renewal. Now there was a red-and-white striped pole across the road and a tent at the roadside. The car stopped and the Prince woke up.

"Where are—oh, yes. What on earth is that?"

"Customs barrier, *Altesse*. French customs.

"Saint Simeon! It was never here before."

A man came out of the hut and walked up to the car; before he had time to say anything the driver leaned out of his window and addressed him.

"Remove your Maypole, Alphonse. This is His Highness the Prince of Sainte-Roche and the Chevalier Robert."

The man came to attention, saluted, and swung the pole up out of the way; the car passed on.

"A milestone on the road of history," said the Prince. "France acknowledges the existence of Sainte-Roche."

The car went on to the gateway towers of the broken bridge and there stopped.

"His Highness," said the driver, "wished the car to stop here?"

"Of course, there would be a resounding crash if you didn't. Scrap iron down on the rocks, your car."

"Not now," said the driver, and moved on slowly through the archway.

The Prince looked, sat up, and stared. "But there is a bridge," he said.

"A temporary bridge, *Altesse*," said the driver. "The Commission caused it to be put." He drove the car on slowly.

"This bridge," said the Prince, "feels oddly light as it were."

"*Altesse*," answered the driver, "it has not, naturally, the rock-like solidity of a genuine bridge, but it will carry far heavier weights than us. It is like the temporary bridges we used during the war." He drove on across the ravine.

"And what happens——"

"There is a road, *Altesse*, rough but serviceable. The Commission caused it to be bulldozed. Your Highness will desire me to drive on?"

"Certainly. How far does it go?"

"To the town, naturally. The Commission said that this access was to be made first in order to get their vehicles in as soon as the work starts."

"I see," said the Prince in a rather stifled voice. "Does it really go all the way to the town?"

"Certainly, *Altesse*. I myself drove a party to the town last week. Journalists, *Altesse*."

The car entered upon what used to be the track through the forest. It had been a bridle path when the Prince had last traversed it, a green lane. It had become a raw yellow scar with the scrape marks of the bulldozers still plainly visible. It was rough and uneven and soft in places; the car rolled and tilted.

"The Commission," said the driver, picking his way, "say that this will be a good road when it is properly made up, *Altesse*."

The Prince threw himself back in his seat and his brows met.

"The Commission this, the Commission that," he said in a tone the driver could not hear. "It is time I came home, Robert. Whose Principality is this, mine or the Commission's?"

"Your Highness signed the agreement yesterday——" began Brown.

"But this work was done long before that."

"Your Highness has momentarily forgotten the clause which gave retrospective permission for preliminary work to improve the access to Sainte-Roche." The Prince turned a blank face upon him and Brown went on. "Yes, indeed, if I may venture to recall the clause in question to Your Highness' mind, it was Paragraph 19, section C, sub-section (f). I took the liberty of reading the draft to Your Highness for approval on the day when it was originally mooted, Your Highness."

"Oh. Yes. I remember now. I was thinking about something else at that time. You are right, Robert." The Prince's scowl lifted and he broke into a laugh. "I don't know what I am losing my temper about; it certainly needed doing. Perhaps I am missing the mules. But, Robert, if I was taken aback, what must my people have thought? Especially the Galliennes, for they have lost their livelihood."

The car rounded a bend in the road and overtook a string of mules. They were in pairs, and upon each mule were two large drums slung pannier-fashion. The Galliennes were leading them as of old; when the Prince's car passed they waved their hats and cried a greeting, grinning widely.

"They look cheerful," said the Prince. "Do you notice, Robert, that every single man of them has a new shirt?"

The car did not pass through the town but turned off by a road leading up to the Palace; this was always passable, since waggons used it to take up supplies. The driver blew his horn, the main door of the Palace was wide open, and the old seneschal in his official dress stood in the doorway. The Prince sprang out of the car, Brown paid off the driver, and the luggage was carried into the hall. The Prince of Sainte-Roche had come home.

Brown had expected some sort of ceremony with or without trumpets. He was mildly surprised and the Prince saw it.

"We are not supposed to leave the country," he explained. "So nobody sees us off and nobody welcomes us back. If we are not seen about the place we are officially 'resting.' It is all in the archives. My great-grandfather used to 'rest' for a couple of months every year in the days of the Third Empire. He had friends in Paris, they say. Seneschal, I am hungry."

After lunch the Prince walked into the town to show himself and hear the news.

The arrival of the Prince in Paris to sign the agreement had reawakened public interest in Sainte-Roche, and one British newspaper took the trouble to send a correspondent there to write half a dozen articles upon various aspects of Sainte-Roche. He was a red-haired young man named Parker and he was an enthusiastic fisherman. He went back to his lodgings in a

Bloomsbury side street to pack; his landlady heard packing noises and came upstairs.

"Are you off again so soon?" she said. "It's only the other day you came back. Let me fold your shirts, for pity's sake; do you like going about looking as though you kept your clothes in the rag bag and for all you know you might be going to meet some quite nice people for a change though I do believe you prefer talking to all the oddest people you can find and heaven knows where you do find them. Here, let me come."

"It's the odd people who tell the odd stories," said Parker. "That's why I cultivate them. They it is who enable me to pay your bills instead of living in sin at your expense——"

"Mr. Parker! Really!"

"Well, it's a sin to obtain goods and services without paying for them, isn't it?" He took down his fly rod from the wall, slid it out of its holland case, and went over it carefully. "It is the odd people who buy my clothes, my beer, my cigarettes——"

"There's a button off this shirt. When are you starting?"

"Today. Two-thirty from Victoria."

"I'll sew it on while you have your lunch. Have it here today? I've got a nice piece of steak. Haven't you got a clean tie at all? You'd better go out and buy one; there is time. What else is to go in here? Socks and handkerchiefs; give me your shaving kit. You'd better take a fresh cake of soap."

" 'You are my heart's delight,' " sang Parker. "Fly book, spare casts—where's that new line? Ah. Can you get these in too? Oh, sit on it; that'll change its mind."

"Where are you going to this time, Mr. Parker?"

"Sainte-Roche."

"Where there's that handsome young Prince. I saw his picture in my paper the other day. I do hope you get some decent digs and no fleas or even worse. You can't trust these foreign places though of course they can't help it I suppose—see how they've been brought up—and I'm sure I'd never trust myself to eat anything not knowing what their kitchens are like——"

Parker had been recommended to stay at The Goat but when he eventually reached Sainte-Roche, having covered the last stage on a builder's lorry, he found that The Goat was uninhabitable with pipes, bathroom fittings, plumbers, painters, and paper hangers.

"But I put you up, yes! It is only to find a room." Tonnerre looked wildly round the yard as though there might be a spare room or two lying about. "I have it, there is the little room over the bar—it is only that a man is putting the hand-basin in. It will be all right, Monsieur need not to take any notice of him—it is not as though Monsieur was a lady visitor, then indeed I would not suggest it——"

But Parker brushed him off and went to The Hunter; proprietor, Jules Gobain. It was a small place indeed; there were only four bedrooms for guests and the furnishings were meagre, but it was clean and Madame Gobain could cook. Parker wandered about the town, talked to people, and wrote a couple of articles; then, in pursuit of agriculture, he went for a walk down the valley. A mile outside the town he came to a sizable stream with a bridge over it; he leaned over the parapet to look into the water and did not believe what he saw. He rubbed his eyes and looked again and then went back at a trot to The Hunter for his rod and some information. He had found Gobain's French surprisingly different from that which is spoken in Paris, but with patience and goodwill on both sides they managed fairly well.

Fish? Certainly there were fish, Gobain said. They were in the river and Sainte-Roche ate them on Fridays, being a good Christian community.

Parker wanted to know where and from whom one asked for permission to fish the river. This proved a little difficult because Gobain could not conceive of a place where people were not allowed to fish.

"You want to fish? Why not? Go, then, and fish, monsieur. A permit? What for? Does anyone own fish, then, while yet they

are swimming about? What an idea. Let Monsieur fish where-
ever he likes; no one will object. Shall I ask Eugene Dompierre
to lend Monsieur his net?"

"Net?"

"To bring ashore the fish."

"Ah yes. A landing net. I did not bring one. Who is Eugene
Dompierre?"

"He is a farm worker every day except Thursdays. On Thursdays he is a fisherman."

"On Thursdays—oh, of course. In readiness for Friday."

"Precisely, monsieur. When we of Sainte-Roche are tired of
fish we have eels from the millpond instead."

"Where does Eugene Dompierre live?"

Gobain pointed out the cottage and added that Dompierre
was probably at home for lunch at the moment. Parker walked
to the cottage, found the man there, and explained that he
wanted to be shown the best spots for fishing if Dompierre
could spare the time to show them to him, and he rattled some
loose coins in his pocket.

"This evening, monsieur? At a little after four, if that will
suit Monsieur?"

"In time for the evening rise."

"Pardon?"

"Where shall we meet?"

"At the bridge at the end of the lane from The Hunter?
Good. Does Monsieur wish me to bring the gear also?"

Parker assented and left Dompierre to his meal.

When they walked by the river that evening, Parker was surprised to find that the places commended by Dompierre were
level stretches of the river where the bed was reasonably flat and
unimpeded by large boulders, as free of rocky outcrops as of
long deep pools such as he would himself have chosen. At last
Dompierre stopped.

"This is far enough," he said grumpily. "What sense is there
in so much walking?" He swung a sack off his shoulder, up-

ended it, and shook out the contents, a long narrow net of the proportions of a tennis net. "Will Monsieur cross the river or shall I?"

When the horrid truth dawned upon Parker, considerable time was wasted while he explained that he wouldn't think of catching fish in that barbarous manner but in the proper way with a rod, a line, and a fly. When this new idea, helped out by a demonstration, eventually penetrated the mind of Dompierre, he was not impressed.

"What?" he said. "One at a time? And so slowly? How long does it take Monsieur to catch a fish in that manner? It is easily to be seen that Monsieur never has to supply a whole town with fish all in one evening. So hard the work, too!"

"It is for the sport," explained Parker.

"Ah," said Dompierre darkly, "the sport. I see." He retired to a grassy bank, turned his back upon the river, and lit a pipe. Parker was much too happy to care. The trout were unsophisticated in the matter of flies, but once hooked they fought like tigers; since Dompierre would not help in landing them Parker had his hands full.

Eventually Parker hooked one of a size unbelievable in that water and played it up and down a long pool until it was hard to say whether fish or fisherman was the more exhausted, since his tackle was too light for a catch of that size. However, at last he manoeuvred it into the shallows.

"Dompierre!"

"Monsieur," in a drowsy voice.

"Get that cleek of mine and come and land this fish."

"I was asleep," said Dompierre, getting up slowly. "What did Monsieur want?"

"That—that hook with a handle—be quick!"

Dompierre brought it to him.

"Can't you—oh——"

Dompierre threw down the cleek with a contemptuous look, waded noisily into the shallows, threw himself upon the fish and brought it ashore. Parker, beaming and gasping, came up to gloat over it.

"It's nine pounds if it's an ounce."

"When we catch fish like that, we throw them back."

Parker goggled at him.

"So big as that," said Dompierre, "they are too coarse to be good. The little ones, they are the best. This one, he is an old man, he is tough. We go home now?"

Parker's first act, when he got back to The Hunter, was to set up his Press camera with its delay-action shutter and take his own photograph holding up the big trout. His next was to sit down at a corner of the dining table and write an article for his paper upon Fly-fishing for Trout in Sainte-Roche.

In due course the article appeared with his photograph beside it; it was read by, among many others, a lean man sprawling untidily in an armchair at his club. When he had read it twice he sat up and looked round.

"I say, Curtis. Have you seen this?"

His friend came across and read the article.

"Giles Parker," he said, and peered at the photograph. "Yes, I've met that fellow somewhere. He's quite good. Writes articles in *The Field* sometimes."

"He knows his stuff, does he?"

"Oh yes."

The first speaker refilled his pipe.

"What about going there," he said, "instead of Carinthia next week?"

"It 'ud be a change," said Curtis, "if Manton agrees. He was in the club—I saw him come in." He put his finger on the bell; when the servant came in he said: "Oh, Fryer, if Mr. Manton is still in the club, would you ask him to come in here for a moment?"

Apart from Tonnerre's French workmen, the first strangers the Prince saw in the town were three men in worn tweed suits with flies in their hats.

"Who are those gentlemen?"

"Englishmen, my Prince," answered d'Ecosse. "They have come here to fish in the river."

"Indeed? It seems a long way to come, does it not, for that?"

CHAPTER XV

Progress Hits Sainte-Roche

Prince André strolled on and came presently to The Goat, practically unrecognizable behind dazzling new paint. In the yard at the side were stacks of water pipes, fixed handbasins not yet fixed, two glittering baths and a sink of such dimensions as to enable it to be used as a third in emergency, and other fittings even more useful but less elegant, especially when upside down. The Prince stopped to observe this display, and Tonnerre rushed out to greet him.

"My Prince, I hope Your Highness had a pleasant rest."

"Excellent, thank you. You are busy here."

"I went to Py and said that I wanted my hotel modernized. This is it."

"I see. All this looks to be a costly business, Tonnerre."

"Yes, my Prince, but I told the Six I would do it all on my own and I have."

"You were, I believe, practically the only citizen of Sainte-Roche to acquire any foreign currency from our earlier visitors."

"That is so, and now I'm spending it in order to satisfy later visitors, if I make my meaning plain."

"You do. What is that boy doing sitting at that table?"

"Counting money, my Prince."

"How nice for him. Your money?"

"The boy," broke in d'Ecosse, "is my best pupil, Guillaume Tarri. He has always had a natural flair for arithmetic."

There was a small shop in the town which sold pottery ware

of a primitive and useful kind: mugs, pots, plates, dishes, and kitchenware. It was made in a village a few miles down the valley where there was a deposit of suitable clay, and a strictly limited family concern worked it. The product was of a pleasant deep cream colour, and some of the more ambitious tableware was decorated with freehand designs in primitive colours by a middle-aged spinster of the Corbet family who had been crossed in love in her youth and had taken to art as a counter-irritant. The result was something like the ware made at Quimper in Brittany, but wilder. The war correspondents and later the American Commission of Enquiry had taken a liking to the untutored fancies of the star-crossed lady and bought quite extensively, paying in all their various currencies.

This brought Sainte-Roche face to face with one of the more tiresome aspects of modern life, the varying value of different currencies, for Madame Grand-Jean Corbet who kept the shop had run out into the market square with her first half dollar and shown it to everybody, crying: "What is this? What is this?" It was handed round, rubbed, bitten and spat on for luck, but nobody knew what it was.

"Go, you, to Monsieur d'Ecosse," they said at length. "Show it to him. He is a schoolmaster; it is his business to know about such things."

"It is a fifty-cent piece of the United States of America," said d'Ecosse, laying down his magnifying glass.

"I was sure you would know," said Madame Grand-Jean Corbet.

"An interesting coin," said d'Ecosse, handing it back. "The bird upon one side depicts the American eagle and the female form upon the other represents an idealized figure of Liberty getting up early to see the sun rise."

"I daresay," said Madame, "but what is it worth?"

"In Sainte-Rochean francs?"

"But naturally!"

"Currencies vary in value, relatively to each other, from time to time. It would be necessary to find out the present-day value of the United States dollar vis-à-vis the Sainte-Rochean franc."

Madame Grand-Jean stamped her foot.

"And, in the meantime, I am selling my goods and I have no means of knowing whether I am giving them away for a tenth of their value or——"

"Or what?"

"Or not."

"I must find out," said d'Ecosse. "This is a matter which will become increasingly urgent. Do you return tomorrow morning and I will tell you."

"Tomorrow morning early," said Madame menacingly, and went away, taking her coin with her.

D'Ecosse went out to find Marcel Avril.

"Have you by chance a recent copy of a reliable and informative newspaper? French for preference."

"I had a copy of *Figaro* only four days old but I lent it to the curé. Was it perhaps some piece of news——"

"A list of international currencies," said d'Ecosse, and told him why.

"This predicament will recur," said Avril, scowling horribly. "Let us consult Monsieur le Curé."

They found him in his bare little parlour sitting in a patch of sunshine with a large pair of spectacles upon his bony nose and reading even the small advertisements in the week-old *Figaro*. D'Ecosse explained his need.

"Ah," said Father Denys. "Yes. Here it is."

He turned to the appropriate page, found the list, and showed it to them.

"But it does not," said d'Ecosse, "mention the Sainte-Rochean franc. That, no doubt, is because there have been no dealings in it lately." He brooded, tapping his teeth with one fingernail.

"In the old days," said the curé, "was our franc equivalent to the French franc? I believe not, am I wrong?"

"Many years ago," said d'Ecosse, running his finger down the list and doing mental arithmetic, "many, many years ago. But when the French franc fell soon after the first world war, we abandoned that parity."

Marcel Avril leaned forward eagerly. "Did we, then, maintain a rate of our own or establish parity with some other currency?"

"The French franc," brooded d'Ecosse, "is at a pitiably low rate, even worse than it was at the time of which I speak. We could not possibly return to that, we who have so much we need to buy from abroad. We pinned our franc at that time to the Swiss franc, which appears to have remained stable." He laid down the *Figaro* and turned a calm authoritative look upon Avril. "I think that for the present we must maintain that rate."

"You are the Chancellor," agreed Father Denys, "but, in point of fact, any change would have to be authorized by the Six, would it not?"

"Certainly it would."

"Whereas, if no change is made it will be possible to begin changing money at once."

"That is so, my father."

"How convenient, then," continued the curé, "that the currency with which we chose to be affiliated should be one which has maintained its value."

"That is so," began d'Ecosse, and suddenly threw in his hand. He looked the curé full in the face for the first time for ten minutes and blurted out: "Can you conceive of any more horrible task than that of explaining to Latour, Durand, and Tonnerre the details of international currency and thereafter of persuading them to give the Prince sensible advice in the matter?"

"No," said Father Denys, "I cannot. But it would be easy to consult the Prince."

"I always intended to do that—I propose to go up to the Palace now," for this was before the Prince went to Paris.

"I am not sure," said Avril timidly, "that I quite follow the argument. Were we not, in fact, at parity with the Swiss franc?"

"No," said d'Ecosse, slowly turning red. "We had a rate of

our own which varied almost from day to day. We tried at one time to hold it at two different rates, one for use when we wanted to sell something and the other for when we wanted to buy something——"

"No!" said Avril, clutching his head. "Please stop."

"At which point my predecessor in office went out of his mind, and then the bridge fell down so it did not matter," said d'Ecosse. "Now the bridge is up and we have it on us once more." He sighed.

"If I may advise," said the curé, "I think you should go to the Prince, taking this list, and suggest parity with the Swiss franc. Should he ask, say that I support this suggestion."

The Prince took an immediate interest in the problem. "You must anticipate being asked to change, not only American money, but also French, Spanish, German, English, all the lot," he said.

"Certainly, my Prince. Taking the Swiss franc, it will be simple. Having to fix an exchange rate of our own as against all these varying currencies——"

"Oh, please," said the Prince.

"Explaining it to all members of the Six——"

"D'Ecosse, I beg of you."

"—who may have views of their own about what the rates should be, my Prince."

"It is part of my duty," said the Prince very firmly, "to protect my people from anxiety, terror, and embarrassment. And also, of course, from making fools of themselves in public. I shall do so on this occasion. The rate of exchange will remain at parity with the Swiss franc, as before."

"As the Prince commands," said d'Ecosse happily.

Long before Prince André returned from Paris, foreign coins had become commonplace in Sainte-Roche. D'Ecosse soon found that money changing took up far too much of his time and he called in the boy Guillaume Tarri, one of those "calculating boys" with a freakish gift for mathematics who crop up from time to time in the most unlikely soil. Guillaume's parents were practically illiterate, but he would extract the cube root of 24,389 in his head. To adjust sliding rates of international currencies would be child's play to him. D'Ecosse showed him the list cut from the *Figaro*, told him what was wanted, and left him to get on with it.

Work started at The Goat, and the French workmen found lodgings in cottages in Sainte-Roche for which they paid in francs, as also for their drinks, cigarettes, and other incidentals. Young Tarri left school to attend to his business, and one day he came to d'Ecosse.

"Monsieur, excuse me. Who pays for all this work I do?"

"Sainte-Roche."

"Oh. Monsieur, excuse me. Should not those who benefit pay for this service? Sainte-Roche, excuse me, is poor."

"That is true and your suggestion appears to be equitable."

"Thank you, monsieur. Excuse me, how much? Five per cent?"

D'Ecosse had consulted the curé upon this very point and was therefore ready with an answer.

"I understand that five per cent is the usual charge."

"Thank you, monsieur. I will put up a notice to that effect. Excuse me, but could you tell me what my office should be called?"

"The name," said d'Ecosse without a smile, "should be proclaimed in several languages. *Bureau de Change. Wechsel. Wisselen.* I will write them down."

"Thank you, monsieur."

Tarri set up a table outside The Goat, and under the three headings a notice hung upon the wall behind him. *Discount 5%. G. Tarri.*

When Giles Parker came to stay at The Hunter another line was added to the notice.

"Travelers écheques cassed."

The Prince walked across to the table and the boy stood up.

"Well, how is business? Are you kept busy?"

"More busy every day, if it please the Prince."

"Excellent. But are you not much exposed to the weather here? What happens to all your little bits of paper when it rains and the wind blows?"

"Excuse me, the Prince. I have taken the Widow Frachot's front room upon the street along there. I start there next week. Hitherto it has not rained, excuse me."

"Excellent. May you prosper."

"Tell me, d'Ecosse," said the Prince as they walked away. "For what does this boy change his foreign coins? I thought that we were short of Sainte-Rochean currency."

"It is coming out, my Prince. People send for things they need from Py and they buy French francs to pay for them. Look, my Prince, at the draper's shop across the square. The stuff for dresses and curtains comes from Py and the draper demands cash in payment. He will not now take eggs for stockings."

"And the boxes under the beds are being opened at last, eh? To think that we despaired of getting this done. That boy Tarri should soon be rich on his five per cent. He can lend it to the rest of us at a further five per cent. I hope he is honest, d'Ecosse."

"I have told him that if he slips but once the Six will close him down and start a national bank. He replied that it would be foolish to cheat when his living depends upon people knowing that he wouldn't."

"He will be the richest man in the country soon. One of these days he will have a palace in Venice," said the Prince, who had looked at illustrated papers while he was in Paris, "a palatial yacht at Cannes, a castle in Spain, and a mansion in London. Perhaps he will invite me to stay. As his guest, I mean."

"It would be too much honour for him," said the scandalized d'Ecosse, but the Prince only laughed.

"Stranger things have happened," he said.

On the following day there was a meeting of the Six in the Great Hall of the Palace. The Prince gave an account of the negotiations for the American loan and the Six passed a resolution of thanks and congratulation for his efforts on their behalf and the Prince said that the Chevalier Robert had done most of the donkey work, don't you know. The Six said yes, naturally, since that was the purpose for which he had been appointed Foreign Secretary, but they passed another resolution in formal terms appreciating his services.

Brown bowed and the Prince raised one eyebrow. He had already learned to assess the mood of a meeting almost before it started, and it was plain that this one was not going to run upon oiled wheels.

"Who has matter to bring before this Council? . . . Louis Durand, postmaster, speak your mind."

"My Prince, I should like to know what is to be done about the post office. It is not like it used to be at all—people come in all the time. I had three in at once yesterday afternoon. It's all those foreign workers and the Englishmen at The Hunter, always writing letters and wanting stamps to stick on them. We shall run out of stamps soon." He paused and looked round the Council. "I may be old-fashioned, gentlemen, but to me the proper way to sell stamps is by the sheet, not in ones and twos. That is retail trade, like selling fish. Then there is a gang of people flood in on the evenings to see if there's letters come for them—again it's those foreigners mostly. It all makes so much work, I have had to hire a boy who has just left school and can still read and write to serve behind the counter. I am paying him out of the stamp money. Have I the Council's approval of that? If there is much more business comes in I shall have to hire another boy—it will be too much for one."

Somebody growled: "Unless you do a job of work yourself for once," in a voice so gruff and low as to be barely audible, but the Prince dropped on it instantly.

"Order. Any Councillor having anything to say will address me and that only in his due turn. Louis Durand is speaking. Continue, Durand."

"My Prince, I do work. I assemble the letters, put them in the new bag, and send them to Py by any lorry which is going there if there is one—sometimes there isn't and the letters must wait. I receive the incoming bag from Py and sort the letters into pigeonholes in alphabetical order to be called for. I open the office in the morning and lock it up at night. I set out the stamps for the day; if they are all sold I must get out more. I had a parcel to despatch on Tuesday and there are no official postal rates for parcels. Happily my wife had a sheet of a Swiss newspaper which came round the meat; since we are using Swiss francs for money—not exactly that—the same sort of francs—I thought I'd better use Swiss postal rates too. I hope I have the Council's approval for that? They were printed on the newspaper."

He stopped, apparently for breath, and the Prince intervened to say that it would be as well to settle that point before proceeding further. Would someone propose that Sainte-Roche adopt similar postal rates to those of Switzerland? Proposed by Marcel Avril, would anyone second that? D'Ecosse, our Chancellor——

"My Prince, in an organization called, I believe, the European Postal Union, are not all international postage rates the same?"

"But I've only got the Swiss ones," said Durand angrily, and added: "my Prince" as an afterthought.

"I do not know, d'Ecosse, the answer to your question," said the Prince, "but surely it is immaterial. If the rates are all the same the Swiss will use them also; if they are not, what the Swiss use will do for us, will it not? Is there a seconder for Avril's motion? Thank you, Father Denys. Those in favour?"

The vote was unanimous.

"Durand," said the Prince, "the word is still with you if you so wish."

"Yes, my Prince, thank you. Could I have a new date stamp, please, for stamping the letters? I can get the day and the month on ours but the years don't go on beyond 1943, and one of those Frenchmen asked me had we all died that year and not found it out yet? Insulting. No manners."

"A little crude, perhaps," agreed the Prince. "I suppose these things are not very expensive? If the postmaster orders a new one and pays for it out of the stamp money, there is no need for a resolution of this Council. Agreed? Good. Anything else, Durand?"

"Yes, my Prince. Nothing will induce me to use that devil-inspired——"

"Durand."

"I beg your pardon, my Prince. That unsatisfactory telephone. I got a shock out of it yesterday that threw me against the counter. It is dangerous and I won't use it." He sat back with a bump, and the Prince looked round the table.

"Marcel Avril, you generally work this death-dealing instrument, do you not?"

"Yes, my Prince. Frankly, I am not an electrician and I know very little about how it works, but I have never got a shock from it."

"Would the difficulty be met if you, Avril, personally instructed Durand's young assistant in the use of it?"

"I have, but——"

"But he can't reach it," said Durand, bouncing forward, "my Prince. He is not tall enough."

"Let a stool be provided," said Prince André. "A wooden box will do. Is that all, Durand? Very well. Does anyone wish to comment upon the postmaster's report?"

CHAPTER XVI

Here We Come

Apparently no one wished to comment upon the postmaster's report; it is possible that they knew that their frank opinions of Durand and his work would not be in accordance with the Prince's strict standard of Council decorum. After waiting for a few moments of silence he started again.

"Who has further matter to bring—Henri Tonnerre, innkeeper."

"My Prince, I don't know if I do right to bring this matter before the Council——"

"If not, the Council can always decline to hear you, Tonnerre."

"I suppose so, my Prince. Though my guest rooms are not yet ready for use I have got the dining room going, and many a one who has to sleep elsewhere is glad to come in for an occasional meal or a little glass of something at the bar and talk to their friends. It is high-class trade, that is the point, and will be more high-class as time goes on and we get more visitors. Not wishing to cry down anyone else as is honestly doing their best for visitors, but there's no question my hotel is the best in the place, and since my dining room's been done up there's many say there isn't a prettier room this side of——"

"Tonnerre. The Council applauds your initiative and wishes you success, but——" The Prince paused.

"I beg pardon, my Prince. I let my tongue run away with me, there's no doubt, and always did. What I wanted to say was how that class of trade demands the best wine and there's no doubt we make good wine in Sainte-Roche, but the way the price has gone up is something wicked with the farmers charging"—he carefully did not look at Jean Latour—"half as much again and more. It isn't only the wine either, it's milk and butter and eggs, anything off the farms as is supplied to The Goat has gone up to the moon. I know people are free to charge what they like, as if they charge too much people don't buy and thus greedy people learn sense, but it seems to me that all the farmers are in this together where I'm concerned. What is so unfair," said Tonnerre, colouring up until tears came into his eyes, "is it's only me as is charged these horrid prices. They haven't gone up for ordinary people who buy—it's only me. It isn't fair, when I'm doing all I can to bring trade into the town, for people to get together to overcharge me. My Prince, I protest. Can't the Council stop it?"

He sat back and there was a short pause until Latour leaned forward upon the table and looked at the Prince.

"Jean Latour, farmer, speak your mind."

"My Prince, I was hoping that some of us as have been better educated and understand finance and that would speak up about the principle of the thing. Although I have been person-ally attacked over this table——"

"Latour."

"My Prince? With respect, you did not stop Tonnerre."

"I was about to say, Latour, if you will permit me, that in my opinion the attack was not personal but aimed at all farmers, though it is true you represent them here. Tonnerre made it quite plain, to my mind at least, that his complaint was against all the Sainte-Rochean farmers alike, and it was this which pre-vented him from applying the usual remedy for unsatisfactory service by dealing elsewhere. If you, Latour, will speak for the whole farming community in reply to this charge, the Council is ready to hear you, but I will have no personalities bandied across this table. Latour, do you wish to continue?"

"I beg the Prince's pardon. The—the case is this. Those who

165

entertain visitors for a financial return get paid for what they supply," said Latour slowly, taking time to arrange his thoughts. "They are in a different position from ordinary people buying supplies for their own use in their own homes. At least, so some of us think. When we see the price of a glass of wine go up to double or even more what it used to be, it don't seem right that only those who actually sell it should take all the profit. Why shouldn't us who produce the stuff do a bit better out of it too? As for not raising the prices to ordinary people, well, they are no better off than they were before all this started. How can they afford to pay more? That is what we farmers think." He sat back.

"Thank you, Jean Latour, for a very clear explanation of the farmers' point of view. That is the sort of considered statement which I always hope to receive from this Council whenever questions like this arise," said the Prince, and Latour coloured with pleasure. "I agree with a suggestion made by Jean Latour that here there is a question of economics upon which we should seek help from those who have studied such matters. Chancellor, have you any light to throw upon our darkness?"

"My Prince," said d'Ecosse, "I only wish I deserved your confidence better than I do. From what I have read in history, there are always difficulties whenever a country changes its way of life. As we are doing. And there will be more changes and more difficulties for us to face. As I see it, if all goes well with us the country will prosper, and all the people in it will prosper also if we arrange things properly. But at the beginning we shall not all prosper at the same pace. Those who deal directly with the visitors are the first to feel the benefit. It is for us to see that it is passed on as quickly as possible. For example," he smiled, "I can imagine that my salary as schoolmaster will come a long way down the list for improvement. And rightly, since unless prices rise generally I can live on my salary. It is the very poor whom we must protect."

"Thank you, Chancellor. Er—Father Denys, our beloved curé, speak your mind."

"My son. As the Chancellor has indirectly suggested, this is the time to put Christian ethics into practice. To be generous and not grasping, to share our benefits among our fellows, to protect the poor, that is obvious and we all agree. As to how this can best be done I am not wise enough to say. The obvious thing is to keep down prices, but if there is more money in the country I believe that to be impossible, if I remember the economics I learned at school. Someone more familiar than I with present-day affairs must advise us."

"Father Denys has described our goal," said the Prince. "Who will tell us how to gain it? Henri Tonnerre."

"My Prince, if we want someone as knows outside affairs there's only one who really knows, the Chevalier Robert."

Brown was standing, as formerly, behind the Prince's chair. Before they came to the meeting the Prince had said that his Foreign Secretary should sit at the table.

"I thank Your Highness most profoundly for the honour he suggests, but may I beg to be allowed to decline?"

"Really, Robert? Why?"

"Most inadvisable, if I may say so. I am a stranger here; it would, if I do not presume, be a serious mistake if I were to put myself so forward."

"You think they won't like it."

"Just so, Your Highness. I am an incomer and should keep my place."

"As Foreign Secretary?"

"A temporary post only, if Your Highness remembers."

"Oh. Yes, of course. You think they might unfrock you?"

"If I showed signs of presumption, Your Highness, yes."

"You may be right. Have it your own way, Robert. Let tact be our watchword."

The Council's tepid acceptance of the vote of thanks to the Foreign Secretary showed Brown just how right he was.

"Tonnerre has suggested," said the Prince, "that the Chevalier Robert be consulted. Those in favour—no, I want a seconder, please. D'Ecosse, thank you. Those in favour—that is unanimous. Chevalier, can you advise us here?"

Brown moved forward to the table and bowed.

He agreed with everything that Monsieur le Curé and the Chancellor had said. "Like doctors, they have completely diagnosed our trouble; now it is to find a remedy. Instead of trying to deal with the trouble as a whole, by price restrictions or some such device, would it not be possible to break it into small pieces and deal with them separately? If, for example, all those who were now being paid more for their goods and their services"—Brown paused and looked apologetically round the Council—"that is, already, innkeepers and those who let rooms, farmers and those who supply goods, the post office, the shops in the town, the newspaper office which has many times multiplied its editions and its sales——"

The Prince's slow grin widened, a laugh spread round the table, and the curé lifted his hand.

"Father Denys, our revered curé."

"My son, I ought not to be omitted from this list. The French workmen are good Catholics and our church has also benefited."

"Continue, Robert," said the Prince.

"It would seem, with respect, that everyone has already benefited except our schoolmaster, as he has already said," went on Brown. "I would venture to suggest, with the utmost diffidence, that it might sometimes be possible to pass on the profits in the form of higher wages to employees. This would immediately spread the benefits to the poor. In this way, and being careful on all hands that prices do not rise more than is reasonable, the transition period may be as smooth and easy as possible." He stepped back to his place.

"Has anyone any comments or questions—yes, Henri Tonnerre."

"My Prince, it was only to ask if those who take the most trouble and risk their own money, like me, shouldn't get an extra reward beyond those who do nothing but put up clean curtains to their windows?"

"Robert?"

"In the majority of foreign hotels, Your Highness, there are two bars as a rule. One is more comfortable, better furnished, more expensively decorated than the other and sells a greater variety of liquors. This is usually called the cocktail bar in these modern days. The other bar is quite separate and is much simpler and more homely; as a rule it has a separate entrance. The point is that in the cocktail bar the drinks cost more than they do in the ordinary bar, even if precisely the same liquor is supplied. One pays for comfort and elegance of décor. If one does not wish to pay extra one uses the ordinary bar."

"But, my Prince, would anyone pay more for wine than he need?"

"Robert?"

Brown smiled gently. "For psychological reasons alone, yes. For prestige, for social purposes. Also, of course, for comfortable seats, shaded lights, and warmth in cold weather."

"Well, there you are, Tonnerre," said the Prince. "Comfortable chairs and elegance of décor, and you can charge what you think your customers will stand. But put in another bar at the back where simple folk who are not getting their salaries raised, like our schoolmaster the Chancellor, can still afford to go. For the rest, let each of us behave like honest men and good Christians and all will yet go well. Eh? Has anyone anything to add?"

No one had, and the curé beamed generally upon the Council.

"Who has further matter to bring before this Council? D'Ecosse, our Chancellor."

"My Prince, a matter for the information of the Council, though I do not know that any action is necessary. Guillaume Tarri, who runs our Bureau de Change, informs me that he is getting an increasing number of Spanish pesetas offered for exchange. There is little or no demand for pesetas as yet—they will have to be sent into France to be changed, but that is not the point. It seems that the smuggling into Spain is increasing. There was always a certain amount of tobacco run over the mountains into Spain for barter, but not much. Now that Spanish currency can be changed here, the practice is increasing, and I am told that two or three Sainte-Rochean men have been caught by the Spanish frontier patrols and jailed for short terms."

"How does the law stand, Chancellor, will you remind the Council?"

"My Prince, Sainte-Roche has no restrictions on the import or export of any article, nor could we enforce such a law if we had one, since we have no police or frontier patrols of any sort."

"No. They are breaking no law of ours."

"None, my Prince. Only the Spanish import regulations."

"With which the Spanish authorities are perfectly capable of dealing, no doubt. Has any Councillor any comment to offer on this report? Jean Latour, farmer."

"Only to say, my Prince, that these men know perfectly well what they are doing, and if they are silly enough to get caught they must abide the consequences."

"I am inclined to agree. Any further comment? No, then who has further matter to bring before this Council? No one, it seems. In that case it only remains for me to thank you for your invaluable counsel."

There followed the time-honoured response:

"Which is no more than our duty."

Adam K. Hopkins finished his business with his hotels in Switzerland and eventually arrived in London accompanied by a still rather absent-minded daughter.

"Yes, I know we could stay at the Hopkins and be waited on like royalty with all charges on the house," he said, "but I just don't want to. Let's go stay a few days in one of those historical old hotels. I want to watch things and see what keeps them ticking. I want to know what they've got the Hopkins chain hasn't got and, barring a bedroom Charles the Second slept in before the battle of Bannockburn, which cuts no ice with me as you know, the Hopkins chain shall have it, whatever it may be. So I've booked a suite at the Savoy, which they tell me is quite a place, and if you'll tell me what you like about it that we haven't got, we'll have it, Betty. You watch things too, and tell your old dad; I'd appreciate it."

But apart from the rooms being quite unnecessarily vast by the Hopkins standard and a certain *je ne sais quoi* about the service, Betty had little to report.

"Yes, I know what you mean about the service," said her father. "It isn't showy, it's just there. I don't believe I've seen anybody run since we came in here, and yet when you want anything it's been done already. I don't know whether it's the staff or where they get them if it is, or if it's the management, and where do they come from? As for the rooms, the size is simply ridiculous." He looked disapprovingly round their sitting room, which looked out upon the river. "In any of my hotels they'd get four rooms into the space this one takes up, and then they'd all have everything. What it must cost them for floor coverings is just staggering, and there's a dozen square yards and more in the corners of this one room that's never stepped on. Sheer waste of space."

Betty agreed and looked out of the window and the telephone rang. Adam K. Hopkins got up from his chair and answered it; it seemed to be a report from somebody about an order for kitchen utensils for hotel use, and Mr. Hopkins was deeply interested. His daughter noticed this, hesitated a moment, and then opened a copy of the *Illustrated London News* which lay upon her knee.

It was not quite a new one—it was in fact a fortnight old. Betty had picked it up at her hairdresser's to look at while waiting for an appointment, and had found one item in it which interested her so much that she had unrepentantly purloined the paper. The item was an excellent photograph of a dark and handsome young man in an official uniform of some kind embellished with a quantity of silver lace and the stars of several Orders. His face, with a look half friendly and half shy, was perfectly familiar to her, as was the air of completely unconscious authority, that of a man who has been notable for so long that he is unaware of it. It was, in fact, a portrait of the enigmatic André Dubois of Paris, the man who would not talk about himself. The caption below the picture was explicit enough.

"His Highness Prince André Amadeus Joseph Theodore of Savoy, hereditary ruler of the Principality of Sainte-Roche, who is in Paris to negotiate American aid for his undercapitalized country."

Miss Hopkins looked at the portrait for a long time, and a variety of expressions pursued each other across her face.

Her father finished his conversation and hung up the receiver, Betty closed the magazine without hurry and turned towards him. He dropped into the chair opposite hers.

"Well, that's another thing settled. Another two or three days and I'll be through here. What have you been doing today, Betty? Shopping?"

Betty said that she had gone with that nice woman in the next suite to see the marvellous pictures in the National Gallery.

"That's right, enjoy yourself. There must be something in this art business—look at the people who spend so much on it. I'll have to look into it sometime. When I've finished here, Betty, where would you like to go? Back home again?"

"Isn't there anywhere else in Europe you want to go?"

"Well," he said, rubbing his chin, "there's Austria. There isn't a single Hopkins hotel in the whole of Austria. I'd need a lot of information first, though."

"I guess, Dad, Austria's full of hotels already. It's been a great tourist centre for years."

"That's certainly so, but are you thinking a Hopkins hotel wouldn't pay there? We thrive on competition, Betty. You pick a place in Austria, anywhere you like, and I'll put a hotel there, and if it isn't paying in two years——"

"Oh yes, I'm sure it would. I was only thinking it would be much more fun for once to start in a new place where there aren't any hotels at all. Start right in on the ground floor and show what the Hopkins chain can do with a clear lead."

"You mean, find a fresh place nobody's thought of and work it up into a tourist centre? Why, yes, that would certainly be an interesting thing to do, but where would it be? See, Betty, I've been over here quite a bit, but I don't know Europe like my own yard back home and I guess most of the really good spots have been worked on already. You've given me an idea, though. I could send some scouts out."

"Do you remember, Dad, that Mr. Mathews we met in Paris who had something to do with American Foreign Aid? He was at that cocktail party at the American Embassy——"

"Morris M. Mathews, yes. He gave me his card. I've got it somewhere. He was talking about some place he'd been to look at; I've forgotten the name, Saint something—what was it now?"

"He was talking to me about it," said Betty. "He said it was so lovely it was out of this world. Terribly sweet but quite primitive with one tiny inn where they stayed, and the cooking was marvellous. They'd all been cut off from the world because a bridge fell down——"

"That's right. Saint something——"

"Sainte-Roche."

"Sainte-Roche. Wasn't there a Prince or something from there in Paris about the time we were there? There was some talk about him."

"I think there was," said Betty.

"Well, you've certainly started me thinking. If I could get on to Mathews, but heaven knows where he is now—these fellows are all over the place. I'll put American Express on to it, and if they don't know they can find out. Good cooking, eh? Well, that's certainly something. Suppose we take a run down there, Betty, if it isn't too awful, and have a look for ourselves? If we don't like it we can leave again next day."

"Of course we could."

"I'll call American Express right away and have them make full enquiries." Hopkins crossed to the telephone and picked it up. "Is that the desk? Could you get the American Express for me, please? O.K., I'll hold on." He turned, holding the receiver to his ear. "That was a bright suggestion of yours, Betty. Looks like the Hopkins brains aren't going to die out for a while. Betty, if this means you're beginning to take a personal interest in the business, it's worth all the rest. That's my girl." He turned sharply. "Is that American Express? This is Adam K. Hopkins. Listen, can you——"

Betty looked away out of the window and her fingers tightened upon the *Illustrated London News*.

"Sainte-Roche," she murmured inaudibly, "here we come."

CHAPTER XVII

The Photographer

In Sainte-Roche the busy days slipped past as the community adjusted itself gradually to changing conditions. The Foreign Aid Commission experts came back to set in train the improvements they themselves had suggested; Morris M. Mathews, Economic Adviser, spent long hours conferring with the Chancellor while the children had an unscheduled holiday, for no man can be in two places at once. Edward K. Spenlow of Roads and Communications stood over his foremen while they took levels and marked out roads, and the farmers of Sainte-Roche wailed aloud when their workers left them to earn better money with pick and shovel along the highways. Mr. Spenlow also had interviews with Louis Durand, postmaster, on the allied subjects of letters (delivery and collection) and telephones.

"We have a telephone," said the postmaster stubbornly.

Mr. Spenlow sighed, and the interpreter girded his loins, for he was beginning to know Mr. Spenlow.

"Listen," he said. "To call that thing a telephone is a misuse of a quasi-scientific term. The point is that in a place this size you don't want a telephone. You want a small exchange here in this office with connections to the Palace, the hotels, the outlying farms, and so on. Then they can speak direct, through this office, to Py or Perpignan or Paris, or London or New York if you want to. Or, of course, to each other."

"What about?" said the postmaster.

After an hour or more of this sort of thing—conversation carried on through an interpreter is always slow—Mr. Spenlow walked down to The Goat, entered the bar, and ordered a little restorative. He was leaning heavily upon the counter, wrapped in wordless misery, when Donald Farson, Housing and Education, walked in.

"Hullo, Ed. What's wrong?"

"I'm resting. I'm sitting trying to remember just what it is the postmaster here reminds me of and I've just got it. It's the long, pale face of an albino donkey whose mother was frightened by an extractor fan so he can only move backwards. If at all." He drained his glass.

"Have another. 'Allo, monsieur! Encore," said Farson, indicating Spenlow's glass. "For me, too."

"Thanks, Don. That man——"

"Oh, cheer up. These people are fine guys, all things considered. You know, you don't make allowances. You have to put yourself in his place. How'd you feel if one day when you were back home in Dallas, quietly fixing your wife's washing machine, a bunch of guys from Mars walk in and tell you you ain't seen nothing since you were born and you don't want to bother about electric power any more because from now on everything's going to be run by the inexhaustible alternating magnetic currents of force derived from the spinning vortices of the cosmic universe—how'd you feel?"

"Better," said Mr. Spenlow.

The Prince also found that there was a good deal for him to do. Day by day he walked about among his people explaining, encouraging, and reassuring. Yes, yes, these new ideas seemed very strange, but everyone would be much better and happier presently and in a little while they would all wonder how on earth they had managed before. Of course Durand had some followers especially among the older people, but they were in a minority and in any case the movement had started and could not now be stopped. An alarming idea. Prince André sat on the churchyard wall one morning talking to the curé.

"You seem a little anxious, my son. Is anything amiss?"

"Not really. At least, I don't think so. Sometimes, Father, I ask myself whether I am not merely leading the gallop of the Gadarene swine."

"You are certain to be assailed by such doubts. This is a great new experiment."

"Yes, but I am experimenting with the well-being of my people."

"No, my son. For we could not go on as we were. If you had not done this there would soon have been no well-being with which to experiment."

"That is perfectly true and I think they are the better for it already. More alive, more interested. There is always some new thing."

"The latest craze," said Father Denys, "is to have one's photograph taken. There is a photographer in the town, had you heard? I have not, myself, fallen before his importunity as yet, but I think that nearly everyone else has. He must be very prosperous."

"Oh, is he that dark little man in a velvet jacket and a beret, with a short beard all over his face—more or less? A Frenchman, is he? I saw him the other day with a camera, but I took him to be one of the workmen."

"He speaks French," agreed the curé, "but he came in from Spain over the hills with boxes of gear on mulebacks. The Galliennes brought him in; they told me about it."

"Indeed? Perhaps he is a Spaniard, then," said the Prince, who was not interested. "I must go down to the Widow Vallance—the Americans have strung a telephone wire past her cottage and she thinks it will bring down the lightning. They say it won't, I hope they're right."

He walked on and turned into the market square. Quite suddenly there was a roaring noise approaching quickly with loud hoots, and everyone ran in all directions. Children screamed and scattered, dogs barked and jumped over walls, hens squawked and panicked, and a large respectable Renault swirled through the turmoil. The driver saw the Prince and turned towards him; since his control of the vehicle was plainly uncertain the Prince abandoned dignity and leapt into a shop doorway. The car pulled up six inches away and the grinning face of Jean-Alphonse Gallienne leaned forth from the window.

"Gallienne! What is all this?"

"An automobile, Your Highness. As you see, an auto of the most magnificent. She is secondhand but she is splendid. We bought her in Py."

"I see. A little change from your mules."

"Yes, indeed, my Prince. Mules are too slow now. A taxi service to Py and other places will soon be needed, and we Galliennes will supply it—who else? So we are learning to drive, if it please the Prince."

"I agree it is advisable, but why down the main street?"

"Because it is the only smooth road in all Sainte-Roche, and not only that—it is for the advertisement. If people see us go up and down they will remember us, Your Highness."

"I am sure they will. Tell me, did not the man who sold you the car also teach you to use it?"

"He brought it this morning, Highness, and spent quite a long time explaining the mechanics. Then one came and said that there was a lorry going to Py if he wanted a lift back today, so he said that any fool could drive a car, it only needed practice, and he ran away and went off on the lorry. So we are practising, Your Highness."

"Be very careful, Gallienne. It is easy to kill people with a car. Go slowly and with great care."

"As the Prince commands," said Jean-Alphonse. He put the car into gear with grating noises and drove impulsively away.

D'Ecosse emerged from a stout gateway and looked after the car.

"My Prince, when I see that I ask myself what we have done."

"I know. I also know what we must do. We must organize some police with white batons to control the traffic. I watched it in Paris—fascinating. When the policeman holds up his baton all men know that they must stop at once."

"Jean-Alphonse must practise stopping," said d'Ecosse thoughtfully.

The Prince did his utmost to abate the panic of the Widow Vallance and returned to the Palace, where he found his personal manservant pressing his master's trousers.

"Robert—Chevalier Robert, Foreign Secretary of Sainte-Roche, what the devil are you doing?"

"I am attending to Your Highness' wardrobe as is my primary duty," said Brown primly. "I have been honoured above my place by the additional duties to which Your Highness is good enough to refer, but I understood them to be of a temporary character to meet a fiscal emergency, if I may so put it. My post as Your Highness' personal man, however, is, I trust, permanent, if I may be permitted without presumption to indulge such a hope."

"I had an English tutor, Robert," said the Prince, sitting on a table and swinging his legs. "My father's idea was that I ought to be able to converse freely with the English-speaking peoples of the world. He would have done much better if he had provided me with you."

"I am more gratified than I can say——"

"Then don't say it. Tell me, Robert, do the English upper class really talk like you?"

"Not in the least, Your Highness. On the contrary. Their manner of speech is much more easy and uninhibited than would be considered fitting for a man in my position."

"Oh, is it. How difficult for the foreigner. Robert, if I had a reason for wishing to learn to speak ordinary good-class English——"

"The Queen's English we call it, Your Highness."

"A charming phrase. Could you teach me, Robert?"

"If Your Highness so desires."

There came a knock at the open door and the seneschal stood there.

"May it please the Prince——"

"Go on."

"There is a man who has come to ask if he may be allowed to make pictures of the Palace and of some of its principal rooms. He says that he will take the greatest pains not to intrude upon Your Highness in any way."

"He'd better not! Make pictures—is he an artist?"

"I could not say, Your Highness. He carries a black box and a thing with legs——"

"Ah yes. The photographer. Robert, have you seen the photographer? He has been much about the town these last few days."

"Yes, Your Highness. A small dark man with a beard. He speaks French, I believe. He looks like a southern Frenchman, a Basque perhaps." Brown lifted the Prince's trousers and began to fold them; the seneschal's eyes rested upon him with approval and the Prince noticed it.

"As Foreign Secretary, Chevalier," he said formally, "is there any objection to this foreigner walking about my grounds and photographing my house?"

Brown put down the trousers and straightened his back.

"Did the man say for what purpose he desired to do this?"

"He said he would make postal cards for sale to the people here and also to tourists," said the seneschal. "He says that tourists always buy postal cards with pictures."

"That is quite true," said Brown, "they do indeed. Since Your Highness deigns to consult me I should think there would be little harm in his taking views of the principal rooms and of the outside of the Palace from various points. He should be closely escorted all the time, especially within doors, if Your Highness approves."

"Yes, I do. You heard that, seneschal, and you can tell him yourself. Put on someone to follow him about and see that he does not enter the private apartments. One of the senior footmen will do. The man must keep out of my sight."

"As the Prince commands," said the seneschal, and went away.

"What are you laughing at, Robert?"

"Your Highness may remember that the journalists who came to see the battle took many photographs in the town, and when the women and children posed before the cameras the journalists paid them small sums. So when this man asked who would like their photographs taken, they all came up willingly ——"

"And then expected him to pay them!"

"Precisely, Your Highness. He seemed surprised and even pained, but as he spoke fluent French I did not feel called upon to intervene."

"No, quite right. Let him untie his own knots."

During the following day or two the Foreign Secretary, going about his duties in the Palace, occasionally caught a passing glimpse of a small dark figure in the act of vanishing round a corner or disappearing down a corridor. The photographer was encumbered with a satchel slung from his shoulder presumably containing his gear, and he carried an extending camera perched upon the top of a tripod, having its head draped in a black focussing cloth lined with red. Behind the photographer, wherever he went, there followed an attentive and distrustful second footman close upon his heels.

"I shouldn't think the photographer will give any trouble," said Brown to himself, and went on brushing the Prince's coats.

The train from Paris set down at Perpignan such passengers as wished to travel from there to Py on the single-line slow local, which in due course reached Py.

"Two hours," Adam K. Hopkins said, stepping down upon the platform. "Two hours to travel thirty-five miles. Betty, why didn't we fly from Paris to Barcelona and take a charter plane there? At any of those long-forgotten wayside halts I would have hopped out and whistled up a plane if you hadn't been with me. All right, all right, I'm not peeved so long as you like it."

"Dad, you said you wanted to slip into Sainte-Roche without anybody noticing you till you'd had a look around. Don't tell me you think they wouldn't notice a man stepping out of a helicopter in a place like that."

"It's your guess they'd think I was the Archangel Michael coming to wind up the whole concern, huh? Well now, where do we hire a taxi?"

The stationmaster asked where Monsieur wished to go and Hopkins guessed correctly what he had said.

"To Sainte-Roche."

The stationmaster nodded emphatically and led the way to the station yard where an elderly and dignified Renault stood gently palpitating. Jean-Alphonse Gallienne had just driven the three English fishermen from Sainte-Roche, not only without accident, but even arriving in time before the local returned to Perpignan. He was justly uplifted and said so to his younger brother who had accompanied him.

"Thou seest, Paul-Alphonse, there is no difficulty. Soon we shall be performing this journey daily and thinking nothing of it."

"Monsieur Gallienne! Monsieur Gallienne!"

"It is the stationmaster who calls," said Jean-Alphonse. "I come, monsieur."

"Two travellers with baggage," said the stationmaster, "for Sainte-Roche."

"Do you speak English?" said Hopkins, but Gallienne shook his head. However, he pointed at the Renault, said: "Sainte-Roche," and picked up the baggage.

"He seems to understand," said Hopkins, "so I suppose it's all right. Get in, Betty."

They drove off in a series of swooping curves which induced Mr. Hopkins to cling to the side of the car and appeal to his Maker for protection. Jean-Alphonse, however, improved with practice.

During the three or four weeks which had passed since the Prince came home from Paris, great progress had been made with the modernization of The Goat. The china fittings which had been lying in straw in the yard were all in position and had been connected with the main water supply as soon as the Commission's workmen, under the supervision of Donald S. Farson, had repaired the broken aqueduct. When, therefore, the Galliennes' Renault pulled up at the door of The Goat, Tonnerre was able to offer to visitors rooms which may have been small, low-ceiled, and of odd shapes but were also gay with new wallpapers and shining with fresh paint. Besides, most of the windows now opened, which must have surprised them.

There were, naturally, certain language difficulties, but what does language matter when a landlord can point with pride to two, yes, two bathrooms? There were other refinements, too, and Tonnerre, beaming delightedly all over his fat round face, practically levered the Hopkins family into four tiny rooms, one after another.

"It works," he said, for he had fathered a few useful phrases from his American visitors, "it works, look." He stretched a substantial arm past Betty's shoulder and pulled a chain. "It works, yes," he chanted above the resultant torrent's roar, "splendid, yes?"

Betty retired with a severe attack of giggles, but Hopkins patted him upon the shoulder and said that it was just swell. The Hopkins family engaged rooms and moved in. When at lunchtime Mathews, Spenlow, and Farson came in, the lounge sounded just like home.

Hopkins was not a man to announce his purposes prematurely. He said that he had finished his business in Europe with a few days to spare, so, since Betty had taken a fancy to see this Sainte-Roche place, they had made a little trip down there. It was interesting to visit a place still in the virgin simplicity of a rural area completely untouched by the rush of modern life, and the scenery was certainly something.

Mathews agreed and Hopkins asked who ran the place—wasn't there a Prince Somebody?

Mathews said that certainly there was and that Prince André was a good fellow, one of the best. Hopkins snorted.

"I suppose he stands around giving orders and all this benighted peasantry fall on their knees and say 'Yes, Your Royalty' to whatever he says. I've heard of these little kings."

"Not in this case," said Mathews. "There is an elected Council called the Six, like a town council but with more powers. They represent various interests—farming, commercial, and so on—our landlord Tonnerre is one of them. He's a wine-grower."

"Oh, is he one of them? What, the fat man? Well, you do surprise me. Imagine them having that much democracy here. Who are the others?"

Mathews told him.

"Well, well. I suppose some of them speak English?"

"No. Only the Prince and his Foreign Secretary. Look, Hopkins, if you want to talk business with any of these people, maybe I could lend you my interpreter. He has hours off getting paid for doing nothing while I'm writing reports and so forth."

Hopkins backed off, metaphorically speaking. His idea was to buy a piece of land upon which to erect a hotel without anyone getting to know about it till the deed was through and the walls up to first-floor level at least. If he employed the Commission's interpreter he might as well publish his views in the Press, and as for the Prince's Secretary, whoever he might be, he was on the opposing side anyway.

"That's very nice of you, Mathews," he said earnestly, "and I appreciate your offering to spare your man when you're so busy. No, no, I'm not on business; this is just a little vacation. No, I only thought I'd like to talk to one of the natives about things generally and what makes the place tick. It doesn't matter a bit. Let it ride, but thank you all the same. Hello there, Betty! Come and take your old dad for a walk."

They went out together. Mathews looked after them with sardonic amusement and Spenlow noticed it.

"What's the joke, Morris?"

"Adam K. has just informed me that his visit here is merely a short vacation and has no business significance at all."

"From which you infer?"

"I should think he's probably scheming to buy the whole Principality, erect a dozen large hotels and a casino to end all casinos, and run the joint as a sort of Pyrenean Monaco."

"Changing the name to Hopkinsville?"

"I shouldn't wonder."

"Don't worry. The Prince will take care of him."

CHAPTER XVIII

A Piece of Land

"Betty," said Hopkins, "you learned to talk French at school, didn't you?"

"No, Dad, I certainly did not."

"What? But I'm darn sure you did. I remember——"

"Listen, Dad. When I was at school I had a lot of lessons in French. I can read it easily and I can even write it not too badly, but speak it, no. I found that out in Paris. What I say is all right but nobody knows that except me because they don't understand one word of it. Not one. And when they speak to me it's even worse—I don't even know what their noises sound like. Might be Arabic or Sioux. No, that's not right. I do know a few words of Sioux. I'm sorry, Dad, but for talking French I'm a dead loss. I did not learn to speak French, and I mean 'speak.' "

It did not take them long to walk round Sainte-Roche, since it is not a large town and is reasonably compact. Hopkins looked keenly about him and finally came to a stop to lean against the gate of one of Jean Latour's pastures.

"You can't build in the town," he said. "There isn't room. Not unless you pulled down about twenty houses, and then it would be cramped. No garden."

"Besides," said Betty, "they wouldn't like it."

"That's so. Those fields leading up to the woods are too steep; what it would mean in the way of terracing is nobody's business."

"It would spoil the view."

"What, my hotel?"

"No, no. All that terracing there. It wouldn't look right."

"You may have something there, and when it comes to aesthetics I'll admit Adam K. Hopkins may have something to learn. But what is more to the point, all that terracing will eat up as much money as the hotel itself, and though I don't mind spending money I won't waste it and never did. Of course, the ideal place is up there where the big house is," and he nodded towards the hillside behind the town.

"But that's the Palace, where the Prince lives!"

"So Mathews was telling me. I wouldn't want the house, only the site, but I don't suppose he'd sell," said Hopkins regretfully.

"Of course not, Dad. It's his home. He wouldn't want it pulled down."

"I wouldn't, in his place, and that's a fact. These meadows behind us here"—he turned to survey Latour's acres—"lie too low. Begin digging foundations there and you'd start a spring every few yards," in which Mr. Hopkins was perfectly correct. "All one water table, this valley floor. No, there's only one place for our hotel, Betty, and that's up there."

She shaded her eyes and looked up where he was pointing. A spur of one of the eastern hills ran out into the valley behind the church. It was steep and thickly wooded, but some hundred feet up a bluff of bare rock showed through the trees which stood back above it.

"There's a big shelf of ground up there if I'm not mistaken," said Hopkins. "Let's walk up there and take a look at it."

"I suppose nobody will mind?"

"They'll have to get used to seeing me around," he said simply, and led the way across a meadow into the woods. There was, in fact, a forester's track up to the shelf and beyond; since the guns had been dragged up that way for the battle, the path was well marked. They walked up without difficulty, since the way was no more than reasonably steep, and came out upon a natural shelf some three acres in extent and in shape like a banana. Betty stopped to look at the view, which was breath-taking; her father strode eagerly about pacing distances, examining the soil, and staring up into the trees behind, all in silence. At last he came across to her, threw an affectionate arm about her shoulders, and ceremonially kissed her upon the forehead.

"This," he said solemnly, "is it. It may not be the finest hotel site in Europe, because some of them have what it takes and here there isn't a lake, which is a pity. But Adam K. Hopkins knows a site when he sees one, and this is it. What's more, it's the only site in this place that's worth a whoop; there is no other. Yeah, I know we haven't seen down the valley, but that's too far from the town anyway. Betty, when you said to me, 'Dad, why don't we go look at Sainte-Roche,' you started something. Well, that's settled. Now all I've got to do is buy it from whoever it belongs to and start building. I'll call Foster this evening to drop whatever he's doing and come here right away."

"Foster?"

"My architect. Come on."

Betty went, wondering what life had in store for a girl whose Prince, continually on her doorstep in Paris, had become completely invisible in his native haunts. She had assumed that it was only necessary to come to Sainte-Roche and stroll carelessly about. Round the first corner—or the second or even the third—she would come face to face with Monsieur André Dubois. He was in residence at the Palace, everyone said so. He was in the habit of strolling about his town, everyone said so, but hitherto the only glimpse she had had of him was of a smooth dark head and a pair of slim shoulders on the topmost terrace a bare half mile away as the lovebird flies. Mathews had pointed him out.

"See up there? That's the Prince."

"Oh? Doesn't he ever come out?"

"What, down here? Oh yes, quite often. He just strolls about talking to people, you know."

Patience, then, and wait. After all, she had only been in Sainte-Roche for about nine hours. Tomorrow would do. She retired happily to bed.

Adam K. Hopkins went into the bar, ordered a drink with

Mathews' help, and sat in a corner sipping it, smoking a cigar, and wondering what to do next. Two simple questions: who owns that land? and how much does he want for it? and he could not ask either of them.

Presently another man came into the bar, exchanged greetings with the Commission in English, and sat on a high stool to talk casually with Tonnerre behind the bar. Presumably that incomprehensible noise was French; anyway, the fat man understood it. The Commission drifted away to play cards on a table in the far corner. Hopkins finished his glass, went up to the bar, and addressed the stranger, a small bearded man wearing a velvet jacket and a beret slung over one ear.

"Excuse me, but didn't I hear you talking English just now?"

"Certainly you did. Can I help you somehow?"

"If you'd help me order a drink? I'm not so keen on all this wine and I can't say what I want to."

"Course I will. Here goes," and with his help matters were arranged more or less to Hopkins' satisfaction.

"Queer stuff they drink in these parts," he said, tasting the Sainte-Roche version of Calvados. "I'd say this is pretty powerful. Are you living here?"

"Oh no. Only a short business trip. I'm a photographer," said the man, and told Hopkins about the picture-postcard scheme. "I'm the first in the field, and when the tourists start coming I should be on to a good thing."

"Probably," agreed Hopkins. "There'll be plenty of tourists here soon or I miss my guess. I wouldn't think there's another camera in the country."

"Only those the Americans carry, and they're not for business."

"In the meantime," suggested Hopkins, "I guess there's quite a market in taking photos of the natives?"

"I'm working it up," said the photographer, "but to start off they expected me to pay them for the privilege."

"Well, what d'you know! Why?"

The photographer explained, to Hopkins' amusement.

"I guess you soon told them. You English?"

"No, French. Excuse me, I should have told you before, my name is Pasquet. Henri Pasquet."

"Pleased to meet you, Mr. Pasquet. My name is Hopkins, Adam K. Hopkins, and I am an American."

They shook hands, Pasquet said that most of the foreign visitors appeared to be Americans, and Hopkins said that that was to be expected. Whenever a new opening offered itself, America would be there first. "You'll excuse me asking a somewhat personal question, but if you're finding things a bit tight as of now——"

"I'm not exactly rolling in money," said Pasquet.

"I was wondering if you'd like to do a little job for me, strictly on business terms?"

"What is it, Mr. Hopkins."

Hopkins explained that he was really in Sainte-Roche on business. "You'll keep this strictly under your hat, Mr. Pasquet?"

"Of course. I'm a businessman myself."

Hopkins edged his chair nearer and explained in low tones that he was keeping his plans dark because he also wanted to be first in the field. He wanted to buy a piece of land and he wanted an interpreter whom he could trust not to babble. "I am a man well known in my line, Mr. Pasquet, and if it got around that Adam K. Hopkins was buying land in Sainte-Roche there'd be a dozen more rushing in to spoil my game. You get me."

"You bet," said Pasquet.

"I want to know who this land belongs to and what he wants for it and I don't want my name to crop up in it. Will you act for me? You can talk to these people. Well?"

Mr. Pasquet agreed at once, and the two associates put their heads together and talked for a long time.

Early next morning Pasquet came to The Goat while the Hopkins family was still at breakfast.

"This is my daughter, Betty, and you can talk in front of her.

She is in on this with me. Mr. Pasquet, Betty. I was telling you we met last night."

Mr. Pasquet bowed over Betty's hand and sat down.

"That shelf of land," he said, "is the property of the Principality of Sainte-Roche."

"What does that mean in plain English?"

"Tell you the truth, I haven't a clue. Laws about owning land are different in most countries, and I've no idea what they're like in Sainte-Roche. It isn't privately owned—I made out that much. Most of this land in the valley does belong to one owner or another; Jean Latour, for example, owns his farm, and Tonnerre owns this hotel. When it comes to the mountains and forests, they belong to the state. The foresters who look after the forests are the Prince's men and take their orders from him. That shelf of land is inside the forest, so it belongs to the state too. As to whether they ever sell any of it or even can sell it if they want to, I couldn't find out. I am sorry not to be more definite, Mr. Hopkins, but you told me not to say much at first."

"That's right, I did." Hopkins retired into thought and Pasquet waited with an occasional understanding smile at Betty whenever she looked in his direction, so she remarked that the view was beautiful and turned her chair to look out of the window.

Hopkins returned to life.

"So my bit of land belongs to the state. Who would you say acts for the state in this locality? The Eight or whatever?"

"The Six—yes, I should think so."

Hopkins finished his coffee and pushed back his chair.

"Then we go call on the Six. Tonnerre here is one, they tell me. Call Tonnerre."

Tonnerre came and was told that Monsieur Hopkins here wished to buy that shelf of land up there on the hillside—it was visible from the window—to build himself a house on it, so entranced was he with the valley of Sainte-Roche.

Tonnerre said that that, of course, was perfectly understand-

able. He himself had never been able to comprehend how anyone could endure to live anywhere else, but as for that piece of
land—he shook his head. It was the Prince's.

"But I was told it belonged to the state," objected Hopkins.

"Same thing," said Tonnerre.

"Oh, is it."

Tonnerre went on to say that he only wished he had a piece of
land to offer to the so friendly Monsieur, but all he owned was
this hotel and his vineyards further down the valley. They,
Monsieur would realize, were Tonnerre's livelihood.

"But can't I buy from the Prince?"

Tonnerre didn't know. He had never heard of the Prince's
house selling their land. Asked whether they could if they
wanted to, he did not know at all. Reminded that he was one of
the Six and ought to know, he begged Monsieur to excuse him.
An innkeeper is a busy man, especially in the mornings, and he
bowed himself away.

"Well, that's one washout. Who's the next?"

"Oh, Dad," said Betty, "you've annoyed him."

"Then he can forget it. It isn't a crime to want to buy a piece
of land. Coming with us, Betty?"

But she made an excuse and went for a walk by herself without meeting anyone she knew except Don Farson investigating
drains.

Hopkins and Pasquet went out, and since the first place they
came to was the post office, they turned in. It was occupied at
the moment by a half-grown lad with red hair. It had sometimes
occurred to Brown, seeing numerous redheads on his walks
abroad, to wonder how large a retinue the Jacobite General
Kennedy had brought with him. D'Ecosse's ancestors, certainly.
However, to return to Hopkins' quest.

Pasquet asked if Monsieur Durand was sufficiently at liberty
to spare them a few moments of his valuable time, and the lad
called to him. Durand drifted out and looked vaguely at them
with his extraordinary pale eyes which never seemed quite to
focus on anything, and Pasquet repeated his opening gambit

about the gentleman who was so enthralled by Sainte-Roche that he wanted to buy a piece of land and build himself a house on it.

"I have a piece I could sell," said Durand.

"Not just any piece," said Pasquet. "There is a certain strip which has——"

But Durand was not listening. "Come with me," he said, and led the way through the house and out into the garden at the back. At the end of the garden there was a small square paddock a little over an acre in extent.

"I would sell that," he said, "if the price were good enough."

"But there is no access from any side," said Pasquet, looking round it.

"That is why it is difficult to sell," said Durand mournfully.

"That cabbage patch," said Hopkins indignantly. "Ask him about my piece up on the hill there."

Pasquet obeyed and Durand said he didn't know about that. Asked to whom it belonged, he said "to the state." Asked whether as one of the Six he was not in a sense the state, he said "no." Asked who was, he led the way back through the house in silence and showed his visitors into the post office. Asked to whom a man should apply who wished to buy a piece of land belonging to the state, he retired into his own apartments and closed the door after him. A key turned audibly in the lock.

Since Hopkins also appeared at the moment to be struck dumb, Pasquet suggested calling upon the curé. "He's an educated man, of course. A real gentleman, like."

"You don't say," said Hopkins dreamily.

The curé was polite but unhelpful. He had never heard of anyone buying land from the Prince. Since the only land the Prince could be said to own—apart from the Palace and its gardens and so forth—was the sort of mountain land which no one would want to buy, this was not surprising. In any case, the Prince did not really own it privately, qua landowner, but only in his public capacity qua Prince of Sainte-Roche. "At least, that is how I understand the situation. That is, no doubt, why there is this confusion in men's minds as to whether the land belongs to the Prince or to the state—it is the same thing. *L'Etat, c'est lui,* to adapt the saying of Louis XIV."

Hopkins, through Pasquet, thanked Father Denys adequately and went on to see Marcel Avril. It was not a good day for that call, because the Sainte-Roche *Bulletin* was to come out on the following day and the editor was busy at the printing machines. Yes, the land belonged to the Prince; no, Avril did not suppose for a moment that it was purchasable; no, he owned no land himself and if he did he would use it to enlarge his own cramped premises. Good morning, gentlemen.

"Seems like we're getting no place fast," said Hopkins gloomily.

"There's Monsieur d'Ecosse who is Chancellor of this Principality."

"What's that mean?"

"He runs all their money business."

"Then why didn't we go see him first?"

"Because he was in school. He's also the schoolmaster too. He'll be free now—there are the kids running home to dinner."

D'Ecosse received his visitors with courtesy but also with reserve, for he did not much like the look of either of them. That photographer did not inspire confidence, and though d'Ecosse had liked all the other Americans he had met, this one seemed the sort of man about whom he had read in books. Tycoons, were they called? He begged them to be seated, told his wife to keep the dinner hot, and listened carefully to Pasquet's introductory remarks. After a pause for thought he answered them, waiting between each sentence for Pasquet to translate it.

"I know the shelf of land of which you speak. It is of no agricultural value because it is separate and difficult of access. It is crown property. Whether the Prince could sell it if he wished, frankly I do not know without searching the archives for a precedent. That would take time and I am a busy man."

"Ask him," said Hopkins angrily, "if he means that nobody

can ever build a house here because nobody can sell him a piece of land to build on?"

"Oh no," answered d'Ecosse. "New houses are built here from time to time, naturally, and Sainte-Rocheans can buy land from each other if they agree to do so. When it comes to selling land to a foreigner, however, the Prince's consent is necessary even if the land is not crown property. Sainte-Roche has always been chary of admitting foreigners as permanent residents."

Pasquet translated and there was a short pause while Hopkins digested this and Madame d'Ecosse clattered plates in the next room.

"I thought this place was supposed to be hard up," said Hopkins. "Yet, when a man comes and wants to do them a bit of good, they won't have it."

Pasquet produced a politer version of this in French.

"It may appear so," said d'Ecosse, "but, thanks to the un-exampled generosity of Monsieur's fellow countrymen, we hope that our financial problems are in a fair way to being solved."

"Has he got any land of his own to sell me?"

"No, monsieur," said d'Ecosse firmly.

"Washout," said Hopkins briefly, and rose to his feet.

"There's still one more of the Six," said Pasquet as they walked down the road together. "Jean Latour, a farmer."

"You can have farmers."

CHAPTER XIX

The Jewels of Sainte-Roche

"There's only one thing left to do," said Pasquet. "You must pop up and see the Prince yourself."

"I won't," said Hopkins.

"But he's quite a nice bloke."

"I know. Mathews and the others have told me about him."

"Then——"

"Listen. I am a good Republican and I don't give a darn for any of these princes and dukes and little tin-pot God Almighties. I've met them back home, calling themselves Imperial Highnesses and looking for a handout. When I started my first hotel back home in the States, I had one as a doorkeeper. Said he came from Russia. Well, here this one's top dog still. D'you suppose Adam K. Hopkins is going up there cap in hand begging him to kindly allow me to buy a strip of his land for six times what it's worth? Think again, laddie."

Pasquet did so.

"Suppose," he said, "just suppose I could persuade him to sell the land, what would there be in it for me?"

"Twenty per up to two grand, ten per up to three, and five per anything over. I won't pay over five grand."

"It's a deal."

"Go to it," said Hopkins graciously.

The photographer Pasquet had his own reasons for not wishing to meet Robert Brown face to face; he had managed to avoid it so far, and, thanks to a good growth of beard and a continental style of dress, he was not readily recognizable at even a short distance. He walked away out of the town by a path into the woods and sat down upon a bank in the sunshine to think.

He could not believe that there would really be much difficulty in persuading the Prince to sell that strip of useless land in view of the quite absurd price Hopkins was prepared to pay for it. Not only that, but there was all the money Hopkins' tourists would bring into the country. Why, the Prince ought to be glad to give that bit of land to a man like Hopkins. Dammit, he ought to pay Hopkins to build there. Now, thanks to the American's idiotic objection to approaching the Prince, he himself looked like getting a nice cut out of it and, of course, the other things as well. It was only the difficulty of paying repeated visits to the Palace without ever meeting Brown. Nearly impossible, that. As Foreign Secretary, Brown would probably be called in. On the other hand, it was out of the question to put through the deal without going to the Palace——

He stopped abruptly and the last thought repeated itself in his mind. Put through the deal without going to the Palace.

He sat there in a patch of sunlight, smoking one cigarette after another and working out details in his mind. Rubber heels, no. Not unless one went to Py for them. No need, there was new linoleum on his bedroom floor. If one cut a piece from under the cupboard no one would notice it. Some good quality paper. Avril might have some at the office. A photographer might well need some for mounting portrait photographs. A few sheets of official paper would be better—probably d'Ecosse had some. Betty Hopkins could read French. So long as it sounded official. André Amadeus Joseph Theodore by the Grace of God Prince of Sainte-Roche hereby declares—acknowledges—graciously consents in consideration of a payment of four thousand five hundred United States dollars to give and bequeath—no, that came in wills.

He got up at last, stiff and a little chilly, and walked slowly back to his room, still revolving formal but gracious phrases in his mind.

He dropped in at the bar of The Goat that evening for a short drink and a few private words with Adam K. Hopkins.

"He's nibbling."

"What, the Pr——"

"Sh-sh!"

"Oh! Well, you don't say!"

"I do, then. Look, it's all that Six lot that's against the sale; you know what these yokels are like—anything new's wrong, you get me, but he's got more sense. But if anything slips out the deal's off. Not a word to anybody, mind that."

"I get you."

"It's a bit dicey still but here's hoping. Of course, I have to lay on the soft soap, 'Your Supreme Highness' gracious kindness' and all that." Hopkins screwed up his nose and Pasquet said all that didn't matter so long as the job went through.

"I guess that's so."

"Look, maybe you won't see me much these next few days. Don't worry, I'm working."

"I understand. You take your time, and if you pull this off you won't find me ungrateful."

"Mind, now," warned Pasquet, "not a word to a soul. Not even your daughter. Good night."

He returned to the small room in the Widow Frachot's house where he lodged, and shut himself up. He told her that he had a great deal of work to do in mounting and touching up photographs; he had got behindhand with them. He would stick at it till the job was done. Once one got behind with a string of orders—Madame would understand——

Madame sympathized. No one should disturb Monsieur, who was without doubt an artist. She was more right than she knew; born under a happier star he might indeed have been an artist of some reproductive kind, an etcher or an engraver.

The Prince was sitting upon the churchyard wall—a favorite perch of his since childhood—watching his little world go by and talking to d'Ecosse.

"Fourteen out of twenty," said Prince André suddenly.

"Twenty what, my Prince?"

"People in the last five minutes—I've been counting them, and fourteen of them foreigners. D'Ecosse, what have we done to our poor little country? We are changing not only the lives but the minds of my people, and the old, simple ways are going forever. It frightens me sometimes."

"What else could we have done?"

"That is what Monsieur the Curé says, but the responsibility remains mine."

"On the whole they are well behaved," urged d'Ecosse, "even the foreign workmen. I have heard that there is even a lady now with the American party at The Goat."

"The wife of one of them, presumably."

"I do not know who she is, my Prince. She cannot speak French so she does not talk to any of us."

"There are plenty of Americans for her to talk to, are there not? It has begun already then, d'Ecosse, a foreign enclave in our midst. However, I suppose they will all go away again when the various works are done."

"One of the Americans was asking about land to build a house on," said d'Ecosse. "He came to me, the photographer acting as interpreter."

"I can't allow that. There's no land to spare in this valley."

"No indeed, my Prince——"

"Tourists, yes," said the Prince decidedly. "Permanent residents, no. I think I shall keep out of the way for the present."

A few days later the Prince told Brown that he was having two guests to dinner that night.

"Very good, Your Highness."

"One guest will be the Reverend Father Denys."

"Yes, Your Highness."

"And the other will be yourself."

Brown started.

"May I entreat Your Highness to excuse me? I am most

highly honoured but the—it would be most unsuitable for me, most undesirable. My place is behind Your Highness' chair, not at your table."

"You sat at meat with me in Paris, Robert."

"Ah yes, but I was then your Foreign Secretary, whereas——"

"You still are. That is the point. Father Denys and I have certain matters to discuss upon which we want your advice."

"I am at all times at Your Highness' service, but——"

"Robert."

There was a very brief pause.

"As the Prince commands," said Brown.

The Prince laughed and clapped him on the shoulder.

"The servants will have to get used to it," he said. "You are not in their service, you know."

Brown smiled suddenly.

"No, my Prince."

The little dinner party took place in the private dining room and was lighthearted and even merry in spite of the seneschal who tended to loom over them. The curé remembered his days as a lieutenant of cuirassiers with a dry wit which surprised Brown into speaking of the second world war. He was even more astonished to find that his hearers knew practically nothing about it. He forgot himself and was perfectly at ease.

"There were two men who passed through," said the curé. "Your Highness will hardly remember? They were escaped prisoners of war."

"I remember being furiously angry because they had gone through and I had not even seen them; I had measles," said the Prince mournfully. "No one told me about them until they had gone again. You saw them, my father?"

"I found them," said the curé, "sitting in my garden eating my gooseberries. I took them in and my good Eulalie, now at rest, fed them. I have never seen men eat like that, never. Then they slept for thirty-six hours and after that went on into Spain. I hope they reached home safely. One of them, I remember, looked from my window and said something in

English about a place called Avilion—it was poetry, I think. I know so little English; so stupid of me."

"Was it this?" said Brown, and changed into English:

". . . *the island-valley of Avilion*

"*Where falls not hail, or rain, or any snow,*

"*Nor ever wind blows loudly . . .*"

"I think that was it," said the curé.

"He should come here in November," said the Prince briskly. "Robert, do you like snow?"

They sat on at table over coffee and brandy, the seneschal removed his brooding presence at a word from the Prince, and a little silence fell. The curé broke it.

"Robert, my son."

"Yes, Monsieur le Curé?"

"There will be a meeting of the Six in a few days' time."

Brown turned his eyes upon the curé and waited.

"They will make a suggestion to you which the Prince and I hope very much that you will accept."

Brown opened his mouth, shut it again, stubbed out his cigarette, and looked down at his hands.

"It is becoming plainer with every passing day," said Father Denys, "that the old days of isolation are over. Sainte-Roche is back in the world again, and, with transport as it is today, it will never be so remote as it was even before the bridge fell down. We shall need someone who is used to modern ways, who can speak several languages, who has travelled and knows many cities and how men think and speak and transact business. The Six will ask you whether you will be that man."

"Are you suggesting," said Brown in a voice like a croak, "that I should be His Highness' private secretary? I ought to tell you that I do not consider myself fit for such a post. I do better as I am, in obscurity."

"The Six want a man who can speak for them with authority, here and abroad. They want a man they know and trust."

"The Six do not really like me, you must know that—at least, some of them do not. I am a stranger here, and country people don't like strangers."

"You are mistaken, Robert," said the Prince calmly. "It is not to you as a man that they object, it is to your status as a paid servant in my household. This is not snobbery; it is due to a long tradition that a member of the Prince's personal staff shall not hold any position of authority in the state. Apparently it is thought that in that case the Prince might be able unfairly to influence his actions and decisions."

"Purely theoretically," said the curé, "the objection seems to me to be justifiable. Under certain circumstances, the man's position might be intolerable."

"Oh, I agree," said Prince André, "in theory. But it does rather make one wonder what some of my illustrious forefathers were like, doesn't it?"

"When I was a rackety young subaltern," said Father Denys, "I remember an entertainment in rather dubious taste called the Dance of the Seven Veils." Brown looked across the table at the saintly old man with such an expression of stupefaction that Prince André laughed aloud. "Unless you saw this act when you were in Paris, my son——"

"No, I didn't——"

"Then I had better add that it is an exhibition of progressive disclosure. It is sometimes a pity when History is inclined to join the dance."

"But, monsieur," said Brown, "it is not always evil which is uncovered by honest historical research."

"Indeed, no," said the curé readily.

"In the case of my family here in Sainte-Roche," said the Prince, "one gathers that they were without exception dutiful, virtuous, and wise."

"Quite so," said Father Denys, and took a little more brandy. When the others had stopped laughing he went on: "I see you have taken my point; somewhere here is the foundation upon which this prejudice was built. Robert, my son, if I may call you that as it were unofficially, what the Six propose to ask you is this. Will you accept the post of Foreign Secretary permanently in place of the post you hold at present as His Highness' personal attendant?"

Every trace of amusement was wiped from Brown's face and he slowly shook his head.

"Unless, of course," he said, "His Highness is dissatisfied with my services?"

"Don't be a fool," said the Prince.

"In that case, Father," said Brown, "I must beg to be allowed to refuse. I am not fit for this office."

"There is no one else, my son. You are a man of good birth and education. I was once a man of the world, and there is no mistaking these things. We have no one else in the whole country who——"

"Listen," said Brown desperately. "I am not fit for this office; I mean that literally. I am not the sort of man who should be employed in this way. I do not wish to tell you my history because it is past and done with, but if you knew what I am you would never suggest such a thing. Is that plain enough? All I ask is to be allowed to stay here as the Prince's servant; after what I have just told you you ought to send me away. Now, then."

"Robert," said the Prince.

"Your Highness?"

"Those rather wordy documents appointing you Foreign Secretary, Chevalier of the Order of Saint Simeon Stylites, Chevalier of the Star of the Pyrenees and all the rest of it, where are they?"

"In the strong room, Your Highness. There was such a rush for the preparations for going to Paris that I put them in there at Your Highness' suggestion, if you remember."

"I do, yes. Did you ever read them through?"

"Why, no," said Brown. "I beg Your Highness' pardon, but there was so much on hand——"

"Go and get them, Robert, will you? Here are the keys."

The so-called strong room of the Palace was actually a small storeroom about six feet by twelve. It had immensely thick walls and a solid wooden door and was almost filled across the far end by a vast and heavy old-fashioned safe. The strong room was on the same floor as the room in which dinner had been served; Brown had only to walk along a carpeted corridor to find the strong-room door on his left. At the end of the passage there was a door which led out upon the terrace. It was closed against the chill of the night air.

Brown's mind was occupied with the proposal which had just been made to him. No recollection crossed his mind of that other occasion when he had been sent alone to fetch the ruby pendant for the Six to see. Then the temptation to seize those almost fabulous jewels and run had been so great as to weaken his knees and bring out the sweat on his brow. Tonight he was not even thinking about them.

He unlocked the heavy door and set it wide and lit a candle which stood upon a little shelf inside the door in such a place that its light would shine into the safe when that, in its turn, was opened. Then he unlocked the safe door; it came open with a soft suck of air, and the candle flame wavered. The papers he wanted were upon a high shelf, all together in a large envelope endorsed on the outside with his name.

He took it out and laid it upon the top of the safe while he closed the door. He had to step back to allow the wide door to swing past him, and as he did so he bumped into something hard against his ribs.

"You can leave that," began a low voice just behind him, but Brown was too quick for the speaker. The safe door was shut and locked and the key in his pocket before the man had finished speaking. Then he turned round and found himself face to face with the photographer.

"What the hell d'you think you're doing here? Get out of this room."

The photographer laughed. "My disguise must be good if you don't recognize me close to, though there isn't much light here. Calls itself a Palace and only candles!"

"Fishy Pike!"

"That's right. Didn't think you'd done with me, did you? No, don't move or this'll go off. Nice little job, don't you think? Bought it in Spain. That lumpy bit on the end is a silencer, in case you don't know. Now, open that safe and give me those jewels and I'll let you live."

Brown's mind raced. If he could keep this fellow talking someone was sure to come—the servants—but they would be at their own supper. Someone would come to clear the table. No, not until the Prince left the room; the Prince might come himself—no, kind heaven, not the Prince, this man was dangerous. But Fishy always loved talking——

"You fool," said Brown, "you'd never get a mile from the Palace, and if you did, murder is an extraditable crime. You'd be hunted down through every country in Europe—run, rabbit, run. Anybody seen a running photographer?"

"If you didn't recognize me as has known me for years," said Pike reasonably, "how do you suppose anybody else will? All I've got to do is bury the camera and shave my face and where's the photographer? Hadn't thought of that, had you? And don't you turn up your nose at my photos neither; I was a street photographer once and I give satisfaction. Good, they are. Now you unlock that safe and hand out the lolly or you'll stop one."

"Going to share out with George?"

"Share with George? What, when he refused to come? Not likely. George went straight home from Paris as the busies told him, like a good boy, and he's in London now trying to keep himself in comfort robbing kids' money boxes. I don't know. For me, George is all washed up. A man who'll run away and leave a job half done is no sort of use to a man like me. George has had it and now I'm all on my ownsome and all I get's my own. Like you. You put one over on me in Paris, I'll give you that, selling that ruby thing on the level to get yourself trusted —very clever—and come back here to have the keys hung on your belt to help yourself whenever you like. You always were clever, I'll hand it to you, but you aren't going to freeze me out and scoop the pool yourself, you dirty double-crosser, you! Been in the game for years, you have; don't try to put it across me you've turned over a new leaf, jailbird," snarled Fishy, working himself up. "Gone pi, have you? Got religion or somefink? Open that door!"

"Certainly not," said Brown. "I told you before I am going straight now and this country is my country from now on——"

"I'll count five while you stand there and think what a bullet through the head feels like. One. I'll put it—two—through your jaw so's you can't—three—talk. Four——"

Pike, in his excitement, had moved forward till he was almost within reach——

Brown sprang at him and seized the arm which held the revolver. It went off with a noise no louder than a champagne cork popping, and a violent struggle began. Brown was the stronger of the two, but Pike was still armed, when suddenly his head went back as something came from behind him across his face. Brown hit him hard in the wind and then, as he doubled up, even harder under the jaw. Pike fell to the floor and the gun skidded across the room. The Prince, pale with excitement and breathing hard through the nostrils, stood in the doorway.

"Did I do the right thing, Robert? I thought if one pulled a man's head back with one's arm round his face, one broke his neck. It was so, was it not, in that film we saw in Paris?"

"Your Highness," said Brown, snatching up the gun and dropping it in his pocket, "Your Highness——"

"Well? He is not dead, is he? He is making the most peculiar noises." The Prince stepped back and glanced along the passage. "Ah, here are the servants. Corbet! Dompierre! Tarri! Quick, here."

They came running.

"This man," said the Prince, indicating the writhing form of Fishy Pike at his feet, "is an intruder who was trying to rob the strong room when Monsieur Robert caught him. He is not much hurt. Tie him up and take him—ah, seneschal. Here is a burglar. Have we a dungeon?"

"No, Your Highness, no, that is, there were some cells under the Town Hall, but the hinges of the doors have rusted, Your Highness."

"Difficult," mused the Prince while Pike, still crowing and holding his midriff, was dragged to his feet by the servants. "Take him away, search him for weapons, and tie him up while I decide what is to be done with him."

"As the Prince commands."

Pike was dragged away down the corridor and out of sight. The Prince turned his attention to Brown, who was leaning against the wall with his face in his hands.

"Robert! I thought you were unhurt, what is it?"

"Your Highness," said Brown, standing to attention, "heard what that man said?"

"Come along," said the Prince, and took him by the arm. "I think a little brandy will do us both good."

Brown blew out the candle, shut the strong-room door and locked it quite mechanically, like a man whose mind is full of other matters. They walked back to the dining room, where the curé was standing with his back to the fire. He looked from one to the other as the Prince poured brandy into three glasses.

"Father Denys."

"Thank you, my son."

"Robert. Drink that."

"As the Prince commands," said Brown hoarsely, and sipped it.

The Prince sat down, picked up his glass and held it up.

"To your health, Robert," he said. "Sit down, please."

"If Your Highness will excuse me, I should prefer to stand. I have something to say."

"Very well," said the Prince. Father Denys sank into a chair, covered his mouth and chin with one long thin hand, and watched the Englishman from under his thick eyebrows.

CHAPTER XX

The Prisoner

"All that that man said was perfectly true," said Brown in a completely unemotional voice. "By the way, I am assuming that Your Highness heard at least something of what was said?"

"When I came actually within earshot the subject of his remarks was someone called George."

Brown thought back for a moment and then said that in that case His Highness had heard most of what really mattered. He looked at the curé, but the old man merely waved his hand vaguely and told Brown not to bother about him.

"He called me jailbird," said Brown. "It was quite true—I have been in prison. My father is, I suppose I may say, a man of good standing; I am his only son. He intended me for the diplomatic service, but I was wild at school and got into trouble at Oxford. I was sent down. That finished the diplomatic idea. My father—I don't blame him—thought that stern measures were needed. He turned me out of the house. This was in 1940, so I went into the Army. After the war I tried one thing and another and lost my gratuity. I don't want to make this too long. After some rather trying years I was lucky enough to become personal manservant to a gentleman who had a flat in town— London, that is. I was happy there for three years. He had interests in gold mining in South Africa; something went wrong and he had to fly out there at a moment's notice. He died of a stroke in the middle of a board meeting. When things were settled up I was accused of having stolen a piece of silver left in my charge. I could not prove I had not, so I went to prison."

Brown paused to take another sip of brandy.

"In prison I met a man; when I came out I met his friends. That man tonight is one of them. They got me another similar post with forged credentials. At this point I may mention that the recommendations I sent Your Highness were forged also. To return to my second post. There was a burglary there one night, and some valuables were taken. I did not see the burglars, but they had benefited by a piece of information which I had told my friends. So I guessed who the burglars were. I went to them and taxed them with it; they admitted it. I said I was going to the police and they laughed at me. They had copies of my forged references. They pointed out that the police would naturally assume that I had taken that post to pave the way for the burglary, and, that being my second offence, I should go to prison for a long time. I did not go to the police.

"However, my employer was not quite satisfied in his own mind about me and he dismissed me. After some time these men approached me again, being sure in their own minds that they had me under their control. They said that they had known for a long time about some immensely valuable jewels in a place called Sainte-Roche, but that there seemed no way of getting in here until they saw an advertisement in the London *Times* for a manservant here, when they immediately thought of me. Once more they forged my credentials, and, since by then I was once more out of money, they paid for my outfit and all that I needed.

"Your Highness tonight heard Pike suggest that I was working my way into a position of trust here in order to abscond with the jewels upon some convenient occasion. I have no means of disproving it, and, with a record like mine, I will not insult Your Highness by offering impassioned denials.

"Now, unless Your Highness wishes to take action against me for the forged credentials, may I go?"

The Prince turned to the curé and said: "Father Denys?"

The old man emptied his brandy-glass, sat upright in his

chair, folded his hands on his knees, and began to speak in his usual placid and kindly tones.

"Robert, my son. I might perhaps begin with a mild reproach against you for thinking that because we are primitive and remote we are also deplorably silly. However, let that go. Your father was——" Father Denys mentioned a name in full and also an address in Dorset. The name was not Brown.

Brown turned white and leaned over the back of the chair by which he was standing.

"I really think, Robert," said the Prince, "that you had better sit down. One man gasping at my feet is enough for one night."

Brown sat down heavily.

"It all started," said the curé, "with the Englishman among that party of journalists who came to see the battle, if you remember. He remarked to d'Ecosse in his very limited French that it was surprising to find a man in your position who had had a university education. He mentioned Oxford."

Brown lifted his head.

"How the—how did he know?"

"I have no notion, but you did spend an evening together which was reasonably alcoholic, did you not? We were curious, I admit it, and then I noticed the ring you habitually wear. Heraldry used to be a hobby of mine, and the arms are not, I think, those of Brown. I made a sketch of the arms you bear and sent them to a friend of mine in Paris who supplied your rather unusual surname. Further enquiries in England filled in the picture.

"We were very thorough but tactful, my son. Very discreet indeed, believe me. We found someone who knew your father, that stern disciplinarian. It is no business of mine to comment upon your father's actions, and I shall not do so. We examined in detail the evidence in the case of the stolen piece of silver, and we were not convinced of your guilt. The same applies to your complicity in the burglary—the affair looked suspicious but that was all.

"Finally, of course, we verified your credentials."

The old priest paused and looked round.

"Brandy and soda, my father, after all that talking?"

"Thank you, my son."

The Prince supplied him, and Brown lifted his head out of his hands to ask when this enquiry took place.

"Between the battle and your visit to Paris, my son. It all took considerable time, you will understand."

"Before we went to Paris with the rubies. His Highness the Prince knew all this at that time?"

"Oh yes, Robert, I knew. And when someone rang up the police to denounce you for selling the rubies, I realized your bad friends were still after you. One of them came to our hotel, did he not? I believe you had him thrown out, Robert?"

Brown said nothing and Father Denys went on.

"You see, by that time we knew nearly as much about you as anyone. As for the forged credentials, what else could a man in your position do if he wished to start afresh? I agree that perhaps in the burglary case you should have gone to the police with what you knew, but you had already served one sentence which we thought you might not have deserved; you were hardly to blame for not risking another.

"In short, the Prince and I decided to proceed on the assumption that you were either innocent throughout or at least only partly to blame and had determined to do better in future. In a word, we trusted you and we were right, I am happy to say. Events tonight proved that, if further proof had been needed, Robert, my son."

Father Denys leaned back in his chair and sipped his brandy and soda, the Prince lit a cigarette, and there was silence for a space until Brown spoke again, hesitantly and with an effort.

"Does that mean, then, that I may—that I am to be allowed to go away, that is, to go free, not to have any charge brought —laid against me?"

"Well, no, in a sense," said the Prince. He got up to stand by the fireplace with his elbow on the mantelpiece. "You see,

Robert, if we do that, Sainte-Roche will still lack a Foreign Secretary and that would be intolerably tiresome."

Brown stood up gradually, like a man who is not sure whether his legs will support him, and stared at the Prince as though he had not understood a word of what had just been said.

"I beg Your Highness' pardon?"

"No, I am not tight, Robert, nor is the reverend father. Sainte-Roche needs a faithful Minister, and I want a friend."

"I understand English, Robert my son," said the curé, "much better than I can speak it. Tonight I heard you tell that man that this country is now your country, and I saw you willing to die to defend its treasures. Such a servant any country might be glad to own."

"Chevalier," said the Prince, "will you stay with us?"

"Yes," said Brown.

There came a knock at the door at exactly the right moment to release an emotional tension. Brown relaxed, Father Denys leaned back, smiling, and the Prince flickered his cigarette ash into the fire.

"Come in!"

The seneschal entered.

"The prisoner has been searched and secured, Your Highness. He had a—a sort of folding dagger upon him but no firearm. He is calmer now. Does Your Highness wish to see him?"

"Ah, the prisoner. We were speaking of other things and have not yet discussed the prisoner. Come back in a quarter of an hour, seneschal."

"As the Prince commands," said the old man, and went out.

"Well, do we want to see the prisoner? Father Denys? Robert? No, nor do I. The question is what we are to do with him. This house has a range of wine cellars but not what any connoisseur would call a dungeon; and though there are cells under the Town Hall, the doors have fallen from their hinges from disuse. We have no police and therefore no police station. It is very awkward to have a thing like this happen."

"I have sometimes wondered, my Prince, what is done with evildoers in Sainte-Roche."

"We outlaw them, Robert, after trial, if they are obdurate. No one will speak to them or look at them or sell them anything or give them food or employ them or pay them any debts. They are not allowed to live in any house, even their own. It is as though they were dead and as ghosts walking about. As a rule they break down and submit to public penance and the making of restitution, but sometimes they leave the country and we hear no more of them. We do not have much crime in Sainte-Roche."

"It sounds mild," said Brown doubtfully.

"It is a dreadful punishment," said the curé quietly.

"It is only for serious crimes, of course," said the Prince. "Minor offenders are fined. I fear that neither of our punishments will serve in this case. If we merely conduct him to the frontier and let him go, he might come back. Would he, Robert?"

"He is very persevering," said Robert dryly.

"Do not let him go," said the curé. "Allow him to escape."

"You are our well of wisdom," said the Prince. "Go on, please."

"I suggest you give him an uncomfortable time. Oh, no brutality, but a hard bed in one of your gloomier cellars. Bread and water for diet. No questions answered—still better, no one should speak to him. He might be told that he will stay there until the Prince has made up his mind what punishment to inflict. The Prince's power is absolute. After two or three days the jailer should be careless with his keys, one evening after dark. We must not make it too difficult for our prisoner to get clear away."

"It would be quite too exasperating," said the Prince, "if some of my faithful subjects captured him and brought him back."

"My Prince, are you allowing it to be known that it was the

photographer who was caught here tonight?" asked Brown. "I suppose it cannot be kept quiet altogether."

"I believe my household will do what they are told," said the Prince, "but some story may have leaked out already. The man was very well known, and he has been up here with his camera—all my staff saw him. I will have in the seneschal and hear what he has to say. An unknown man if possible, Robert? Yes. I will see what can be done. Father Denys, before you go, a little more——"

"No more, my son, thank you. If I have any more brandy tonight I shall be telling the world I was educated at St. Cyr."

"But you were, Father, were you not?"

"Indeed I was." The old priest smiled at Brown, who threw up his hands in a gesture of surrender. "Now, if I might have a servant and a lantern, it is time I went to bed."

"With the Prince's permission," said Brown, "I will be the servant with the lantern."

He took the curé's arm down the dark terrace steps and through the sleeping town, but of what they spoke between themselves no one will ever know.

Pike was locked up in a cellar dimly lit, even at midday, by a tiny window not nearly big enough for him to pass through even if it had not been barred. The cellar had a strong wooden door with a grilled aperture in it through which he could see his villainous-looking jailer sitting at a table with a lantern on it, for the passage outside was completely dark.

Pike talked incessantly at first, but nothing that he could say aroused a flicker of interest in the jailer, who merely yawned, leaned back in his chair, and went to sleep. Pike asked what was going to happen to him and was told that he would know soon enough when the Prince had made up his mind what punishment to give him. When he shook the cellar door and howled through the bars he had a pail of water thrown in his face. He was told that if he gave trouble they would put him in irons.

"It's an outrage," roared Pike. "What, handcuffs in a locked cell?"

"Not handcuffs. Leg irons with a ball on a chain. The armourer welds them on so you don't pick no lock."

Pike thought he had better behave. He meant to escape if given the smallest chance, and one cannot escape in leg irons.

He had for a bed some planks screwed to battens which raised them a few inches from the floor, he had a rather smelly horse blanket to cover him, and his diet was bread and water. Also there were rats which so terrified him that he scarcely dared to sleep. If this was not already punishment enough, what more would the Prince do? His only comfort was that they had returned him his own possessions except the flick-knife. He had his passport and his money, even cigarettes and a lighter. He rationed himself severely in cigarettes; there was no telling when he would get any more. His only chance was somehow to outwit the jailer, who did not look too bright; this place would drive a man out of his mind. Hopkins must wonder what had become of the helpful Pasquet. There were those beautiful certificates of sale all ready and all that money waiting to be picked up. Watch the jailer, watch him, watch every move.

The jailer was not particularly expert and he was alone. He was a big man powerfully built; perhaps he thought that it was not necessary to be so careful with a weaselly little rat of a man whose neck he could break with one hand. So Pike thought, for he had no illusions about his own physique. He could not know that the jailer was acting under the Prince's own detailed orders and that these included looking stupid and taking small avoidable risks.

On the evening of the second dragging interminable day, when Pike already felt that he had been entombed for at least a week, the jailer came down with supper for the prisoner, and he brought it on a tray. The time was between seven-thirty and eight in the evening, and it was already dark.

"Thank the Prince for his mercy," said the jailer, "you are to have soup tonight."

There was a bowl of soup on the tray and a wooden spoon to eat it with, two thick slices of bread, and a jug of fresh water. The jailer held the tray with one hand; with the other he put the key into the keyhole with the customary "Stand back, there," unlocked the door, and pushed it open. As he tried to withdraw the key, the things on the tray began to slide and Pike said: "Oh! Be careful!"

The jailer grunted, left the key in the lock, and advanced into the cell to set down the tray upon the stumpy wooden stool which was all Pike had to sit on.

Pike said hungrily: "It smells good," and came forward as it were involuntarily. The next moment he had skipped round the jailer, out of the door, and had locked it behind him.

The man let out a roar of baffled rage which did not worry Pike at all, for he knew that yells from the cellars were inaudible upstairs. He ran on silent crepe-rubber-soled feet along the twisting passage and up the stone stairs. The door at the top was ajar. He listened intently and heard only distant kitchen clatterings and the sound of cheerful voices not very near.

There was an outer door only three paces away and that was on the latch.

Pike opened this door just wide enough for him to slip out, tiptoed to the other, and lifted the latch cautiously with his fingers. The next moment he was out in the darkness and free. He had the whole night before him: his supper was the jailer's last duty before settling down for the night, and the jailer was locked up.

The third footman, grinning widely, came out of the larder from which he had been watching through a ventilating grille to see the prisoner go by. He went to the seneschal and reported.

"Prisoner escaped, sir."

"Good. Go down and see if Jacques is all right."

Jacques had occupied the time of waiting by drinking the

prisoner's soup—it would have been a pity to let it grow cold. He was released.

The seneschal went up and reported to the Prince, who was glad to hear it. "Send Jacques to me."

Jacques came up and stood to attention just inside the study door.

"Well done, Jacques. How villainous you do look—you will be glad of a shave. A tiresome duty, I fear."

"Only dull, Your Highness."

"No doubt. Take forty-eight hours' leave and this to celebrate it with."

"I thank Your Highness."

"That is all."

Jacques went off to spruce himself up before going out to enjoy himself on the Prince's *douceur*. He also had found the two days rather long.

Pike pattered down the terrace steps and froze behind a bush while some of the house servants went by. He went by back lanes to his lodging at the Widow Frachot's, slipping from shadow to shadow because, for all he knew, every Sainte-Rochean had heard that the photographer had been caught in the act of robbing the Palace strong room. If Hopkins had also heard, it might be awkward, but Pike thought he could talk his way out of that. A mistake, so natural when Monsieur could not speak French.

He reached his room without meeting Madame Frachot; when he came out again a quarter of an hour later, washed and changed and tidy once more and with his precious papers in his pocket, he hoped to avoid her again. However, just as he opened the door to go out, she approached it coming in.

"Ah, Monsieur Pasquet! What a pleasure. I have been quite anxious these two days."

Pike's heart swelled with relief. The story was not generally known, then. If there had been even a whisper Madame would have heard it. He apologized volubly.

"I have been round the outlying farms taking my pictures. Your people here are so kind—they would not let me go. Such hospitality!"

He went on, reassured. Anyone from the Palace, from Prince to scullery maid, must be avoided with unfailing agility, but apart from them there seemed to be not much to fear. He wound a scarf round his face as a precaution against Palace dwellers. All the same, he would be wise to collect the loot from Hopkins and get out quickly. Even if the general public of Sainte-Roche did not know about him, there might be many who did. The Six, for example, and Tonnerre was one of the Six. Better ask Hopkins only for his commission and let the capital sum go, although the idea of losing all that beautiful money as well as the jewels made him feel quite sick.

Still, anything was better than going back to that awful cellar. And, of course, the rats . . .

Besides, the promised commission would mount up to a nice little sum.

He sidled round The Goat in the shadows and had another stroke of luck. The door opened and Adam K. Hopkins came out upon the doorstep to look at the night.

CHAPTER XXI

Bill of Sale

Pike sidled along to Hopkins' elbow and whispered.

"Mr. 'Opkins? Sh-sh, now. I've got it."

"Pasquet? Well, if that isn't——"

"Quiet! Could we slip up to your room? Who's in the bar?"

"Tonnerre and some of the natives. Why, what's——"

"Quiet, keep your voice down. Tonnerre's one of the Six, don't want him thinking things. Anyone in the passage?"

Hopkins turned and glanced through the door behind him.

"Nobody about, come on."

They walked fast along the short passage and ran up the stairs. Hopkins threw open his bedroom door, Pike scurried in, and Hopkins was following when a voice in the passage stopped him.

"Dad! Are you——"

Hopkins turned back.

"Look, Betty, I've got to see a man on business. Tell you all about it later, can't stop now. You run on down and talk to Don Farson or something."

He entered his room and shut the door behind him.

Betty raised her eyebrows and walked thoughtfully down the stairs. There was no doubt that Dad was up to something, and that something must be that piece of land. He might even be arranging to meet the Prince.

Betty had begun to feel as though the Prince were being withheld from her by some malign anti-matrimonial agency.

She had twice seen him in the distance, walking away at a
pace which she could not match without actually running after
him; once he had passed the hotel in the early morning when
she was not even half dressed, and once, the worst of all, he
had come walking down the street towards her when she was
with her father. Betty hastily dragged her parent into the Corbet
pottery shop, for it was no part of her plan to bring him face
to face with André Dubois without previous explanations having been made.

But at any time they might meet—why not? Now it looked
as though a meeting were imminent.

Betty turned into the lounge, and there was the Foreign
Secretary talking confidentially to Tonnerre. He looked round
and saw her and his face lit up; she recognized him at once
and went to meet him. Two minutes later they were sitting
at a table in the corner talking earnestly together.

"But I did write to him, at the Hotel George the Fifth. To
Monsieur Dubois, of course."

"Yes, but there was another Monsieur Dubois in the hotel
and His Highness did not receive your letter."

Five minutes later they were talking like conspirators.

"If I don't meet him before my father sees him there will be
the most awful mess. Have you heard anything about this bit
of land?"

"Absolutely nothing."

"But you would, wouldn't you?"

"I'm quite sure I should."

"I can't think what else Dad would be so steamed up about.
Mind you, I don't know, he hasn't told me a thing, but we
seem to be staying on here, and I don't know what else it
would be for. And if they meet, Dad will be so rude!"

"His Highness," said Brown, "is coming down tomorrow
morning. There is to be a ceremony about starting work on
the power station. He is to cut the first sod."

"Tomorrow morning, oh! That'll ruin it."

"I think so too." Brown looked at his watch. "If I might venture to suggest——"

"What?"

"It is not yet nine P.M. and a beautiful night now that the moon is up. Miss Hopkins, if you would accept my escort to the Palace, it is no distance, and the Prince is at home this evening——"

"Oh. But wouldn't that look—I mean, if I go up there uninvited, I mean——"

"I could, of course, go back to the Palace and tell the Prince that you are here."

"And then what happens?"

"He will immediately come here to call upon you."

"And run into Dad on the doorstep."

"I should think that is more than likely."

Betty looked down at the table for a full minute and then rose to her feet.

"Wait for me while I get a coat."

"I am quite sure that you are doing the right thing."

In the meantime, Pike and his client were sitting at Hopkins' dressing table with a most convincing document spread out between them. It was quite beautifully written in a formal hand in French and started: "To all and sundry to whom these presents may come, André Amadeus Joseph Theodore, Prince of Sainte-Roche, sends greetings. Take notice that——" and so on, to the effect that the said Prince did sell and transfer by purchase, including all rights and revenues therefrom, the strip of land known as Belle Vue of one hectare and thirty-seven square metres, together with access thereto, to Adam Kysh Hopkins of New York in the United States of America to have and to hold in perpetuity, without let or hindrance, from this time forth forevermore, in proof of which the said Prince did hereto set his hand and seal. There followed a large round stamp none the less impressive for being a little blurred in places, and across it was written an indecipherable scribble barely recognizable as André if one knew what it was meant to be. Below this was the signature of a witness in a neat English hand: Robert Brown, Foreign Secretary, and the date.

Below again a note: Agreed Purchase Price four thousand five hundred United States Dollars.

Pike read all this out to his client, translating as he went along, and his voice conveyed a simple pride in his achievement, which was, indeed, entirely justified. The deed was beautifully written and imposingly worded, and Pike had every right to be proud of it. He had, after all, done it all himself singlehanded, and it was a very nice job of work. Hopkins slapped him on the back.

"A very nice job indeed, and when I think you worked it all yourself singlehanded I take my hat off to you. I can see you're proud of it, and you have a right to be."

Pike stopped breathing. Hopkins sprang impetuously to his feet.

"Yes, you've done a good job. I only wish I could see the faces of those Six guys who tried so hard to stand me up over this when they learn that I've gotten it after all——"

Pike drew a long breath, and his head was singing so loudly that he missed the next few sentences of the Hopkins jubilate. His ears cleared as Hopkins was saying: "—a good mind to take this down right now and show it to old man Tonnerre. That'll teach him not——"

"No, no! You mustn't do that—you'll ruin everything. The deal isn't through till you've paid for it and got the——"

Hopkins laughed shamefacedly.

"There now, doesn't that show what a fool a man can be when he gets excited? Call myself a businessman! I ought to be ashamed of myself and I am, Pasquet, I am. Well, well. What happens next?"

"You've only got to go up to the Prince with your cheque and get his official receipt and the thing's done. You can publish it in the Sainte-Roche *Bulletin* then, if you like."

"Not me. Adam K. Hopkins is going to stay nameless for

quite a while yet. Now I'll just go tell my little girl and then——"

"Mr. Hopkins. Don't think I'm trying to rush you, but I've had some worrying news from home and I'm leaving just as soon as I can get away. If you don't mind me asking——"

"You want your cut and you have earned it. I'm sorry if you've got troubles back home—I hope it's not serious. Let's reckon up, now." Hopkins scribbled some figures on the back of an envelope, muttering to himself. "Well, I make it five hundred and seventy-five dollars—how's that? Call it six hundred dollars, suit you? Take a cheque, or how? Would it be all right if I pay you in hundred-dollar bills?"

Pike thought this an excellent idea.

They parted with mutual satisfaction and Pike went down the stairs with his wallet comfortably lined, if not so fat as, with a little more luck, it should have been. Never mind, one must cut one's losses sometimes, and something over two hundred pounds was a lot better than the Prince's dungeons. He would go back to the Widow Frachot's for his gear and then get in touch with the smugglers to put him over the Spanish frontier.

He was in the act of passing through the hall when the door to the lounge opened at his elbow. Pike looked round and found himself face to face with his recent jailer, who ought to be still locked up with the rats for company——

Pike uttered a startled yelp and bolted like a frightened cat.

Across the square in the shadows towards which Pike instinctively steered there stood the Gallienne Renault with the engine ticking over. The car had had starting trouble and this was serious, since it ran down the battery and there was no means of getting batteries recharged unless one went to Py. A kindly lorry driver had taken pity upon the inexperienced Galliennes and spent some time doing the necessary adjustments. When at last the Renault was "ticking over like a watch" they left her running to make certain that the cure was lasting, and went round to The Hunter for a drink. They were returning to the car when they heard—for The Hunter was down a side street—the car door slam shut and the engine roar up. They broke into a run and came out in the square just in time to see the Renault move off at a rapidly increasing speed out of the square and up the road and take the left-hand turn by the school.

"Who has done this?" cried Jean-Alphonse.

"Some friend borrowed it for a joke?" suggested the lorry driver.

"Impossible," said Paul-Alphonse. "None of our friends can drive an auto in all Sainte-Roche."

They rushed across the road in a body and charged into The Goat, crying: "Our car, one has stolen our car."

"Decidedly," said Tonnerre, leaning so far over the bar that his feet must have been off the ground, "decidedly we must have a policeman. Who took it?"

"We did not see—some evil stranger——"

"Calm yourselves," urged d'Ecosse, "calm yourselves. He will be stopped at the Frontier."

"But if he damages our car——"

"Who can it have been?"

The babble of enquiry continued, the only one who took no part in it being Jacques the jailer, who said nothing, for he was sure that he knew who had taken it. But the Prince had said that the affair of the imprisoned photographer was not to be mentioned, so he did not mention it.

Pike drove the car along the only road upon which it was possible to drive a car, that leading to the new bridge and the French frontier. He did not stop to consider where he was going; anywhere out of Sainte-Roche would do him. The fact that he had not been chased across the square he put down to Jacques's being a slow thinker. Took a long time for the penny to drop. Probably standing in the doorway still, looking out into the night, poor boob.

Hopkins sat down and brooded over his beautiful certificate of sale for a few moments and was then seized with an urgent desire to show it to Betty at once, immediately, this minute. He folded it up, put it in his pocket, and knocked at her door. No answer, and he rushed downstairs. The lounge was full of excitable Sainte-Rocheans shouting, jumping about, and waving their arms. These foreigners, always blowing their tops over something. There was no sign of Betty nor of anyone else who could speak English—none of the Americans. Probably all gone out for a stroll together. He went to the door and looked out; it was a lovely moonlit night. He looked up at the Palace above its terraces. There were lights in many windows, and the sight of them gave him an idea. Why not settle the business tonight? No time like the present.

He went back to his room for his cheque book and his cards, his coat and hat, and walked out again into the moonlight. It was not so very late.

He plodded steadily up the four flights of stairs and arrived rather breathless at the top. The Palace, after all, was nothing like so big as many of his hotels.

"Princes, phooey," he said aloud, and pulled at the great iron ring which awoke a clamourous bell.

He was shown into a small room which had long french windows giving upon the terrace; there was a cheerful wood fire burning in the grate, and the room was comfortably if rather stiffly furnished. Hopkins approved of it; it was all rather like an old-fashioned but good-class hotel, the chairs matched each other, and there were expensive-looking pictures on the walls. A man could be comfortable sitting here. In point of fact it was a little-used anteroom, and the Prince had never sat in it in his life.

There had been something of a holdup at the front door, and none of the servants had understood Hopkins. However, he had sent in his card, and after a few minutes' waiting he had been shown in here and a chair pushed up to the fire for him. He smiled, nodded, and sat down, and the servants went out leaving him alone. He wondered whether one could smoke there and decided that it would be better manners to await permission.

Presently the door opened again and a short, rather stout man entered and bowed to him.

"Mr. Hopkins?"

Hopkins got up.

"That is my name. Do I address the Prince of Sainte-Roche?"

"No, sir. My name is Brown and I am His Highness' Foreign Secretary."

"Pleased to meet you, Mr. Brown. Sounds to me like you might be English."

"I am English by birth. In what way can I serve you, Mr. Hopkins?"

"Well. I wanted to see the Prince."

"It would probably help if you would be so good as to tell me your object in seeking this interview."

"Well, it's about this little deal of ours, Mr. Brown."

"Deal?"

"This sale. I got your very fine document this evening and I thought we might as well finalize it right away. I'll bring my architect out here for the preliminary survey and plans. So I've brought my——"

"But——"

"——cheque book up with me, and if the Prince will give me his formal receipt we'll be all set."

"Mr. Hopkins, I am very sorry, but I have not the faintest idea of what you are talking about."

"But for goodness' sake, Mr. Brown! It's got your signature on it, hasn't it?"

"On what?"

"On this."

Mr. Hopkins produced the certificate of sale and, without letting it out of his hands, allowed Mr. Brown to see it. "That's your signature, isn't it? You're Foreign Secretary, aren't you?"

The Foreign Secretary read the document with enthralled interest.

"So, as I was saying," went on Hopkins, "I've come up to pay my four thousand five hundred dollars, which I may say, in my opinion, is plenty, but if Adam K. Hopkins wants a thing he——"

"Excuse me just one moment," said the Foreign Secretary, and hurried out of the room.

He stood in the passage and thought; if he had followed his first impulse he would have put his head under a cold-water tap, but that untidies the hair. The Prince was not to be disturbed. He was talking to Betty Hopkins in the study, and if the Palace had caught fire every one of the Prince's servants would have dealt with it first and informed the Prince at some convenient later time.

When Hopkins' card was given to Brown he had at once jumped to the conclusion that Hopkins had missed his daughter, discovered where she had gone, and come up to reclaim her. Brown had gone to the anteroom armed with resolution to prevent Hopkins from interfering in the Prince's affairs, even if it involved doping his drink or having him abducted by alleged bandits. To be greeted with smiling politeness had taken Brown aback, but to be shown that astonishing certificate of sale was completely unexpected, for he had entirely forgotten Betty's vague story about a business deal. If there had been such a thing, he would have known about it.

Pike had forged it, of course; Brown was familiar with his work, and the Foreign Secretary's signature was a most convincing copy.

Brown went along to the study door and listened but could hear no voices. One wouldn't, anyway—the door was far too thick. He raised his hand to the panel and dropped it again.

But if he did nothing, Hopkins would not. He was a determined and enterprising man and no respecter of persons, especially princes. He was annoyed already. If something was not done there would be a noisy scene. The only possible thing was to go back to Hopkins and postpone him somehow until the morning. What an hour to call, anyway. Brown turned on his heel and went back to the anteroom.

Hopkins, already annoyed, very soon tired of waiting. He strode impatiently about the room and then parted the curtains to look out at the night. The lighted room, reflected upon the window glass, baffled him. He passed between the curtains and drew them together behind him. Ah, now, that was something. The moonlight was brilliant, the terrace was like a stage setting, and the backdrop was composed of dim mountains suitably arranged, a valley clothed in forest, and the little lighted windows of the town to give it human interest. A magnificent setting for the Belle Vue Hotel.

Two figures came strolling along the terrace very close together. A man and a woman, their arms were about each other and her head was on his shoulder. They so completed the theatrical scene that at first Hopkins approved heartily. They looked just right.

Then they drew nearer with the moonlight on their faces, and Hopkins realized that he knew them both. The man was that idle waster André Dubois, last seen in Paris, and the girl was Betty Hopkins.

The french windows flew open with a crash, the young man started, the girl screamed, and the infuriated parent charged out upon the terrace.

"What—what—what," he began, and choked. "Dubois! What the hell are you doing here?"

The young man placed the girl's arm more closely round his neck, pressed a comforting hand upon her hair—her face was against his chest—and turned a calm regard upon Hopkins.

"I live here," he said, and smiled.

"Betty!" roared Hopkins. "Stop that this minute and come here to me."

The young man stroked her hair.

"My own," he said in his stilted English, "I think it more wise if you introduce me."

Betty turned round with her chin up.

"Father, this gentleman is His Highness the Prince of Sainte-Roche."

"What!"

Hopkins felt rather than heard someone close behind him. He looked round to find Brown at his elbow and not looking at all suavely diplomatic. The terrace seemed to be filling with figures, men in livery, men in green tunics with silver badges. The Prince also noticed them.

"I think," he said again, "we talk more private indoor, eh? This way."

He drew Betty's hand through his arm and led her towards the study window with Hopkins following behind. In the doorway the Prince turned.

"Robert," he said, "I want you. The men can go."

The terrace emptied of figures; the Prince escorted Betty to a chair and moved to his favourite place before the fire with his shoulder against the mantelpiece. Robert shut the windows and drew the curtains; Hopkins stood in the middle of the room, very red in the face from various emotions.

CHAPTER XXII

The Prince and Betty

Pike drove out of the town, as fast as he dared, by the only road practicable for a car. He was not much troubled about whither the road would take him—his one idea was to get away from the place he had just left. Once across the frontier and he would probably be in Spain. He had the impression that Spain practically surrounded Sainte-Roche. Probably the frontier officials would be in bed. He breathed more freely when he was out of the valley and driving through the woods.

Sainte-Roche had no road barrier at the frontier; why should they since they had neither customs nor restrictions upon exit or entry? The French, however, took matters more seriously; since Sainte-Roche had awakened from its twenty-year trance there must be frontier guards and customs and currency officers, a red-and-white pole for them to let down across the road, and a new shed for a customs office and to shelter the men on duty. It was very new—it had only been finished the day before and the paint was still tacky.

It stood a little back on the French side, over the brow of the hill past the frontier marking post; the sergeant in charge and his one assistant were standing outside admiring it in the moonlight.

"This is better," said the sergeant. "It is dry, weatherproof, and warm now that we have the stove lighted."

"What had you before?" asked his assistant, for this was his first turn of duty there.

"A tent, lately. At first we wore our cloaks when it rained.

Now we can be indoors in the dry except when there is traffic. You need not look so superior; there is much traffic during the day with the lorries going through."

"But at night?" asked the assistant, amusing himself by swinging the pole up in the air and down again.

"At night, not so much, it is true. Sometimes the Sainte-Roche taxi to Py."

"Sounds exciting," drawled the assistant in a sarcastic voice.

"We are not here to be excited; we are here to perform our duties."

"But if there are no duties——"

"Listen! There is something coming from Sainte-Roche. It sounds like the Gallienne's Renault. He will probably have a passenger. Put the bar down."

"I leap to obey," said the assistant.

Pike came out of the woods and crossed a bridge. The road was better here and he accelerated. The car shot through an archway and a clump of trees and roared up the rise beyond. Over the crest the road twisted, and there, at once, was a red-and-white pole across the road and people waving lights.

He jammed on his brakes and the car skidded on loose gravel; as the two officials leapt for their lives the Renault charged through the barrier, swerved, and crashed into the hut, which collapsed. The car rolled over, throwing Pike out in the road, and immediately burst into flames.

The sergeant and his assistant picked themselves up.

"You said you wanted excitement," said the sergeant reproachfully. "Are there people in the car?"

"One man has fallen out," said the assistant. "I do not see anyone else."

They dragged Pike away from the flames. The sergeant saw that the ruins of the hut had also caught fire, and the sight exasperated him.

"You have wrecked our post, you—you——"

Pike, who was only stunned and extensively grazed, struggled to rise, so the sergeant sat upon him.

"Lie there, scoundrel," he said magnificently, "until the police come to drag you to jail. Dupont, mount your bicycle and——"

"How can I? It's in there," objected Dupont.

"But," gasped Pike, "what have I done wrong? Anybody may have an accident. I skidded."

The sergeant considered this and found that it was true. "Driving dangerously," he said, and paused. "You were driving much too fast," he added, and rose to his feet. What, precisely, did one do in the case of a man who had wrecked a customs post by accident? The sergeant fell back upon routine. "Your papers, please."

Pike sat up shakily and handed over his passport, which the sergeant examined by the light of the leaping flames.

"Aha, I have you!" he cried. "*Rentrée Prohibée!* Now you shall go to jail after all! For this is France, monsieur, let me tell you."

"Oh no," said Pike weakly, "it can't be. This is too much."

The sergeant smiled.

"Monsieur is perfectly right, it is."

"Betty," said Hopkins, "what is all this? I told you I wouldn't have you mixed up with that Dubois."

"He isn't a Dubois, he is the Prince of Sainte-Roche. I told you so just now."

"When I were in Paris," said the Prince, "I call myself Dubois for to avoid fuss. Then you say you do not like princes. But, sir, when I marry your daughter she will be Princess of Sainte-Roche."

"Who says you're going to marry my——"

"I do," said Prince André.

"I do," said Betty. "Mother will be delighted."

Hopkins wilted and recovered himself.

"Well, I'm not. Betty, you come along with me and I'll talk to you when we're alone. She's under age," he added triumphantly, "so if you think you can marry her without my say-so, you can think again."

"We are here in Sainte-Roche," said the Prince.

"You're telling me! So what?"

"Here," said the Prince, choosing his words carefully, "our young are of full age when they add up seventeen."

Hopkins emitted a faint hissing noise, and Betty said that one of the things she liked most about Sainte-Roche was that the laws were so sensible.

"On the terrace but now," said the Prince, "we discuss law."

"There is also," said Brown smoothly, "the curious affair of the certificate of sale."

"The what?" said Prince André.

"My piece of land," said Hopkins. "I'm having that. You signed it and I'm holding you to it."

The Prince raised his eyebrows, and Brown explained in French.

"But I have signed no such thing," said Prince André. "I cannot sell my land—you tell him, Robert. My English will not support the strain."

"Then what is this?" said Hopkins angrily, and unfolded his certificate.

"I am sorry, sir," said Robert, "but it is a forgery. That is not His Highness' signature, there can be no sale, and the second signature is not mine."

"So you're backing out——"

Betty rose suddenly from her chair, twitched the certificate from between her parent's fingers, and read rapidly through it.

"Daddy! Did you pay somebody for this? Did you? You did, I can see it. Daddy, you've been made a fool of. Who was it? How much did you pay him—how much—how much——"

"Stop it," bellowed Hopkins. "It's my business what I pay, and I won't be bullied."

The Prince laughed suddenly. "Bullied!"

"Daddy, I'm sorry, but you are an idiot. Most of this—these phrases—come out of the Prayer Book of the Episcopal Church.

233

'To have and to hold . . . from this time forth forevermore'—
Daddy, really! 'Without let or hindrance,' I'm not sure whether
that's the Prayer Book or what the British have on their passports, but——"

By this time Prince André was reading it over her shoulder.

"It is ver' nice, you know," he said appreciatively. "It soun's
good, not?" He changed into French. "Robert, is this the
work of our recent guest, he who writes such charming letters
of recommendation? It is? He is really clever, isn't he? Is that
supposed to be my signature? Robert, find a genuine signature
of mine to show Mr. Hopkins—something official. That requi-
sition for slates for the church roof will do. It's in my desk."

Robert opened a drawer, took out a document headed "By
Order of the Six in Council," and handed it to Mr. Hopkins,
who compared the small neat "André" at the foot with the
illegible scrawl upon his certificate.

"All right," he said, after a pause, "you win and I'm a fool.
Tell me, where's that guy Pasquet now—probably skipped
across the frontier some place. He told me he'd had bad news
from home. I'm losing my grip, that's what." He drooped.

The Prince asked what it was all about, and Hopkins told
him at some length.

"This country shall require hotels," said the Prince thoughtfully. "The Goat, she is too little and The Hunter more so."

"Then you'll sell?" asked Hopkins.

"No. I may not. Robert said to you just now, you know.
The law again." He smiled widely. "There is a way. I may
not sell, but I can give to one of my own family. When you
are papa-in-law it is easy. Embrace me, my angel." He clasped
Betty firmly in his arms and grinned at Hopkins over her
shoulder. "So we are all happy, how nice to think."

"You can't marry her till my hotel's up," said Hopkins
firmly. "That'll fill it if nothing else does."

"How long," asked the Prince, "to up a hotel?"

3